DEEP

A NOVEL BY
DANETTE MAJETTE

A Life Changing Book in conjunction with Power Play Media
Published by Life Changing Books
P.O. Box 423 Brandywine, MD 20613

Library of Congress Cataloging-in-Publication Data;

www.lifechangingbooks.net

ISBN - (10) 1-934230-93-6 (13) 978-1-934230-93-0
Copyright ® 2007

ACKNOWLEDGEMENTS

I would like to dedicate this book to all the woman and men serving our country. Semper Fidelis!

First, I would thank my Lord and Savior for giving me a second chance in life. To my mother, Nellie Best, you have been my rock and I don't know what I would do without you. Thank you for everything. I Love You! My father, Melvin Hester, and step-mother, Patricia Jennings, thank you for your love and support. My wonderful kids, Bryan Majette and Marketa Salley (author of "Her Secret" in Teenage Bluez 2). I love you guys more than life itself. Thanks for promoting my work. My brothers, Ronald Williams and Melvin Williams, I'm so glad we have finally found each other again after all these years. I love you guys. To Keisha and Angie thanks for being such great sister in laws. To my nieces and nephews, your auntie loves you. My cousin, Shelly Majette Carrington, words cannot express how blessed I am to have you in my life. You are always there when I need you and I'm so grateful for that. Oh, and Shawn Carrington, I didn't forget you this time. Thank's for not getting mad at me for hogging so much of your wife's time. My cousin, Rodney Baylor of Black Russian Music Group, thanks for all the love.

To my family, the Majettes and Hesters, thank you all for support. My extended family, Betty Hamilton, Tamika, Karen and Fannie Gordon, Ebony Dudley, and Kevin Levy and Equan. My Goddaughters Andrea Thomas and Patrice McCray. A special shout out to my cousin, Allen Bailey, keep your head up. I love you!

To my girls, Anita Belachew, Tiffany Adkins, Erika Arndt, and Sabrina Wright of ATL, Miss Vay and Tracy from Norfolk, thank you for all your love and support. You guys are the best friends a girl could ask for.

Harold (Smax) Morning, thanks for all the help with this book. My God father, Earl (The Pearl) Taylor, you have been absolutely the greatest. I don't know how I would have made it without you. You are always there for me and I appreciate it so much. Terrence McKinley, thanks for being such a good friend to me. Laron Profit, thanks for helping me have a new outlook on life. I still think you missed your calling to be a comedian. To Lance Griffin, thanks for all the laughs when I wanted to cry. You have proven to be a REAL friend.

To my Publisher, Azarel (A Life to Remember, Bruised and Bruised 2) and Leslie Allen, I can't thank you enough for all the support, time, and energy you have put into this book. To the rest of my LCB family, Tonya Ridley (The

Takeover and Talk of the Town), Darren Coleman (Before I let Go and Do or Die), J.Tremble (Secrets of a Housewife and More Secrets More Lies), Tiphani (The Millionaire Mistress), Mike G (Young Assassin), Mike Warren (A Private Affair), Zach Tate (No Way Out and Lost and Turned Out), Tyrone Wallace (Double Life and Nothin' Personal), Juicy Wright(Flexin and Sexin), Ericka Williams (All That Glitters), you all are all like family to me. Thanks for all the love and support, and let's take LCB to another level this year. To Leslie German, and Cheryl Moody thanks for the feedback on the book. LCB'S Creative Director Davida Baldwin, thanks for the amazing cover and all of your hard work. To Kathleen Jackson, thanks for the final editing. My publicist, Nakea Murray thank you for all of your support. Also to my test readers, Courtney Kinney and Keisha George, thanks for your help and input.

To my fellow authors, Shannon Holmes, Kwan, KiKi Swinson, Shon Majette, JoJo of Street Knowledge Publishing, Hickson, Treasure Blue, Ed McNair, K. Elliott, Chunichi, T.N Baker, Nicolette, and Wahida Clark, let's keep giving it to the readers!!!

To my Nordstrom Family in Annapolis and Pentagon City, especially my boss Frank Androski, Claudia Korrot, Courtney Caughy, Karen Schriever, Loren Donaldson, Kirsten Starlett, Norene Wilson, Denise Payne, Sally Fuller, Erika Burton, Erica Petsche, Shannon Stewart, Amanda Peet, and Karina Slota, thanks for spreading the word and supporting me 100 percent.

My friends, Alana Beard (Washington Mystics), Etan Thomas (Washington Wizards), Howard Tinker and Curtis (Curtbone) Chambers (All Daz Clothing in D.C.), C. Jonah (D.R.U.G.S. Magazine), DJ Joe Stick and Bink One Shot Deal of Norfolk, Jake Blue (Superstar Jewelry in Norfolk), Kelly Fox of Diverse Recording, Audrey Thomas, Willie Savage, Nicole Wiggins, Jodie Adams, Cheryl Vance, Angie and Andre Whitaker, Marcus Gates, Dave Taylor, Kelly Fox. Elonda Dolly, 2 Face the Don and Goldie of Da Grip Boyz, DJ Joe Stick, Tory (D. Frasiers in Norfolk), Big Sam of Norfolk, VA, Michelle Butler, and my dear friends Aaron and Cheryl from Capitol Heights, MD, thanks for the love and support.

A special thanks to the crew at Waldenbooks in Military Circle (Karen, Ron, Patrick and Annette), Karibu Books, DC Bookman, Natti at African World Books, Massamba the King of Jamaica Ave), for all the love you've shown me. You have been my biggest supporters, and I thank you from the bottom of my heart.
Please write to: Danette Majette P.O. Box 471396 District Heights, MD 20753 or www.myspace.com/danettemajette

SOMEONE CALL 911

It was a hot Sunday August afternoon, and Anacostia Park in Washington, D.C. was jumping as usual. Trae and his boys Kevin, Big Paul and Ice Man, were posted at the entrance with their Honda CBR street bikes lined up for everyone to see. Trae was especially proud of the new exhaust he'd just added to his metallic silver beauty.

"Yo', the bitches are out today," Kevin said, as he inhaled one last pull from his blunt.

"I can definitely agree," Trae said, his eyes following a girl's ass as she walked by. The girl turned around and flashed a sexy smile. "Hey gorgeous, what's yo' name?" he asked, licking his lips.

The girl stopped dead in her tracks when she saw Trae's tall and muscular physique. His dark complexion and bald head was an added bonus. "I'm Courtney," she replied, showing her pearly whites.

"Nice to meet you, Courtney. I'm Trae." He sized her up. "Give me those digits, so I can call you," he ordered.

All of Trae's boys laughed because as crazy as his pickup lines were, they always seemed to work.

Courtney didn't hesitate. She recited her digits like she was in a spelling bee, as Trae locked them in his cell phone.

"I'll call you later tonight, a'ight. Maybe we can go get something to eat."

"Oh absolutely," Courtney said, giving Trae a mischievous smile before she rushed off with her friend.

As Trae turned back to his crew, he noticed someone staring at him. The guy looked at him up and down, then clenched his jaw.

"What dat fool lookin' at?" Kevin asked, looking at Trae.

"I don't know. But that nigga better recognize," Trae responded, with an evil look. He tried to remain cool, but the stranger kept sizing him up.

A NOVEL BY DANETTE MAJETTE

"What's up, nigga? You got somethin' you wanna say?" Kevin asked boldly. He was known for not being able to hold his tongue.

The stranger walked over. "Yeah, I got somethin' to say. Tell your man not to try and talk to my girl, if he wants to keep his life," he said, gritting hard on Kevin.

"Your girl?" Kevin asked. "Nigga, obviously she ain't your girl if she was just on my man's dick!"

"Man, fuck you and the rest of your punk ass crew," the stranger replied.

As Kevin and the rest of his boys jumped off their bikes, Trae quickly intervened. He was always the voice of reason and more of a lover and not a fighter. "Don't pop off, shorty, keep your cool," he said to Kevin, pushing him back.

"Yeah, shoorrtty…listen to yo' man," the stranger said, in an insulting tone.

Kevin made a slight turn toward Trae, then came full force with a punch that knocked the guy off his feet. "Nigga, you don't know me," he said, kicking the guy in his stomach as he tried to get up.

After letting out a hearty laugh, Trae stood over the stranger and shook his head. A few seconds later, the guy finally managed to stand up. As he brushed the dirt off his shirt, he tried to take a swing at Trae, but missed.

The calm temperament Trae displayed just minutes earlier quickly diminished as he hit the guy with a hard left. "Never fuck with a South Paw," Trae said, referring to his boxing skills.

Spitting the blood that trickled from his mouth, the stranger looked up at Trae and smiled. "I'll see y'all niggas in the streets," he said, as he stood up for the second time and walked away.

"You better hope we don't see your bitch ass first," Kevin responded.

Trae and his crew watched as their newly acquired enemy walked away.

"That bitch you just met is startin' trouble already. See what happens when you chase women," Kevin added.

"Shit, I'm like Biggie. I don't chase 'em I replace 'em," Trae replied with a huge grin.

They all laughed and gave each other a pound before walking back to their bikes. Determined not to let the incident spoil the rest of their day, Trae and Kevin continued to shoot the shit with their boys.

Moments later, Trae noticed a group of unfamiliar bikers rolling up on them. "Yo', you know them, Kev?" Trae asked, trying to get a better

DEEP

look.

His question was never answered, because gunshots immediately rang out as the bikers drove by. Kevin and Trae took cover behind a car that was parked nearby. Big Paul, who was massive in size and covered in tattoos, decided that hiding wasn't an option. He took off running behind the last biker, shooting him in the back. He was like the bodyguard of the crew.

Not wanting to leave their friend behind, the bikers circled around busting mad shots at Trae and his friends long enough to get their injured friend onto one of the bikes before riding off. People were running for cover, and screaming like a scene from the movie *Godzilla*.

When the dust finally cleared, there were several people crying and trying their best to get the hell out of dodge. Mothers were also scrambling to gather their children, but one mother wasn't so lucky. Her eight year old daughter was lying on the ground bleeding uncontrollably.

"Someone call 911!" a man yelled, as the mother tried to comfort her child.

"Let's roll!" Trae yelled. He and the rest of his crew jumped on their bikes, started up the engines and left.

However, when Trae got a few feet away he stopped suddenly and looked back as Kevin and his boys kept going. He prayed that the little girl would make it. Minutes later, the paramedics arrived. They worked on the girl and tried to keep her conscious, but it was too late. She had already drifted off to sleep.

Trae felt sick. He shook his head as he watched the mother cry uncontrollably. *Damn, I hate that lil' shorty got caught up in this shit*, he thought. After watching the EMT's place a white sheet over the little girl's body, he drove off thinking how his love for women had caused the entire thing.

Getting to sleep that night was impossible for Trae. He laid in the bed, thinking about how a peaceful day with his boys had turned into another tragedy. D.C. was known to have one of the highest crime rates in the country. *I guess we're part of the problem*, he thought. Half asleep, he saw his grandmother out the corner of his right eye.

Those fools you hang around with are going to get you in more trouble than you can handle. You mark my words. They're gonna either land you in jail or six feet under one of these days.

Trae knew his grandmother was right. He hated the fact that a kid had to get caught in the line of fire, but the guy had disrespected him

A NOVEL BY DANETTE MAJETTE

and his crew, so he had to be dealt with. Besides, Trae wasn't about to give up everything he ever wanted in life. Money, power, and respect was something he'd worked hard for, and planned on keeping.

Trae woke the next morning and turned on the television. It didn't surprise him to see that every news channel in the area was covering the young girl's death. What did surprise him was the fact they made no mention of him or his crew. Instead, eyewitnesses concentrated on the biker crew that started the shooting. Usually whenever there was a murder in the city, the police always mentioned his name. The police had been trying to pen things on Trae for years, but luckily nothing ever stuck. He even knew all of the officers at the Fourth District Police Station on a first name basis.

Trae felt sick as the mother of the eight-year old wept during her interview. "This wave of crime must stop. Mothers, I call upon you to help me bring every ounce of pressure on the State Attorney's office to do something about the crimes that have taken over D.C.," she pleaded, wiping away her tears. "We need a plan to get rid of every pimp, drug lord and murderer in this city!"

The reporter signed off, saying the matter was under investigation and there were still no suspects in the case.

"Thank you," Trae whispered, as he picked up the picture of his grandmother, who'd passed away leaving him with no family. "You still watchin' out for me, huh?"

When Trae heard his cell phone ring, he put the picture down reluctantly. He was never in the mood to talk during his personal moments with his nana. He looked at the screen and the word, KEV displayed. "Yo', what's up?" he asked, answering his phone.

"Nothin', nigga. Just callin' to check up on you," Kevin responded.

"I'm cool. I was just sittin' here watchin' the news." Trae glanced at the TV again. "I can't believe that lil' girl died, man."

"So what? People die in these muthafuckin' streets everyday. She's probably better off anyway," Kevin replied coldly.

Trae stared at the phone for a few seconds. It was like he was talking to a stranger. He couldn't believe this was the dude he loved and grew up with all his life. *You're right. I'm gonna end up dead or in jail hangin' around this fool,* Trae thought, as he looked over at his grandmother's picture.

DEEP

AN EYE FOR AN EYE

Later that day, Trae spotted a familiar face out the corner of his eye as he drove down H Street in his Cadillac STS. It had been years since he'd seen him, so to make sure his eyes weren't deceiving him, he circled the block to get a closer look. When Trae approached the familiar person for the second time, his suspicions were confirmed. His eyes grew big as he immediately recognized the man known as Pretty Tony. He watched as the light skinned man, dressed in a designer suit, gators and a large brim hat, stood on the corner shooting the breeze with his friends.

Pretty Tony was older and moving a little slower than he used to back in the day, but other than that, he looked the same; with the exception of the gray hair that peeked from under his hat.

So, the bastard finally got out, Trae thought to himself. As he stopped at a light, his mind drifted off into deep thought, and the memories of his mother rushed in like flooding water.

Trae's mother, Debra, was one of the baddest prostitutes in Washington, D.C. back in the 70's. She was very petite, and walked with a strut that would put the average model to shame. Prostituting wasn't the life she always wanted, but when she got laid off of her government job, she had no other choice. Losing her job meant losing her house, as well as her car, so she decided to leave D.C. for a new life in Tampa, Florida. That's where she met Pretty Tony, who was in the Sunshine State on business.

After dating a couple of days, Pretty Tony promised her that if she moved back to D.C. with him, he would set her up in an apartment. Little did Debra know she would be paying for it with her life.

Pretty Tony kept his promise and got her an apartment when they moved back to the District. However, after paying the bills for two months, he told her she would have to start working for him in order to

A NOVEL BY DANETTE MAJETTE

stay. He knew she didn't have a place to go or a dime to her name. It was all part of his plan to get Debra where he wanted her.

Within a few days, he had her beating her feet for him on 14th Street, a known prostitute district. In return, she got to live in her apartment rent-free, and had access to all the money, clothes and cars she wanted. Sleeping with men she didn't know bothered her at first, but she soon got use to it, and became one of Pretty Tony's biggest moneymakers.

However, things got even worse when she became pregnant a year later. Debra had no idea who the father was, since she was sleeping with different men every night. Scared of what Pretty Tony would do to her if he found out, she kept her pregnancy a secret, which wasn't easy to do with her small frame. However, her secret was revealed, when she went into labor prematurely in the middle of her seventh month and gave birth to Trae.

To say Pretty Tony was angry was an understatement. He dragged Debra and Trae out of the hospital the day after she gave birth, and only allowed her three days to rest before he pushed her right back out on the street...stitches and all.

The whole ordeal was too much for Debra to handle, so four months later, she took the little bit of money she had saved and moved to Virginia Beach without saying a word to anyone. She'd heard several girls on the street talk about the area a few times, and thought it would be a great place to start over.

However, once she arrived, her life after Pretty Tony was rough. She had to take on three jobs that didn't pay much, and for six years, she lived from paycheck to paycheck, trying to make ends meet. After realizing she couldn't make it without Pretty Tony, Debra made the decision to go back to work for him. A year after being back on the scene, she was killed.

The sound of cars honking their horns, made Trae snap back to reality. With his adrenaline pumping, he looked around for Five-0 before deciding to roll up on the familiar man.

When he pulled up to curve, he placed his gun inside the waist of his pants and jumped out the car like it was on fire. As he approached Pretty Tony, he clinched his fists repeatedly. He could feel the anger rushing through his body.

"Yo', what's up, Playboy? Let me holla at you for a second," Trae said, gritting his teeth.

"What you got to talk to me about young fella?" Pretty Tony replied looking at his friends then back to Trae.

DEEP

"Ain't you Pretty Tony?" Trae asked.

"Yeah, how do you know me?"

"My moms used to know you."

"Oh yeah? Well, in that case, you should know my name. Shit, all the ladies know Pretty Tony," the old man said, with a smug look on his face.

Trae shook his head. "No doubt. You used to be the man back in the day. I give you that."

"I'm still the man, Young Blood."

Muthafucka you wish you were still the man. "So look, do you remember Debra Keal?"

Pretty Tony laughed. "Debra Keal! Hell yeah, I remember Debra! She used to be one of the baddest bitches to ever walk these streets. No disrespect, of course. That's just the way it was back then."

Steam was coming out of Trae's ears, but he kept his cool. "Naw, that's cool. She was a very beautiful woman. That's until she got caught up with yo' ass."

"Look, don't come at me like that, Slim. The choice was hers. Debra ain't have shit 'til she got with me. I was the one who put her ass on the map."

Angered by Pretty Tony's lack of remorse, Trae walked up to him and stuck his gun in Pretty Tony's side. "Let's take a walk," he ordered, nudging him along.

Pretty Tony was shocked and angry at the same time, but he knew from the look in Trae's eyes that he meant business. If he had been about twenty years younger, he would've probably tried Trae. But now old and frail, he knew that was out of the question.

"Be cool, Young Blood," Pretty Tony said softly. "Don't do anything crazy." He looked at his friends, to try and give them a signal, but they were too busy talking shit to one another and didn't pay him any attention.

When they reached a safe distance from the hustle and bustle of H Street, Trae pushed Pretty Tony toward a brick wall and cocked his burner.

"She had a choice, huh?" Trae asked.

"Hey, what's this shit about?" Pretty Tony asked, with fear in his eyes.

"Debra was my mother, that's what this is all about!" Trae shouted.

"Your mother? Well, I know you and your sista ain't tryin' to blame me for her death."

Trae raised his eyebrows. "What sista? What the hell you talkin' 'bout? I don't have a sista, dumb ass. All I had was my mother. She was my life. So yeah, nigga, I blame you and for good reason," Trae said, moving closer to him. "See, what you and everybody else don't know is I was home that day. Yeah, that's right, I was home when you came over and blamed her for stealin' from you. My mother was a lot of things, but she never stole a dime from yo' punk ass."

Stunned by Trae's words, Pretty Tony stood speechless.

"Yeah, see I saw you. I saw you stab my mother. And the crazy thing is, you didn't stab her one time. Naw, you hit her up quite a few times, even after she was dead. Now yo' ass 'bout to feel this iron."

Raising the gun to Pretty Tony's forehead, Trae shot off one round. He didn't even wait for his body to drop before he turned and quickly walked back to his car. He also didn't care if Pretty Tony's friends had seen him. All he cared about was that he'd finally gotten the asshole who'd taken his mother's life.

"You can rest in peace now, Ma. I got the bastard!" Trae said out loud.

That night, Trae reminisced about the good times he had with his mother, and how much he missed her and his grandma. However, his trip down memory lane was abruptly interrupted by a sudden knock at the door.

He immediately flew across the living room floor to retrieve his Glock. Ready to put in work, he quickly cocked it, and waited for who-ever was on the other side. For all he knew, it could've been the nigga from the park, or one of Pretty Tony's friends, so he wasn't taking any chances.

"Who is it?" he yelled.

"It's me."

When Trae heard Kevin's voice, he took a deep breath, then opened the door.

"What's up wit' you? Are you paranoid or some shit?" Kevin asked, as he walked in and noticed the Glock in Trae's hand.

"You know I don't fuck around. Niggas out here be actin' stupid," Trae responded, laying the gun on his coffee table.

Trae and Kevin had been best friends since elementary school, and lived two doors down from each other after Trae's grandmother took him in. They were like brothers. If you messed with one of them, you messed with both of them. Trae watched as his tall, slim friend sat on his brand new micro-suede couch.

"What's up, man?" Kevin asked. "Hey, did you hear 'bout that old-nigga that got shot off H Street?"

"They don't have any witnesses, do they?"

"Naw. Why?" Kevin asked, looking at Trae suspiciously.

"You my man, right?"

"Yeah, but what that got to do wit' that old man gettin' shot?"

Trae sat on the other end of the couch. "I know who popped the dude."

"What are you talkin' 'bout?" Kevin asked with a confused expression.

Trae asked Kevin to give him his word that he wouldn't repeat what he was about to tell him. Kevin told him that went without saying. Trae then went on to tell Kevin how no one ever knew who killed his mother, but he did.

"You mean to tell me that you knew who killed your moms and you ain't tell the police?" Kevin asked.

"Why, what were they gonna do? She was a hooker! They could've cared less about her death. That's why I kept it to myself. I've been waitin' for this day for so long. I thought it was never gonna come to tell you the truth."

Kevin stared at Trae for a few moments. It was all too much for him to comprehend.

"I was at home when he killed her," Trae confessed. "See, I was hidin' in the closet, and was gonna jump out and scare her. I used to do that all the time. She would get mad at first then we would sit and laugh about it. While I was hidin', that muthafucka came in and started cursin' and hittin' her like she was a fuckin' punchin' bag. I was about to jump out, but then he pulled out a knife. I was so scared I just froze. I let her down," Trae said sadly.

"Man, what are you talkin' 'bout? You were only seven years old when it happened," Kevin replied.

Trae held his head down. "I know, but if I had just ran out and at least kicked him or somethin', maybe she'd still be here today."

Kevin reassured Trae that he couldn't blame himself for what happened to his mother.

"I know, but I did at first. That's why I didn't say anything. And to tell the truth, I sorta blocked it out of my mind for years, but I never forgot his face. I wanted to remember it, so when I was old enough, I could make him pay for what he did to her. And today was somethin' that I've been waitin' for a long time. I finally got that muthafucka!"

It was all coming together for Kevin. "Shorty, I can't believe the man they found today was the nigga who killed yo' mom?"

"Yeah, that was him...Pretty Tony. I bet that muthafucka ain't so pretty now," Trae said, with a huge laugh.

Kevin stood up and patted Trae on the shoulders. "I'm glad you got your payback. I couldn't even imagine lookin' for a nigga who killed my mom."

"It wasn't easy," Trae replied. "But you know, his ass said somethin' that I didn't understand."

"What?"

"He said, I know you and your sista ain't trying to blame me. I don't have a sista," Trae said annoyed.

"Maybe the muthafucka was on that shit," Kevin responded, trying to lighten the mood, then pulled out a long blunt.

Trae shook his head. "You might be right." He was happy he'd finally gotten his revenge, but saddened that nothing was going to bring his mother back to him.

After revealing the secret that bothered him for years, Trae perked up. "Let's go chase some hoe's," he suggested. The last thing he wanted to do was sit in the house after the day he had.

"Man, I'm wit' you. I ain't had no pussy all day," Kevin responded with a smile.

"It's almost impossible to find a parkin' spot in Georgetown," Trae said, as he drove down several streets like a mad man.

"Nigga we ain't gonna get no play ridin' up in your hooptie," Kevin said, referring to Trae's three year old Escalade. "Why didn't we take the Range?"

"Man, is that all you think about...pussy?" Trae asked.

"Like you don't,"Kevin said smiling. "You just fall in love with your pussy too quick. See, I got my bitches on a schedule like a fuckin' parkin' meter. After their time expires...I'm done."

Trae laughed uncontrollably. "Why don't you find one girl and settle down?"

Kevin frowned at that question. He was a known playboy who, like Rick James, liked to love them then leave. Because of his good looks and naturally curly hair, women flocked to him day and night. It also

DEEP

didn't hurt that he had money. Women could care less about the way he treated them. "Settlin' down is for losers. Not real niggas like me," Kevin said.

"Don't you want someone to come home to at night?" Trae asked, as he finally found a parking spot.

"I do. There's Sherrie, Tonya, Rachel, Connie, and..."

"Okay! I get the picture, toothpick," Trae said, with a huge grin. He knew Kevin hated when he called him that. It was a name that he'd been calling his friend for years because of his slender frame.

"Shut up, nigga! I may be skinny, but I can wrap my dick around my waist," Kevin said jokingly.

"Just wait and see. I'ma find me somebody, man. I need a girl who loves me and not my money. Besides, I'm twenty-seven years old, I need to settle down soon," Trae replied as they got out the truck and activated the alarm. "I'm tired of waking up to a new chick every morning."

"Man, fuck the dumb shit. Just put those bitches out before you go to bed," Kevin said, with a wide smile. "You ain't gonna find no chick that don't care about a nigga with money. I guarantee you right now, if you pull up to a chicken head in a fuckin' Honda Accord, she ain't gonna give you the time of day. But pull up on that same girl in yo' fly shit...I guarantee she'll be hittin' you off by the end of the night."

Trae knew what Kevin was saying was true. Before they started getting money, girls used to laugh at them and talk about their clothes. Now those same girls were all over them. And it was all because of the Benjamins.

After walking into Sequoia's Restaurant and requesting their favorite waitress, they sat down at a table with a beautiful view of the Potomac River.

"So, what are we gonna do now that Yakeem is locked down?" Kevin asked, stuffing a piece of bread in his mouth.

"I don't know, man. Shit ain't looking too good," Trae said, discouraged. He'd been thinking about his supplier a lot lately.

"I got a connect in Jersey, but I don't know 'bout that dude, man. I get a bad vibe when I'm around him," Kevin said.

"Well, that's a sign to stay away from the nigga. Don't worry, I'll figure somethin' out. I didn't bring us this far to have everything go belly up now," Trae replied reassuringly.

"I know you will, you always come through," Kevin responded.

"So, have you heard from Rico's bitch ass?"

A NOVEL BY DANETTE MAJETTE

"Naw, the nigga been ignorin' my phone calls for the past two days," Kevin responded. "You know how he gets when he owe's you money."

"I hate niggas who think they gonna hustle, for free. I see I'ma have to teach his ass a lesson."

"Yeah, we need to show him that school is in session," Kevin added.

As they waited for their food, Trae began to think. *Everything's gonna fall into place. It has to. Besides, I can't stay in this life forever.*

DEEP

A BRIGHTER DAY

The following afternoon, Trae's day started off with lunch at Ben's Chili Bowl on U Street, followed by one of his frequent trips to Neiman Marcus at Mazza Gallerie. Staying on top of his fashionable wardrobe was a must, and he hardly ever wore the same thing twice.

As he drove up Wisconsin Avenue, he saw one of the finest women he'd ever laid eyes on getting off the bus. Shockingly, she reminded him of a taller version of his mother. She stood about 5'6" with long chestnut colored hair that accented her glowing caramel skin. He watched as the woman switched down the street swiftly in her pink Juicy Couture sweatsuit, that showed off her toned body.

Damn, what is a fine ass woman like that doing riding a bus, he thought. Pulling his white Mercedes S550 up beside her, Trae rolled down his tinted window. "Excuse me, gorgeous. Can I talk to you for a second?"

"Yeah, go ahead," the woman responded, as she continued to walk.

"Damn, you can't stop?" Trae asked.

"Look, I don't know you. So, no I can't!"

Trae laughed. He held up traffic as he slowly drove beside her. Normally he didn't bother with women who played hard to get, but this female seemed worth his time.

"You're feisty and I like that. My name is Trae."

The woman hesitated for a moment. "Hi Trae, my name is Karina. Is that it?"

"Nice to meet you, Karina," he said, yelling from his car window. As she kept walking, she could feel his eyes scanning her body. "A'ight, so now that we know each other, can you stop now? You gonna make me wreck my ride."

A NOVEL BY DANETTE MAJETTE

Karina sucked her teeth. "I'm not gonna make you do anything. If you wreck your ride, it's gonna be your own fault, sweetie."

"Is that so?"

"You know it."

After following Karina for a few more seconds, Trae pulled into an empty parking spot and jumped out to continue his pursuit. He was not about to let her get away without making a connection. "So, do you live around here?" he asked.

Karina looked at him like she was annoyed. "No, I don't."

"Annnnddd!" he asked.

"And what?"

"So you're not gonna tell me where you live?"

Karina stopped dead in her tracks "What are you a stalker or something? Or even worse, the police?"

Trae smiled. "That's funny."

"What is that suppose to mean?"

"Nothin'. It's just that I usually ask that question about the cops ."

Karina raised her eyebrows. "Really," she said.

Although Karina wasn't giving Trae the time of day, he was still intrigued with her, so giving up was not an option. "Look, all I want to do is take you out on a date," he said.

"Well, I don't go out with men I don't know," Karina responded, as she started walking again. This time she picked up her pace.

Trae walked briskly beside her, trying to keep up. "How you gonna get to know me if you don't go out wit' me?"

Karina stopped again and looked at him. "Touché."

"Does that mean you'll go out with me?" Trae asked.

Karina thought about it for a minute. Just as she was about to give him an answer, Courtney walked up out of the blue.

"Hey, Trae, remember me?" she asked, eyeing him like he was a piece of candy.

Trae turned around and looked at Courtney, who didn't look as good as she did when he first saw her at Anacostia Park, especially in her all white waiter's uniform. But her pecan colored skin and long dark wavy hair was still an attraction. "What's up," Trae said. "What are you doing around here?"

"I work at the Cheesecake Factory," Courtney answered, pointing to the restaurant. "Why haven't you called me?" she asked, looking at Karina from the corner of her eye.

No this bitch ain't trying to get with him right in front of me. What if I was his girl? Karina thought.

DEEP

"Umm...I've been a lil' busy, shorty," Trae replied hesitantly.

"Oh, my bad. Am I interrupting something?" Courtney asked, being sneaky.

"Actually honey, you are," Karina said, grabbing Trae by the arm. "Are you ready, Trae?"

"Bitch, it's not that serious!" Courtney shouted, getting buck.

"It is that serious. You're being very disrespectful and I don't appreciate it," Karina countered.

"I don't give a fuck what you appreciate," Courtney said, getting up in Karina's face. "Don't get it twisted. I'll fight your ass right in front of my muthafuckin' job. I've been looking for a reason to quit anyway."

Trae broke the two of them up just as they were about to start throwing blows. He grabbed Karina and continued to walk down the street.

"Trae!" He turned around. "Why don't you call me later tonight!" Courtney yelled. She ran her tongue across her lips. "I promise, you won't regret it."

Trae gave Courtney a smirk before turning back around.

Karina felt Trae had disrespected her by talking to Courtney. So after she let him have it, she told him to get lost.

"Why are you mad at me? I don't even know her like that," Trae said, in his defense.

"Whatever! Just go play with someone else, because I'm a grown woman. I don't have time for your games," Karina snapped.

Trae shook his head. He almost had Karina where he wanted her, and now he was back at square one. Courtney had managed to fuck up his day once again.

Man, that broad ain't nothin' but trouble. "Look, you heard when she said I didn't call her. That's because I wasn't interested. She's a lil' girl as you can see, and you're right, you're a woman. The kinda woman I need in my life."

Karina looked at Trae liked he was two short of a six pack. She didn't know much about him, but one thing was for sure...he had game.

"Come on. Give a brotha a chance."

Against her better judgment, she let down her guard. After talking for almost an hour, Trae and Karina finally exchanged numbers.

"Well, I gotta go. I'm late for my spa appointment," Karina said, looking at her watch.

Trae laughed. "You just got off a bus and you're going to the spa?"

Karina placed her hands of her hips. "Look, don't make me take my number back. I'm riding the bus because my car is in the shop, if you must know."

"Okay, don't shoot me," Trae responded with his hands in the air. He then reached in his pocket and pulled out three crisp one hundred dollar bills. "Here, this should cover your day at the spa, and a cab ride home. No beautiful woman, like yourself should be ridin' a bus."

She shook her head. "I'm not taking that. What kind of person gives a complete stranger three hundred dollars?"

"I don't consider you a stranger. You're gonna be my girl," he said smiling.

"Don't be so sure about that."

"Take the money," Trae replied, as he grabbed Karina's hand and placed the bills inside.

Thinking she would be going back and forth with him for hours, Karina decided to keep the money. "Thanks, but I hope you don't think you're gonna be my pimp or some shit by giving me this. I'm not a prostitute."

The comment instantly made Trae think about his mother. "Trust me, I would never treat you like a hooker. There's something I see in you that makes you special."

After talking for a few more minutes, they finally said their good-byes. Trae walked away with a huge smile on his face. Out of all the girls he'd met, Karina seemed different. He knew that if he played his cards right, she really could be the one.

Less than two hours later, Trae called Karina for a date, but she turned him down. As far as she was concerned, it was too soon. Karina's one flaw when it came to men was she never got to know them before she got too involved.

Her last boyfriend, Cory, of three years was a traveling business-man, who would leave for weeks at a time, closing deals for big corpo-rations. It wasn't until days after their four year anniversary that she realized what an asshole he was. On the eve of their anniversary, Karina found a receipt in his car for a ring. Excited that she was get-ting a two-carat marquise cut diamond ring, she kept quiet and waited for her gift.

After a beautiful candlelight dinner, the two retired to the living room in front of the fireplace to exchange gifts. Karina had practiced her surprised look in the bathroom mirror for hours. However, the practice was a waste of time, because as soon as she opened her eyes, they were bigger than a sumo wrestler. Her gift ended up being a picture of them on their first date in a beautiful Swarokski frame. After kissing her, Cory got up and told her he would meet her in the bedroom. That's when she knew something was wrong.

After some careful investigation, she found out the ring wasn't even her size, and had LUV U SAM inscribed on the inside. Karina felt faint, because at that moment, she knew there was somebody else in his life, and that person was more than likely a man.

Three days later, Cory told Karina he needed to go to Connecticut because a deal he was working on was falling apart. After telling her he would be gone for a few weeks, bells started to ring in her head. Hartford was the one city he spent a lot of time in, so Karina booked a reservation on the same flight. Disguised and sitting a few rows behind her man, she felt guilty for going to such great lengths to prove his infidelity.

Once the plane landed, Karina watched as Cory ran straight into the arms of another woman and two children. After watching them greet each other with a kiss, she quickly walked over and asked him who the woman was. With great attitude, the woman informed Karina that she was Samantha, Cory's wife of five years. That's when it clicked, the ring was meant for her, and that Sam was short for Samantha. Karina was furious. His wife then told Karina that she knew all about her stalking Cory, and that she needed to move on because he didn't love her.

The argument started out with verbal exchanges, but after Cory couldn't calm the two women down, it ended up a blood brawling cat-fight. The women pulled each other's hair, scratched, and even ripped each other's shirts off. After several minutes, and a couple of blows thrown his way, he finally got control of the situation with the help of airport security. As they stood, stripped down to their bras, the ladies still continued to exchange words, they didn't even take into consider-ation that there were kids present.

The revelation was a devastating blow to Karina, and she vowed to never let that happen to her again.

A NOVEL BY DANETTE MAJETTE

Trae pursued Karina for weeks, before she finally gave in and agreed to go out on a date. Little did he know, the only reason she was going out with him was because she had him checked out first. This proved to be difficult since they didn't run in the same circles. But after a few phone calls, she managed to find out from a friend that he didn't have a wife, or even a girlfriend for that matter. That was great news, because Karina was actually starting to get lonely for male companionship.

How could a guy that cute not have anyone, she thought to herself.

Stepping out of a sleek black limo, Trae and Karina both held huge smiles as he helped her out. Trae was prepared to dazzle Karina all evening, because he knew that if he wanted her to be his girl, he was going to have to pull out all the stops.

When they walked into the private room Trae reserved at Ruth Chris in Arlington, Karina was stunned. There were several candles lit, and rose pedals were scattered everywhere.

"I can't believe you did all this!" she said excitedly.

"Why? I don't look like the type," he said.

"Umm, not really," she said, with a smirk. "Just kidding!"

Trae laughed as he pulled her chair out.

The night went off without a hitch. Their steaks were cooked to perfection, and the conversation was just as divine. After eating and talking for hours, Trae suggested they take a ride around the city. Karina agreed.

She was amazed at how beautiful the city looked in late September when the leaves were turning colors. It was unusually warm for that time of year, so Trae took full advantage of the weather by taking Karina to Old Town, so they could walk around. Trae stepped out of the limo and escorted Karina to a secluded area by the water, where he had another surprise. As they approached a tall gentleman, he held out a dozen of red roses along with a bottle of Cristal.

"You did all this?" Karina asked, surprised. She watched as the strange man quickly disappeared.

"Yeah, I hope you like champagne," Trae said, popping the cork.

Karina snickered. "Wow, the tough guy has a soft spot."

"Only for beautiful women, and you are definitely beautiful," he said, kissing her hand.

DEEP

Trae handed Karina a glass of champagne. "Let's toast."

"Toast to what?" she asked.

Trae looked at Karina, whose brown eyes matched her beautiful skin tone. "Let's toast to a new friendship," he said.

Karina raised her glass. "To a new friendship."

A NOVEL BY DANETTE MAJETTE

DEEP

NEVER JUDGE A BOOK BY ITS COVER

The next day, Trae went to check on his strip club called Pleasures, located on Georgia Avenue near the historic Howard University campus. The club was one of the many things that Trae had purchased with his drug money. It catered to everyone...from hustlers to businessmen, and employed some of the finest women in D.C. Draped in silk red curtains that hung from the ceiling, and several red leather couches and chairs, Pleasures was the hot spot. There were three bars, a huge VIP section for private parties, along with a main stage and two smaller stages on each side.

As soon as he opened the door, Trae walked in and noticed an unfamiliar woman standing at the bar. He wanted to say she was the most stunning sight he'd ever seen, but he thought that way about all the ladies. With Citizen of Humanity jeans that hugged her ass with perfection, a pair of black stilettos, and a Chanel bag thrown across her shoulder, the woman danced to a Missy Elliot song that played in the background. The way she swung her hips was a rhythm that Trae could definitely dance to.

"Hey beautiful, you lost?" Trae asked, walking up to her. He smiled as he admired her light complexion and beautiful light green eyes.

"First of all, my name ain't beautiful, it's Sommone," she said, with an attitude that immediately turned Trae on. "And yes, I'm lost. I'm looking for the owner."

"Oh, he just stepped out. But I can take you to his office if you want to leave him a note," Trae replied.

She appeared disappointed "Oh, that would be great," Sommone answered.

"Cool, follow me, beautiful. Umm...I mean Sommone," Trae said, with a devilish smile. He turned around and walked down the tight hallway.

When they reached the office, Trae handed Sommone a pad and pen. "So, what do you need to see the owner about?" he asked.

A NOVEL BY DANETTE MAJETTE

"That's between me and him. Just give him this," she said, handing him the paper with her name and number on it.

Before she walked out, Trae grabbed her by the arm and confessed he was actually the owner.

"Oh, so you like playing games, huh?" Sommone asked, standing so close to Trae it instantly made his dick stand at attention. She could tell what she'd been told was true. Trae was definitely a womanizer.

He eyed Sommone up and down. "I'm sorry. I was just havin' a little fun wit' you. My name is Trae, the owner of this spot," he said. "Sit down. What can I do for you?"

Sitting on the plush leather couch, Sommone explained that she had just moved to the area and needed a job. "I use to dance in Atlanta, but my mother died recently, and I needed to get away from the memories," she said.

Trae was a true businessman and never missed an opportunity to make more money, and there was no doubt in his mind, Sommone could do that. Especially since she used to dance in ATL...they were known for their strippers. *Damn, this bitch is bound to bring in a crowd,* he thought, as he looked down at her cleavage that was peeping out of her low cut top. *Yeah, that body alone is gonna bring in tons of thirsty niggas.*

"I tell you what, I'll give you a chance, but don't let me down," Trae said, trying to sound like he wasn't sure.

"I won't," Sommone replied. She got up and threw her arms around him.

I'ma fuck the shit out of you, baby. You just don't know it yet, Trae said to himself.

Just as he was about to get more in depth with his new employee, Kevin walked through the door.

"What's up, man?" Kevin asked.

"Kev, man, this is our new dancer, Sommone," Trae replied. He knew Kevin would be happy, since he was fond of red bones.

"Nice to meet you," Kevin said, trying to figure out where he knew her from.

Needing to talk to Kevin in private, Trae told Sommone that he'd call her tomorrow with her schedule, then escorted her to the door.

"Yo', Trae what's her name again?" Kevin asked.

"Sommone," Trae said, sitting at his desk. He immediately began shuffling through the large stacks of paperwork that had been there for weeks.

"Umm, I think I know that bitch from somewhere," Kevin said.

DEEP

"You always actin' like you know every damn body. You don't know her, she just moved here from Atlanta," Trae insisted.

Trae was sure Kevin was mistaken, so he changed the subject. "So, what's the deal?" he asked.

"Man, I got us a new connect in Miami. All we got to do is get the money to him," Kevin said.

Trae was a little hesitant about dealing with new connects, but he didn't have a choice since his old connect, Yakeem, hadn't been released from jail yet. If he didn't get some product soon, he was going to lose his credibility on the streets, and he couldn't have that. Everyone knew that if they ever needed work, they could get it from him.

"Look, Kevin, since that shootin' shit last month, the Feds have been tryin' their damndest to get at me. So, before we set anythin' up wit' that nigga, I need to have him checked out first."

Kevin agreed. "I'll talk to my connects at the Second District Police Station. It's about time they start workin' for all the dough they bleedin' out of us," he said.

"Man, I couldn't agree with you more," Trae said, nodding his head.

Having police officers on the payroll was an idea Trae came up with when he first started out. It was expensive, but well worth it.

When Sommone walked outside the club, she pulled out her cell phone. Looking around to make sure no one was around, she dialed a number. "Come get me."

Click.

Sommone walked about two blocks, before a Dodge Magnum pulled up beside her. She stopped walking when she heard the door to the passenger side unlock.

"Took you long enough," she said, as she got inside and fastened her seatbelt.

"Did he buy it?" the male occupant asked.

"Like a new pair of Jordans," she said chuckling. "I start tomorrow."

The man passed Sommone a set of keys, and took her to where she would be staying. Before she got out of the car, she looked at her new residence, then back at the driver.

"This is a joke, right," she said.

"You're supposed to be broke. This is broke," he said, pointing to the old apartment building. He could see she was pissed. "Look, if all goes to plan, you won't be here long."

"Well, you just better make sure it does," she said, getting out of the car.

"I will. See you tomorrow, and remember be careful. Trae's no dummy."

When Sommone entered the building, the smell of piss and weed instantly hit her in the face. "No, I need to get out of here sooner than he thinks," she said, as she walked up the short flight of steps.

As she approached the front door, she slowly pulled out the keys. Sommone dreaded what the inside would look like. However, when she opened the front door, she let out a small sigh of relief. The apartment wasn't as bad on the inside. *At least I got some decent furniture.*

After throwing her purse on the couch, she walked into the bathroom and turned the shower on. At that point, she didn't care how stylish the place was. Showers always relieved whatever stress she had. Sommone kicked off her shoes, and slowly took off her clothes before taking off the honey colored wig that she'd worn, just for the occasion. Underneath the hot strands of hair, was a short curly haircut that only had to be brushed. Luckily, she'd gotten her good hair texture from her father, who was white. The shower felt good as she placed her entire body under the hot steamy water. After lathering the soap just right, her mind flashed back to her meeting with Trae. *Damn, he was fine, with a triple threat. Dark, tall and bald, but I can't forget what I'm here for.*

Several minutes later, the water started to get cold. "Shit," Sommone yelled out, "I haven't even been in here long!"

She quickly turned off the water and stepped out the shower, looking for a towel. When she couldn't find one, she walked into the bedroom, dripping wet. At that moment, Sommone realized that she hadn't brought any clothes with her.

What else can go wrong today? Just as she was about to lay in the bed naked, she noticed a Macy's bag on the floor. When she looked inside and saw the clothes, along with toiletries and two fluffy white towels, she smiled. *He always takes care of me.*

Later that evening, Sommone thought about how she was going to pull off the impossible as she laid in the bed. She'd always excelled in everything she committed her time and energy to, but this was going to be one of the most difficult things she's ever had to do.

DEEP

HEAR ME OUT

The following Friday, Trae traded in a night of girls, drinking and hanging out with his boys at H2O nightclub, his favorite spot for another romantic dinner with Karina. It didn't take long for his boys to start calling him pussy whipped, after spending all his time with the same girl, but in return, all he would do was laugh. Little did his boys know, he and Karina hadn't even been intimate yet. This was unusual for Trae, because he could have a different girl every hour if he wanted to. Especially since he was constantly surrounded by tits and ass. It also didn't hurt that he was paid. Girls at the club would do almost anything to have a private meeting in his office, but he often found himself thinking about Karina. That's how he knew he really liked her.

When he pulled up in front of Karina's house, she jumped in the car with a huge smile. "Hey, what's up," she said.

Her peach scented body lotion instantly made Trae's dick hard, but he tried his best to think of something else. "Let's see. Where can we go eat this time?" Trae said, teasing Karina. Deciding where to eat was a challenge for them since she loved seafood, and he was more of a steak and potatoes type of guy.

"I don't know. You decide since you seem to be the picky one," Karina replied.

"I know, how 'bout Morton's Steakhouse? I heard they have great lobster tails." Trae knew it was foul to act like he'd never been there before. It was actually one of his favorite places to eat. He also knew there was a chance of him running into one of the waitresses he'd fucked, but he didn't care. The mouth watering New York Strip was calling his name.

"Sounds good to me," Karina replied.

Twenty minutes later, they walked into the upscale restaurant on Connecticut Avenue, looking like the happy couple. Even though there was a thirty minute wait, as soon as the hostess saw Trae, she seated them right away.

As Trae sat down, he immediately noticed the hard stares from two of the waitresses who stood near the bar. He watched as the two women whispered back and forth in each other's ear. Then one of them had the nerve to bring him a Remy and Coke, knowing he didn't ask for one. Trae tried to play it off by telling her she must've had the wrong table. Pissed, he sent the drink back and made a mental note to set her straight when he got a free moment to call her. *Bitches always hating,* he thought. By the look on Karina's face, she wasn't too amused herself.

They both started out with Caesar salads, then moved on to their entrees. Karina had the jumbo lump crab cakes, while Trae opted for the New York Strip, of course. During dinner, Karina asked Trae what he did for a living. She knew he owned a club, but a club wasn't pulling in the kind of cash to afford all the luxury things he owned, like his beautiful home in Bethesda,Maryland and all his vehicles.

Caught off guard by her question, Trae tried to change the subject, "How's your food?" he asked.

"So, in other words, mind my business," she said, putting her fork down.

"Naw, I'm not saying that," Trae responded.

"Then answer my question," Karina said firmly. The last thing she wanted was someone who played games. Especially after all the drama Cory had taken her through.

"I'm in to all kinds of stuff. Mostly real estate and stocks, but you name it, I'm into it," Trae stated.

Karina could tell Trae was hiding something, but she wanted to give him the benefit of doubt. "Real estate, huh. So, how's the market?" she asked.

Trae was caught off guard again, but kept his cool. "It's good." He knew he should've answered the question with a little bit more detail, but couldn't. *Shit, all I know is how the drug market is doing, baby. As a matter of fact, the price of coke has sky rocketed.*

Karina looked at Trae suspiciously, then went back to her food. As she placed a piece of crab meat in her mouth, she secretly hoped he wasn't lying.

"So how old are you, if you don't mind me asking?" Trae said.

"Didn't your mother ever teach you not to ask a woman her age?"

Trae held a serious look. "No, my mother didn't get a chance to teach me a lot of things."

DEEP

Karina didn't know what that meant, but knew Trae wasn't in a joking mood. "I'm twenty-five. And you?"

"Twenty-seven."

Karina smiled. "So, you're almost at the big 3-0, huh?"

"Yeah, hopefully I make it there."

Karina gave Trae a concerned look. *What the hell does that mean? Damn I hope I don't regret going out with this dude.*

After eating, Trae took Karina straight home. All throughout dinner she stressed over and over how she had to run an errand early the next day, and didn't want to be out late. When they arrived, Trae got out the car and walked around to the passenger side door. After opening it, he extended his hand to help her out.

Before she could even thank him, Trae pulled Karina close and nudged her chin close to his lips. His hands marveling all over Karina's body gave her chills, and almost made her let out a slight moan, but she stopped herself. Taking things slow was her number one priority, so she quickly pulled away and told him goodnight. All Trae could do was laugh. He knew it was only a matter of time before she gave in. He placed a soft kiss on Karina's cheek and walked her to the door. Once she was in her home safely, he turned around, got back in the car and drove away. *Man, I hope this gentleman shit is working in my favor,* he thought.

Karina arrived at her job at Nordstrom's in Pentagon City Mall around eight o'clock that Monday morning. She had worked at the department store for five years and had just been promoted to a manager in the men's department. Every since high school, she had always dreamed of a career in fashion, so helping customers pick out clothing was right up her alley.

First on her list was to re-merchandise her floor, then put away the new shipment. Then she attended her usual Monday morning manager's meeting. However, during the meeting, Karina could hardly concentrate because she kept thinking about her date with Trae. For some reason, she knew he could possibly be trouble, but it was that same bad boy image that turned her on. The only thing she didn't like was the fact that girls practically ignored her when she was with him. But what could she do? He was fine, and even more importantly, paid. A lethal combination for any gold digger.

A NOVEL BY DANETTE MAJETTE

Around noon, Karina's stomach started to do flips as the thought of food danced around her head. She wanted to go to lunch, but since she was the only one in her department, she had to wait until one o'clock. To keep her mind off being hungry, she started on her new schedule. She usually worked nights, but had recently changed her schedule to the morning shift. *I need to keep my nights open for Trae,* she thought. However, her thoughts were cut short when the phone rang.

"Thanks for calling the Rail...this is Karina. How may I help you?"

"You can start by getting undressed for me."

"Excuse me?" Karina asked, about to lose it.

Trae laughed. "It's me. I'm just playin' wit' you."

"You were seriously about to get it."

"I know. I just wanted to call and see how your day was going," Trae said.

Karina smiled as she told him all about her morning. She could tell that he was trying hard to win her over, but it was going to take more than a call to see how she was doing to accomplish that goal.

"So, what do you have planned for tonight?" Trae asked.

"I think I'm going to stay in tonight and catch up on some sleep since you've been keeping me up so late," Karina replied.

"A'ight, I'll let you catch up on your rest, but Saturday night belongs to me."

"You got it," Karina replied. She hung up the phone and continued writing out her schedule.

Right before lunch, a dozen red roses were delivered to Karina's department. When she found out they were for her, she smiled as thoughts of her magical date in Old Town suddenly appeared.

She walked over to the gorgeous bouquet and smelled one of the roses, before pulling out the little white card. As she read the note, which said, "To the future Mrs. Trae Keal," she held the card close to her heart, took a deep breath and exhaled.

"What does it say?" her hyper co-worker, roommate, and best friend, Ashley asked. When Karina proudly showed her the card, Ashley wasn't amused. She'd heard about Trae from another girl who'd already been hurt by him. "Karina, I don't want to be the bearer of bad news, but Trae isn't what you think he is," she pleaded, trying to spare her friend's feelings.

Karina looked at her chubby best friend and smiled. They'd been friends since the third grade. "Ash, there are still some good men left in the world," she said.

DEEP

"Yeah, well Trae ain't one of them," Ashley replied, sliding the card across the counter. "Do you know, Dominique who works in the shoe department...well he used to mess with her too. I can see if she's working today, so she can tell you about it."

"No, I'll pass," Karina responded trying her best to ignore Ashley.

"I'm serious Karina. Trae hit it, then dumped her ass. Dominique said he did another girl like that before her too."

"Don't hate, girl. You'll find a man soon," Karina said jokingly. She knew that would get under Ashley's skin. Besides, she was having a good day and didn't want to discuss the subject anymore.

"Yeah, whatever!" Ashley responded as she walked away.

After lunch, Karina tried to forget what Ashley said about Trae by staying busy. She trained a new employee, in between helping a few of her favorite customers, and then completed her schedule. At five o'clock sharp, she straightened her department, clocked out, and waited for Ashley outside the store. Even though she loved her job, she still looked forward to the end of her shift.

Throughout the entire ride home, Karina could tell that Ashley was still annoyed. It was obvious her friend needed to get something off her chest.

"What's your problem?" Karina asked.

Ashley always had to be the one to get her point across. "I don't have a problem, but you do, and his name is Trae!" she shouted.

Here we go again. "Why do you keep making snide remarks about him?" Karina asked.

Ashley knew even if she told Karina what Trae did for a living, it wouldn't matter and was probably too late. Her friend was already falling for the popular hustler. The flowers and fancy restaurants were all a part of Trae's game to trap her in his web.

When Karina pulled up in front of their apartment, she put the car in park. There was a brief pause before she said, "Trae has been nothing but a total gentleman to me." She then turned to Ashley, who looked like Pocahontas with the long bone straight weave she wore. "He hasn't even tried to sleep with me yet."

"He doesn't have to. He can have any girl he wants!" Ashley yelled.

"Well, he doesn't want them. He wants me! Why can't you accept that?"

Frustrated by Karina's naïve demeanor, Ashley got out of the car, slammed the door and stormed into their apartment. Karina quickly followed behind her,

"Why can't you just be happy for me?" Karina asked, as she walked in the apartment and closed the door.

Ashley stood in the doorway of her room with her arms folded. "If it was any other guy, I would. Trust me, Trae is no good for you," she said.

"What's wrong with him?" Karina asked.

"I don't know. Let's see, for one he's a kingpin."

Staring at Ashley with a blank expression on her face, Karina asked, "What did you say?"

"I said he's a kingpin."

Without even responding, Karina turned around and walked into the bathroom. Staring at her reflection in the mirror, she recalled their most recent date. *His lying ass told me he was into real estate. Damn, why do I always have to attract the dudes who run game?*

DEEP

SOMMONE'S DEBUT

In a room only lit by blinking lights, Sommone strolled out, swirling the tail of her sexy black cat costume. Dancing like she was born for the spotlight, she moved provocatively to the beat of Beyonce's *Kitty Kat* song. Once she was feeling the crowd, she dove off the stage into the waiting arms of a sweaty guy, who was sitting front and center. His groping hands were all over her body.

Sommone wanted to loosen his grip, but she caught a glimpse of Trae out the corner of her eye. *I gotta make this look good,* she thought. So, instead, she climbed back on stage and put on a show that made even Trae throw a couple of dollars her way. Even Sommone had to admit to herself that she worked the pole better than any of Trae's other dancers.

In the middle of her routine, she felt a pair of hands on her inner thighs that began to slide upward.

"Watch it, daddy. My kitty bites," she said, in a taunting voice.

"Well let it bite me, baby," the guy responded, smacking her on the thigh.

Sommone looked around for Trae, but didn't see him. Instead, she saw the faces of dozens of horny men. The guy began to pull on her skimpy outfit until it tore, and then with one final yank, the black outfit fell to the ground. The crowd went wild as her 38C boobs stood at attention. With everyone's eyes glued to her ass, guys immediately ran up to the stage and started throwing money. Her first instinct was to make a quick exit, but she knew she couldn't do that. She had worked too hard to get close to Trae, so she sucked it up and kept dancing. Besides, the countless dollar bills that covered the stage did-n't hurt. *I'll consider that my overtime pay.*

As Sommone bent over and touched her ankles, she shook her ass, and swayed it from side to side. Before ending her routine with a finale on the famous silver pole, one man managed to grab hold of her wig, as he pulled himself closer to her bare tits. Sommone prayed it wouldn't come off, and looked around for Trae again. When she finally spotted him, he just smiled from the sideline as he watched the man drop fifty dollars and let her hair go. Once her set was finished, Sommone picked up her money and hurried past Trae toward the dressing room.

"Hey wait!" Trae yelled. She could hear his footsteps on the porcelain tile behind her, but never bothered to stop. The last thing she wanted was to stand in front of him with only a thong on. When Trae opened the door to the dressing room, he found Sommone standing in front of the mirror with a sexy black lace robe on.

"Damn, you didn't hear me callin' you?" he asked. He was a bit annoyed, because when he spoke, all the girls in his club listened.

"I'm sorry. It's just that this is my first night dancing here, and I'm not quite comfortable being nude in front of you if I'm not on stage," Sommone replied.

How in the hell can a stripper be shy? Plus, it's not like this is her first damn gig. "Well, I just wanted to say that you were great. The fellas loved you," Trae said, standing close to her.

"Thank you for giving me a chance, I really needed this job," Sommone replied, giving him a hug. The smell of her sweaty skin intoxicated him and his heart rate increased as he lost his concentration. All he could think about was how Sommone looked on stage. Especially the way her body moved to the music. It was almost hypnotic.

"You okay?" Sommone asked, noticing Trae's blank expression.

"Yeah…yeah, I was just thinkin' about somethin'."

I know what the fuck you were thinking about. You're so pathetic! You have no idea what I have in store for you, Sommone thought smiling at Trae.

"Why don't you go to my office and relax 'til I get there. Then we can go have a drink at the bar," Trae said.

When Sommone agreed, he kissed her on the hand and walked out the dressing room. *Damn, if it weren't for Karina, I would fuck the shit out of her,* he thought, looking down at the bulge in his pants.

Once in Trae's office, Sommone quickly closed the door behind her, ran over to Trae's desk and began to fumble through his stuff.

DEEP

"Shit, nothing!" she said, closing two of the drawers. As she sat down to open the last drawer, she noticed a beautiful mink rug on the floor under his desk. *That's an odd place for such an expensive rug.* When she pulled the dark colored rug back, she shook her head and smiled. *Wow, this nigga is pretty creative. A safe in the floor is surely better than in the wall,* she thought, as she stared at the expensive Gardall safe. Sommone tried to play around with the push button lock for a few seconds, but nothing happened. She was about to try again, but was suddenly interrupted.

"Surprise!" Karina yelled, as she opened the door. Of course she was the one who was surprised when she saw Sommone in her skimpy attire. "Where's Trae? Better yet, who are you?" she asked, with an attitude.

"Hi, I'm Sommone. I work here," she said, as she stood up from behind Trae's desk. "I think he went to go throw a dude out who snatched my costume off while I was performing."

"Oh, so I guess you were about to perform in here next," Karina said, eyeing Sommone up and down. She couldn't help but be a little bit jealous of her shapely figure.

Sommone was confused by Karina's remark, until she glanced down and noticed that she was still wearing her robe.

"Oh God...no. I can assure you it's nothing like that. I'm..." Sommone stopped talking.

"You're what?" Karina interrupted, with her eyebrows raised.

"Nothing. I'm gonna go. Can you tell Trae I'll see him tomorrow?" Sommone said.

Karina didn't respond. She just gave her a strange look. Obviously, Sommone got the message and left the room quickly.

When Trae finally returned, Karina was sitting behind his desk with her hands folded and her foot tapping against the floor. Surprised by her unannounced visit, he walked over to her and tried to place a kiss on her cheek, but Karina pulled away.

"What's wrong wit' you?" he asked. "I'm sorry if you been waitin' long, but I didn't know you were comin'. I had to deal with this guy that got a little rough with one of my dancers."

Karina folded her arms. "You mean the one who was in here half naked waiting on you?"

"She wasn't waitin' on me," he lied. "Where is she anyway?" *Damn, I forgot I told Sommone's fine ass to wait for me.*

"She left, obviously," Karina said, with an attitude.

A NOVEL BY DANETTE MAJETTE

Trae tried to calm the waters by assuring Karina nothing was going on, but she was still skeptical. The crazy thing was, she was more suspicious of Sommone. Karina sensed she was up to no good. She knew Trae would think it was a jealousy thing, so she kept quiet and vowed to keep her eyes and ears open where Sommone was concerned. She also decided not to confront him about what he did for a living, which was why she was there in the first place. For some reason, she just didn't feel like hearing any more lies.

Sommone had walked three blocks, when a black Yukon pulled up next to her and blew the horn. She jumped in the back seat and pulled her wig off. "Damn, I couldn't wait to take that hot ass thing off," she said.

"What you got for me?" the stranger said.

"Well, I know he keeps a safe under a mink rug in his office," Sommone replied, exhausted.

"Anything else?"

"Yeah, I ran into a girl, who I think is his girlfriend."

"What's she like?" he asked.

Sommone sucked her teeth and sighed. "She acts like one of those high maintenance chicks. She actually thought I was after his dumb ass."

"Little does she know you are. Just not in the way she thinks." They both laughed.

When the driver pulled up in front of Sommone's apartment he turned and told her good night.

"Are you coming in?" Sommone asked, with puppy dog eyes.

"I can't risk it," he responded.

Disappointed with his answer, Sommone opened the door, got out the truck and slowly walked toward her lonely new home.

DEEP

THE NEW WOMAN IN TOWN

Special Agent, Carmen Nichols looked at Trae out the corner of her eye as he held up his glass to toast with his crew. She could hardly wait until it was time for her to make her move, so she constantly fidgeted in her seat. She'd been briefed and debriefed for months about Trae's crew and her role in his organization, so now she was ready for the games to begin.

As Trae held up a bottle of expensive champagne and refilled his crew's glasses, Carmen continued to give him a discreet stare. She settled into a booth across from Trae at club H20, where Trae spent most of his Friday nights.

Look at that fool. Anyone who wanted to kill him could, he's here every fuckin' Friday, she thought.

Trae was known around D.C. to be a notorious drug dealer, so being a few feet away from him without being able to lock him up was starting to bother Carmen. She began to think about her first drug case when she joined the FBI. She had been on an assignment to bring down a huge drug lord in Florida, but instead of locking him up, she let her guard down and fell in love with him.

A week later, when she was on a date with the guy, she missed an important check in with her superior. Had she gone to the meeting, Carmen would've found out that her cover had been blown and that she needed to get out. By the time the Feds got to her, she was already lying in a pool of blood with two gunshots to the chest. If it wasn't for her bullet proof vest, she would've died.

Like the Miami drug lord, Carmen knew she had to be careful, because Trae and his crew were notorious for getting rid of anyone who threatened their camp. If her cover was ever blown, she knew they wouldn't care that she was a woman. That's why it was so important for her to be on point at all times. She learned from her last assignment, that attention to detail was essential, especially since it could save her life. A waitress interrupted Carmen's thoughts.

"What can I get for you?" the waitress asked.

"Just some water," Carmen said.

"Don't you think you should get something to help you look a little more believable?" the waitress asked.

Carmen felt stupid. "Oh yeah, then make it a martini."

"There you go. It's not like you're really paying for it," the waitress said, as she walked back to place the order.

That's Agent Gates for you. Always saying something smart out her damn mouth, Carmen thought. Gates and Carmen had gone to the Academy together, but didn't really care for one another. Gates was a blond bombshell, who was always the brunt of dumb blond jokes. Carmen and several male agents never took her serious, because they thought she made her way up the chain of command because of her looks. Ironically, she was always put on assignments that required a beautiful female agent, and was never put on assignments that could potentially be dangerous.

When Agent Gates returned with Carmen's drink, she winked her eye to let Carmen know that everyone was in place. Carmen sat and playfully sipped on her drink, while keeping a close eye on Trae.

Like clockwork, at two a.m., Trae received a call on his cell phone. Not able to hear the person on the other end of the receiver clearly, Trae motioned to Kevin that he was going outside. As soon as he got up, Carmen followed slowly without being suspicious.

With only one foot out the door, gunshots suddenly rang out as soon as Trae stepped outside. He dipped behind a car, slipped his Glock from his waist, and placed his index finger on the trigger. With Carmen taking cover next to Trae, they both shot back at the vehicle screeching down the street. Like the Secret Service, within minutes Trae's crew ran out to see what was going on. Trying to help Trae to his feet, Carmen asked if he was alright.

"Yeah, I'm okay. Good lookin' out, shorty," Trae said. Leaning up against a parked car, he bent over in an attempt to catch his breath. "What's a cutie like you doin' packin' heat?"

"Forget all that, who was those niggas?" Carmen asked, putting away her piece. She'd been practicing for months on her street dialogue. Hopefully it was believable.

"I don't know. All I know is if it wasn't for you, I might not be standing here," Trae said, staring Carmen in her beautiful almond shaped eyes.

"Don't worry about it. Just let yo' man and them take you home.

DEEP

Until you find out who those muthafuckas were, I think you need to keep them close." Before Trae could answer, Carmen walked away with him eyeing her like she was his prey.

Suddenly, the outside of the club became total mayhem. A dozen police officers rolled up on the scene and jumped out like they were ready for war, as curious spectators looked on. The police tried their best to piece together what happened but were unsuccessful. No one wanted to cooperate.

Trying to get Trae out of there, Kevin ran to the end of the street where his truck was parked, pulled it up in front of the club, then rushed Trae home as Big Paul and Ice Man followed closely behind. "Who was that chick?" Kevin asked, looking around for anyone suspicious. "Did she hold it down for you?"

"Yeah. We could use a chick like that. Niggas won't know what hit them," Trae responded.

Kevin shook his head. "Hell no!" he yelled. "We don't need any bitches in our crew. Besides, they too much trouble."

Trae didn't bother to respond. He knew if they got into a debate it would last forever, so he decided to let Kevin think he was right. Little did Kevin know, he always called the shots and had the final say so.

"Don't worry, I'ma find out who those niggas were and deal wit' 'em," Kevin said, like he was ready for war. This was just the kinda shit he lived for.

"Good, 'cuz those niggas are gonna wish they missed," Trae responded.

An hour later, Trae's crew members, Ice Man and Big Paul knocked on a few doors around one of their drug spots in Southeast, D.C., to see if anyone knew who the shooters were. Trae wanted to know who was behind the shooting because in his mind, they had just committed suicide.

DEEP

TONIGHT'S THE NIGHT

Trae rushed into the front door of his house like he was on a mission. He'd left one of his drug spots extra early, to spend the rest of the evening with Karina, which was highly unusual, because normally nothing came between him and his money. It had been a week or so since someone had tried to kill him at the club, and he wanted to make sure that the heat had died down before he went out with her again. He knew that the dudes who shot at him were live wires, and he didn't want to put Karina in that sort of danger.

After showering and changing into his Armani slacks and a white button up shirt, Trae jumped back into his car and sped off to the Northeast side of town.

A few minutes later, he was double parked in front of Karina's apartment. He took two steps at a time as he ran up to the door.

"Hey gorgeous," he said, kissing Karina on the cheek when she opened the door. "You ready?"

"Not really. I meant to call and tell you that I didn't feel like going out tonight," Karina replied. She didn't appear to be in a good mood.

There was a puzzled looked on Trae's face. "What's wrong? You sick?" he asked.

"I guess you can say that."

They both stood silent for a few seconds until Trae broke the silence. "Cool, we'll just stay in tonight. I'll even cook," he replied, with a face that any woman would fall in love with.

Karina started to pace back and forth, and before she knew it, she was screaming at Trae. "Why did you lie to me?" she asked. Every since Ashley had told her about Trae being a kingpin, she'd held out on her question, but she couldn't take it any longer. She had to know. She was glad that Ashley was out for the evening, because Karina knew her friend would've made a smart comment about Trae being

A NOVEL BY DANETTE MAJETTE

there.

"Lie to you about what?" he asked, pushing Karina back into her apartment for privacy.

When Karina confronted him about what he did for a living, he stood quietly, and mentally prepared himself for an explanation. After a long silence and a few deep sighs, he finally responded.

"I don't have an excuse. I was wrong. I just thought that if I told you the truth, you wouldn't want to be bothered wit' me," he said.

"Well, you're right. I can't be involved with someone like you."

"Some...one...like...me." Trae's face grew hot with anger.

His mood scared Karina. "Trae, I want you to leave."

"I'm not goin' no where 'til you listen to me," Trae ordered.

Her hands started to shake.

Trae moved to the living room and sat down. He immediately began to pour his heart out about how his mother was killed, and how he had to grow up in the streets in order to survive. He felt that was the only way he could get Karina to understand.

"I've never felt this way about anybody in my life. Yeah, I do sell drugs, but that don't have anythin' to do wit' us. I love you!" he yelled, before grabbing Karina and pulling her close. "The only way I'm gonna leave is if you look me in the eye and tell me you don't feel the same way," he said, putting his strong arms around her. He whispered sweet thoughts in her ear, as he sucked and kissed on her lobe.

A chill ran through her body as he moved downward and kissed her lips. He stopped suddenly and looked into her eyes. "Give me a chance. Please," he begged.

Karina's heart was saying no, but her body was saying yes. Even Trae picked up on her vibes. Then he went in for the kill. "If you forgive me, I promise I'll never do anythin' to hurt you." He really did a number on her when he said that, because after his comment, she led him straight to her bedroom.

As they laid naked on her plush queen sized bed, Trae gently opened Karina's legs and positioned himself between her thighs. He slowly moved his dick around her lips until she slowly began to squirm. Anxiously, she reached underneath and forced his dick inside her. Karina had no idea how long their relationship would last, but she wanted him at that moment. Trae could feel her walls tighten as he pushed himself further inside.

"Damn, you feel good," he whispered, out of breath.

Trae instructed Karina to get on her knees. When she followed his orders, he gently rubbed her ass before separating her cheeks,

DEEP

then slid his stiff dick inside her pussy. She moaned as her body arched up off the bed.

"Yes! Yes!" Karina screeched in pleasure.

She began to rock her body, throwing her ass back against him like she had something to prove. He grabbed her hair as she arched her back to give him the perfect angle, which gave him immediate satisfaction. Pumping faster, Trae watched as his thrusts made Karina grip the sheets on her bed tightly.

"Fuck me harder," she grunted.

The sound of Karina's order enticed Trae even more. He immediately flipped her over on her back, and placed her legs over his shoulders.

"Oh...umm...aahhh," Karina moaned.

"Does this feel good, baby?" Trae asked.

"Yes...yes!" Karina responded as she bit her bottom lip.

"Damn, you feel good too," Trae hissed, as he continued to dig deeper inside of Karina's walls.

At that moment, he tried to hold out a little longer, but couldn't. Instead, his body stiffened. "Shiiiittttt," he groaned, until his dick went soft.

Early the next morning, Trae's cell phone rang waking Karina. She turned and gave him a disapproving stare as he quickly checked the caller ID.

"See, I'm not even gonna answer it," he said, turning the phone off, then placing it on her nightstand.

"Good." She turned her back toward him and pushed her naked body up against his.

To Trae's delight, Karina's sex drive was still in full throttle. They made love twice before they even ate breakfast.

DEEP

SURPRISE SURPRISE

Over the next few weeks, Trae's crew was on a rampage. Christmas was only a month away, but spreading good cheer wasn't a part of their plan. Anyone that had ever threatened or looked at them wrong got paid a visit, and it wasn't a pleasant one either. Trae was determined to find out who tried to kill him, and no one was enjoying the chase more than Kevin. Trae had given him full authorization to do whatever he wanted in order to find the culprits. They even set a plan in motion to go back to H20, to see if the same thing would happen again.

The following Friday, Trae went back to his favorite spot, as his boys waited in different cars outside. All throughout the night, he drank and socialized as usual. The last thing he needed was for the targets to realize he was after them too. He even walked outside by himself a couple of times, to see if anyone tried anything, but nothing ever happened. Eventually, Trae decided to end his investigation and motioned for Kevin and Ice Man to follow him inside.

However, as soon as he entered the club, he recognized a familiar face. Strolling over with his third Heineken, Trae sent his crew away and boldly sat down beside the beautiful woman who reminded him of Chili from TLC. With her jet black hair hugging her shoulders and a Bebe sweatsuit on, Carmen sat at a table bobbing her head to the reggae blasting from the club's speakers.

"What's up, beautiful? I ain't seen you since that night you saved my life," Trae said, sitting his beer on the table.

"Oh yeah. What's up? With all the excitement going on, I forgot to get your name that night," Carmen replied.

"It's Trae. What's yours?"

"Carmen."

Trae smiled, noticing her full lips and beautiful skin tone. "So…

A NOVEL BY DANETTE MAJETTE

where you from Miss Carmen?"

"I just moved here from Jamaica."

"Jamaica. Wow, that's sounds excitin'. I lose my mind just visitin', so I can't even imagine livin' there," he responded. "So, why don't you have an accent?"

Carmen was caught off guard. "Oh…well, I only lived there for a few years. I'm originally from Philly," she said.

"Um…interesting," Trae said, in serious thought.

Trae sat and talked with Carmen for hours. Her tough exterior, yet soft interior, intrigued him. He couldn't explain it, but he felt a connection. After listening to what seemed like Carmen's life story, a light bulb went off in his head.

"Hey, give me yo' number. I think I might have a job for you. That's if you interested," Trae said, pulling out his blackberry.

He knew trusting Carmen so soon was unusual for him, but he had a feeling that she was harmless. It also didn't help that she was beautiful. Trae stared at her smooth cinnamon brown skin. Women were definitely his weakness.

Wow, the plan is really working. "Hell yeah, I'm interested. I need to start makin' some dough," Carmen said with excitement. When she smiled, a dimple popped up on the left side of her face.

Trae gave a slight grin. "Damn, you make it sound like you're unemployed or some shit. So now I'm curious. What's up wit' you?"

"Well, I would rather not talk about it here. But let's just say I was involved in a little bit of this and that," Carmen responded.

"Cool, I'll get the details later."

Kevin walked up as Carmen was giving her number to Trae. He knew Trae was up to something, but he had no idea he was offering Carmen a job. Especially since hiring someone new was something they usually discussed with each other first.

"It looks like I just missed something important," Kevin said smiling. The huge Polo shirt he wore drowned his slender frame. He always wore clothes to make him look larger, but it never worked.

"As a matter of fact you did. Kev, I want you to meet Carmen, your new co-worker," Trae responded.

Kevin looked at Trae like he was on crack and quickly walked away.

"Looks like yo' man ain't too happy," Carmen said.

"Oh naw, he cool. Besides, I'm makin' an executive decision," Trae replied, trying to assure Carmen that he ran things.

Trae secured Carmen's info, then went back over to where his

DEEP

boys were sitting. Before Kevin could say a word, Trae ran Carmen's 411 down to him, but Kevin wasn't impressed. He felt something wasn't right with her, and he didn't have any qualms about telling Trae.

"Look, man, I'm not that stupid. I'm definitely gonna check her story out before I deal wit' her," Trae said. He smacked Kevin in the back of his head. "Sounds like you a lil' jealous."

"Nigga, please," Kevin said, with a smirk. "It's just somethin' 'bout that chick, man. How many girls you know just start poppin' shots like that? I mean, she just happened to be right there at the exact time those dudes rode up on you. Somethin' ain't right."

"Trust me, I'll look into it first before I decide somethin'," Trae responded, reassuring Kevin.

Trae and Kevin continued to talk shit and drink until it was last call. When they got ready to leave, Trae made a phone call to Big Paul who'd been waiting outside in the car for hours.

Kevin and Ice Man walked out the door first to check things out before they let Trae come out. When Kevin thought the coast was clear, he motioned for Trae. The streets were empty, not a body or car in sight. That was until a homeless guy came sliding around the corner from the alley.

"What's up youngins? Y'all got some change?" the man asked, barely able to stand.

"Hell naw we ain't got no change, nigga!" Kevin yelled, as he jumped at the man like he was going to hit him. Caught off guard, the man leaped with fear which caused him to fall. Trae's crew laughed wildly.

"Why y'all tripping?" the homeless man asked, guarding his face with his hands.

They continued to laugh, then their attention was diverted to some girls who had just left the club. Along with Trae, Kevin was also a big flirt, so he walked the girls to their car, which was parked right out front. Convinced everything was alright, Trae told Ice Man to go ahead and leave with Big Paul, then waited for Kevin to finish macking.

After the girls pulled off, the homeless man finally saw his opportunity. Instantly, he sprang at Kevin, landing right on him. After pinning him down with his weight, he pulled a .40 automatic out his jacket and pointed it directly at Trae.

"Now what, bitch!" the homeless man yelled.

Trae looked the homeless man in the eyes, which were cold as ice. "Shorty, if it's money you want, here take it," Trae said, pulling out

A NOVEL BY DANETTE MAJETTE

a stack of cash. He was more concerned the man might lose it and shoot him or Kevin.

"Hand it over then walk down the street!" the homeless man yelled.

"I ain't goin' nowhere without my man," Trae said, holding the money up.

"Okay, well give it to me. Then take a walk, and don't try nothin' or I'ma bust a cap in both y'all ass." After Trae handed the man the money, he helped Kevin to his feet. "Get to steppin' and don't turn around," the man said, pointing the gun toward Trae's head.

Carmen watched from a nearby window as the two walked halfway down the street. Kevin, being hardheaded as usual, turned around anyway. Of course, by then the man was long gone.

"Where the hell everybody at?" Kevin asked, holding the back of his head.

"I told them to go home. I thought we were straight. Shit," Trae said.

Trae sat in the front seat of Kevin's Escalade truck in a daze as Kevin vented. He then looked over at his crew member, and started laughing.

"What the fuck is so funny?" Kevin asked.

"Shorty, you got beat down by a homeless dude. How you gonna show yo' face tomorrow?" Trae asked.

"The same way yo' broke ass gonna show yours," Kevin said, finally loosening up.

DEEP

BE MY GIRL

After a long hot shower, Karina made herself a margarita and layed on the chaise in her room. Drowning out the loud sounds of children and sirens, she put in her favorite Luther Vandross CD, closed her eyes and fantasized about Trae. They had been out on a date almost every night for the past three months, and she could tell her feelings for him were starting to become a little bit stronger.

Damn, I hope I'm not moving too fast, she thought. Thinking about Trae caused Karina to place her index finger inside her panties and slowly make her way toward her clit. After making a few circular motions over the sensitive area, she let out a slight moan.

"Wake up, freak," a squeaky voice said, interrupting her.

When Karina opened her eyes, she smiled and blushed bashfully at Ashley before removing her finger.

"You nasty," Ashley said, pointing at Karina. "I guess I don't have to ask you what y'all doing tonight."

"You got that right. I can't wait either, because Trae said he has a surprise for me," Karina responded, kicking her French manicured feet in the air. "Can you believe he's taking me to his house after dinner?"

Ashley gave her friend a look of concern. "I thought he didn't want you to know where he lives."

"He didn't at first. He probably wanted to make sure I wasn't a serial killer or anything," Karina said laughing.

"No, it's not that. He *couldn't* let you come over because his girl probably wouldn't have liked that."

"Ashley, why do you always have to rain on my parade? Trae doesn't have a girlfriend. He would've told me if he did."

Karina began to think that maybe Ashley was jealous of her relationship with Trae, but quickly disregarded it. Besides, even though Ashley had put on a few pounds over the years, she was still equally

A NOVEL BY DANETTE MAJETTE

as beautiful as her, and could get any man she wanted.

However, unlike Karina, Ashley had grown up in the streets, so she was all too familiar with the drug game. She was also suspicious of any guy who wouldn't tell where they lived or gave up their home number. She was familiar with Trae's reputation in the streets, and thought there was no way he didn't have a girlfriend, or even worse, a wife. Ashley tried to stay out of it, but it was hard, because Karina was her girl. Even more importantly, she knew how niggas got down, and didn't want to see her best friend fall into the trap.

"Enough about me and Trae...what about you?" Karina asked. "Did you meet anyone at the club last night?"

"First of all, I would never go to a club to find a man. Second, all the good guys are either married, or carrying around enough baggage to ground a 747," Ashley responded.

"Why don't you let me introduce you to Trae's friend, Kevin?" Karina asked.

"Hell naw. I'm not interested in anybody Trae associates with. I'll let my shit dry up first," Ashley said laughing.

Karina laughed too, but deep down she was concerned about her friend. She even began to feel bad about not hanging out with her like she used to. She had tried on numerous occasions to include Ashley in her plans with Trae, but her invitation was always refused. It was like Ashley hated Trae, but Karina didn't understand why.

Karina looked at her watch. "Oh shit, I'm gonna be late," she said, jumping up. "Come help me pick out something to wear."

"Yeah, I'll help you pick out something alright. I don't care what you wear with that asshole," Ashley responded.

Refusing to let Ashley's comments spoil her evening, Karina smiled as she ran toward the bathroom, looking like a teenager.

When Trae arrived at Karina's house, he was speechless. Wearing a BCBG halter black dress that made her breasts stand at attention and four inch stilettos, it was hard for him to keep his eyes off of her. Every strand of hair was in place, and her make-up was flawless.

"Damn!" Trae said.

"What? Am I dressed wrong for our date?" Karina asked.

Trae shook his head. "No, you look nice."

"Thanks, you don't look so bad yourself," she replied, looking at his tan custom made suit and brown Bruno Magli shoes. She loved the way Trae kept himself dressed nicely, and not like a thug.

"So, are you ready?" Trae asked.

"Yep...Ashley, I'm gone!" she yelled, as she made her way out the door holding Trae's hand.

Once they got in the car, Karina immediately asked where they were going, but Trae kept their destination a secret, saying only that it was going to be the most amazing date she'd ever been on.

After thinking all day, Trae had decided tonight he would make one of the biggest decisions of his life. Even though he and Karina had only been dating for three months, Trae knew he wanted to be with her, and had planned to ask Karina to be his girl.

He was excited as they pulled up to his six-bedroom Victorian style home in Bethesda. He quickly turned off the engine to his car and walked around to the passenger side to open the door for his future wife.

"Here we are," Trae said, helping her out the car.

"Your house is beautiful," Karina responded, as they walked up to the front door.

"Thanks, I'm pretty proud of it myself," Trae responded.

When he opened the door, Karina was in awe, and didn't waste anytime asking for a personal tour. "So, do I get to look around?"

Trae smiled. "Sure come on."

He took Karina on the tour of his home. Not only was it vast in size, but its amazing blend of charm and elegance made the place remarkably glamorous. The main level was graced with hardwood floors, a formal dining room, a library, a huge family room and a spacious kitchen with granite counter tops. Trae's room was also decorated nicely with a spacious king sized bed, a sixty-inch plasma television that hung above a fireplace, and a six zone audio system.

After the tour, Trae escorted Karina into the family room, where he made her a Hypnotic Raspberry Martini. Sitting comfortably on the couch, Karina commented on Trae's house again. As she continued to talk, Trae grabbed her hand.

"I have something to ask you before I lose my nerve," he said, picking up a small wrapped box that was laying nearby. "I know we've only been seeing each other for a short time, but I think it's safe to say that we really enjoy each other's company and that we really like each other, right?" Trae looked Karina directly in her eyes.

She looked at him with a confused expression. "Yeah," Karina answered, twitching around on the couch.

"Alright then. So what do you think about us makin' it official?"

I know this dude is not about to ask me to marry him? "Official can mean one or two things, so what are you saying?" she asked.

"I mean... I want to be with you and only you. I want you to be my girl," he replied.

Karina looked at him like he was crazy. "Are you serious?"

"I haven't been this serious about anythin' in my life," he said, with his pulse beating faster by the minute. To convince her that he meant every word, he pulled a key out of the box and placed it in her hands.

"What's this?" Karina asked, at a complete loss.

"Ah, let's see, that would be the key to my house. I want you to move in wit' me."

Overjoyed, Karina held the key to her heart. She knew how hard it must've been for Trae to let her in since he probably had the same problem she did with trust.

"When do I move in?" she responded. However, as quickly as her smiled appeared it quickly faded away. *Ashley is gonna kill me.*

DEEP

WHAT'S THE 411

Carmen smiled as she entered the FBI building in downtown D.C. through a back entrance and into a service elevator that was reserved for undercover agents. The Feds always took extra precautions to make sure their agents covers were never blown. Despite the constant danger she put herself in, and the risks that were involved, Carmen loved her job. Growing up, she always wanted to be a cop, and often expressed it by dressing as one every Halloween. She even carried around a fake pair of handcuffs, and pretended to arrest her friends when they played cops and robbers. It was a dream that became a reality when she was accepted into the FBI Training Academy, and even more of an accomplishment when she became a Federal Agent. Carmen was determined to make the Bureau proud, and bringing down Trae Keal was sure to give her a few accolades around the office.

All of the agents assigned to Trae's case, including Carmen's husband, Damien, and supervisor Willie, were seated at a conference table when she walked in wearing an All Daz t-shirt and baseball cap. As soon as Carmen sat down, everyone started laughing hysterically.

"What's so funny?" she asked, looking around the room.

"Nothing homegirl. Don't pull out yo' gat," a white spiky haired agent said, throwing his hands up. The whole group laughed.

At that point, Carmen knew he was referring to the urban clothing she had on. "Funny," she said, throwing a stack of papers on the desk before sitting down. "You know I wouldn't normally dress like this."

"Honey, don't pay them any attention," Damien said, as he blew her a kiss.

Willie gave everyone a disapproving stare. He was a very dark and hyper man who stood 6'3. Unlike some of the newer agents, he carried a few extra pounds because of all the takeout he consumed while working long hours on cases like Trae's.

"Alright, everyone settle down," Willie said, peeking over the top of his reading glasses. "As you all know, we've been trying to bring down Trae Keal's organization," he said, pointing to the bulletin board with pictures of everyone in Trae's organization, along with their position. "So, let's recap."

The whole room sighed. They'd been over Trae's case at least fifty times.

Willie looked around the room. "You all can huff and puff all you want, but that's not gonna stop me. I'm gonna go over this a million times if it means one day Trae's ass will be behind bars," he informed.

"Continue, sir," the spiky haired agent said.

"Thanks...now Trae is the piece of shit head honcho of the crew. After his grandmother died, who was caring for him after his mother's death, he needed money. So, I guess since crime paid more than a nine to five, he chose that life. He started off as a runner for Big Charlie before he was killed five years ago, and that's when he started his own crew and took over were Big Charlie left off." Willie pointed to another picture. "Over here we have Kevin Dobson, his sidekick and right hand man. He's a cocky guy from Southeast and the top Lieutenant in the organization. Now this ugly muthafucka right here is Paul Gibson aka Big Paul. He's Trae's bodyguard. And last, but not least, there's Derrick Richardson better known as Ice Man. He's what you would call the enforcer of the crew and will kill anyone without hesitation."

"They're all equally dangerous," Carmen added.

"From the looks of things, I suspect Carmen will be getting a call from Trae soon. Hopefully to confirm her job offer," Willie informed everyone.

"How can you be sure?" Damien asked.

"Well I can't, but it seems Trae's been doing some investigating into Carmen's bogus arrest record. If he likes what he sees, I'm almost sure he's gonna want her to work for him," Willie replied. "And we all know how much Trae Keal loves women, that's why we sent Carmen and her partner to infiltrate in the first place. We figured if anyone could get close to him, it would be someone of the opposite sex," he continued. Willie then went on to explain how Trae liked to keep peo-ple around him who were just as dangerous and crazy as he was. "Carmen, I'll let you fill them in on what you know so far," Willie said, taking a seat.

When she stood up, she told them about the various operations

DEEP

Trae had going on. She also explained how lucky Trae had been in the past by not getting caught, and how hard it would be to take him down.

"He has a high-powered attorney that always seems to get him off on technicalities because there is never enough concrete evidence to convict him. Also, he never touches any of his product. He never even talks about it," Carmen mentioned.

This time the Feds were going to use the RICO Act to prosecute Trae and his crew, since they were selling drugs and committing murder to protect their interests. They even started looking back on unsolved murder cases in the projects that Trae's crew might've been responsible for. All they needed to know was the crew's daily routines...who was selling the drugs, and where they were getting them from.

"This piece of shit has brought nothing but misery to this city, and I want to be the one to take him out!" Willie shouted. The agents stared at one another. "Pardon me, I mean take him down," Willie added.

A few minutes later, when the meeting ended, Willie walked over to the board and stuck a thumbtack in Trae's left eye as all the other agents left the room with the exception of Carmen. More than any other drug dealer he'd gone after, Willie had a deep hatred for Trae.

"Don't you think you're a little obsessed with this case?" Carmen asked. Willie was surprised by her question. "I'm only asking because I don't want to see you do something you'll regret."

"I won't. Trust me, no one knows more than I do how important it is for this to be done right. I've been after this guy for years, and I don't want that son of a bitch getting away with murder again because we fucked up," he replied.

"Don't worry. I'm all over this one, sir," Carmen said with a smile, as she walked toward the door. When she got halfway down the corridor, she turned around and went back into the conference room. "So, how much did you get from Trae the other night?" she asked.

"Couple thousand," Willie replied, with a big grin. "I knew his bitch ass was really weak. I wanted to punch that muthafucka in his face."

"Good work. You almost convinced me you were really homeless," she said, with another smile.

"Well no one knows about that little stupid stunt except you and a few other agents, so let's keep that between us. I could be fired for taking his money like that," Willie said.

"Sure, no problem, but what are you gonna do with it?"

"Let's just say I plan on using it for a rainy day."

Carmen smiled. "Talk with you soon," she said, before turning around to leave.

Halfway down the hallway, Carmen's husband called out her name. She turned around and walked up to him.

"Hey baby. What's up?" she asked.

"I just wanted to tell you to be careful and give you this." He leaned over and planted a kiss on her lips. "I love you," he said.

Carmen and Damien had met at a party given by the Bureau six years ago, and quickly fell in love with each other. A year later, they exchanged vows and white gold wedding bands at a small ceremony in front of the justice of the peace. With both of them being agents, there was no time to plan a huge ceremony.

Unlike Damien, Carmen grew up with her strict aunt in Florida. Damien, on the other hand, grew up with both his parents. Every time Carmen was around Damien's family, she would wonder where her parents were. She tried locating them on several occasions, but was always unsuccessful. During her last attempt to find her birth parents, she became discouraged when she was told by her aunt that she should just leave well enough alone. When she asked her aunt what she meant, her aunt replied that her mother was a slut who didn't know who Carmen's father was. Carmen was furious that her aunt would say such nasty things about her mother, so a few years after graduating from college, she left Florida and went to the Academy.

"I love you too, baby," Carmen said, placing her arms around his neck.

After talking to each other for a few more minutes, Carmen told her husband she had to go. With her being on a special assignment, there wasn't a lot of time to hold loveable conversations. She had to get back on the street, just in case the other man in her life called.

DEEP

MOVE IN DAY

Sitting in her car, Karina took one last look at the apartment she shared with Ashley for years. With her car packed so tight her rear view visibility was blocked. Karina held a constant grin as she headed to Trae's house. Despite her constant arguments with Ashley over the past week, she was still in a good mood. When she pulled up in her 95 Ford Explorer forty minutes later, Trae shook his head.

"Damn, baby did this thing pass emissions?" he asked, laughing.

Karina sucked her teeth. "Hey, it gets me from point A to B," she replied, with attitude.

"I hear you babe. Now close your eyes, I have a Christmas present for you."

"I don't think I can take another surprise. The house key was enough," Karina lied. Inside, she was jumping up and down.

"Trust me, I'm sure you'll like this." Walking her toward the surprise, Trae double-checked to make sure she wasn't peeking. "A'ight open up," he said.

Karina's eyes lit up like a light bulb. "Whaaaat is that?" Karina said barely getting the words out.

"What does it look like?"

Karina knew exactly what it looked like. She just couldn't believe what she was seeing. "Trae, I can't accept this," she stated.

"Yes you can," he said, kissing her on the forehead.

Karina slowly walked over to the shiny new black XJR Jaguar that was wrapped in a red bow. This was truly one of the happiest days in her life. She was in love, moving into a beautiful home, and was now going to be driving a new car.

"Don't be afraid to touch it. Get in, it's yours," Trae suggested. "The keys are already inside just in case you want to take a spin around the neighborhood."

A NOVEL BY DANETTE MAJETTE

Karina was still speechless as she opened the door and sat in the best gift she'd ever gotten. She had to pinch herself as she touched the soft leather seats that felt like butter. "You're spoiling me," she said, playing with the buttons on the radio.

"That's what I'm supposed to do. That's my job. I'm sorry if those other niggas ain't treat you right," he answered jokingly.

"Shut up and hop in," she ordered, before starting up her new ride.

After an hour of joy riding, they returned back to the house to continue with their day. Anxious to get Karina settled, Trae started to unpack her old truck. As soon as they got into the house, he led her to the bedroom.

"Okay, close your eyes again," he repeated.

"Baby please, I can't handle anymore surprises today."

"Yes you can. Close'em," Trae said, slapping her on the ass.

Karina did what Trae ordered. When she opened them, she was floored. Trae had paid a contractor to come in and tear down a wall to the adjoining bedroom to make Karina her own walk-in closet. Not only did he have the closet made, he also had a stylist come in and fill the new space with brand new clothes, shoes and handbags.

"What'chu think?" Trae asked.

Karina jumped into his arms. "Are you crazy, I love it!" she screamed.

"I thought you would."

"Now let me show you how thankful I am."

Karina moved close to Trae, looking deep into his eyes, and kissed him gently on the lips a few times. She then licked the outline of his lips with her tongue. Trae grabbed her ass and pulled her close to him before she pulled back and began to unbutton his jeans. When they hit the floor, she helped him pull off his shirt.

Instantly, Karina nibbled and licked Trae's nipples, causing his hardness to poke her in her stomach. Karina placed her hand on his chest, and ran her fingers up and down his body. She knew Trae couldn't hold out any longer, so she led him to the bed and pulled his boxer shorts off. Her own juices were starting to run down her leg, so she quickly undressed, and began to show her appreciation to her man.

She climbed on top of him and slid down on his manhood slowly, before pulling her pussy back up, resting on the tip of his head. Karina continued this a few times before she began riding his stallion. She jumped up and down on Trae like a trampoline as he grabbed one of her protruding nipples and placed it in his mouth. Back and forth from breast to breast, Trae kept his mouth full, not wanting to show favoritism. He then moved his hand down to tickle her clitoris. Before long, Karina was on the verge of exploding, but before she did, she wanted to make sure her man came with her. Karina removed her man's thickness from inside her kitty.

"No baby, what are you doin'?" Trae asked.

Karina didn't say anything as she turned her body around and straddled Trae with her back to him. He grabbed her ass and opened it up, so he could dig deeper into her cave. Karina dropped low and rocked her hips from side to side. She grabbed Trae's arms to keep her balance, and began to ride his thickness in full throttle. She squeezed her vagina as she went down, so she could feel every inch of Trae inside her.

Moaning and screaming to the joyful pain, Karina's nails dug deeper into Trae's arms. He continued to rub and pinch her nipples as she rode him like a true professional.

"Don't stop, Trae. Aww, ohh," she moaned.

"Karina, umm umm, I'm 'bout to...I'm 'bout to… to cum, baby," Trae stuttered, as he was reaching his climax.

"Come on, baby, I'm cumming with you," she replied.

Karina dropped harder and harder on his penis as Trae stroked and went deeper until he exploded inside her.

He sat holding onto her breast for a few moments then began to kiss her all over her back. "Baby, that was amazin'," he said.

"Yes, it was." Seconds later, she untangled herself from her man, and they walked hand in hand toward the shower.

Before getting in, they stood naked in front of each other, and admired each other's bodies. "Your shape is amazin'," Trae said, looking at Karina's plump round ass.

"Thanks, you don't have a bad body yourself. Especially this huge thing," Karina replied lifting up Trae's dick. "Hey what's this?"

"It's a birth mark," Trae replied referring to the odd shaped mark on his manhood.

Karina smiled. "Are you sure, someone didn't try to cut it off before?"

"Yeah, I'm sure. Now let's get in the shower, so we can get started on round two.

A NOVEL BY DANETTE MAJETTE

That evening, Karina continued to put away her things until going into the kitchen to fix dinner. She scrambled around the unfamiliar place, trying to find everything from seasonings to the pots and pans.

"You alright in there?" Trae asked, from the living room.

"Yeah, I'm just trying to find my way around this huge kitchen," she responded.

"Don't worry, you'll get used to it," he said laughing.

She was still fumbling through the cabinets when she ran across a small package. It was wrapped tightly in newspaper and was light in weight. Looking to see if Trae was coming, Karina carefully opened the package and almost dropped it from shock. She had never seen it in person, but knew it was cocaine.

What the fuck? she thought. She started to yell for Trae to come into the kitchen so she could ask why he was not only risking his freedom, but hers as well by keeping it in the house, but when she looked around at all the new things he bought her, she quickly decided against it.

She made a decent living at Nordstrom, but it was nothing compared to the new life Trae had given her. So she figured she would let this one transgression slide. Despite how strong she used to be when they first met, Karina was turning out to be one of the girls who let their men get away with just about anything as long as he kept providing.

Two hours later, they sat down and talked over dinner.

"Damn, babe, I ain't never tasted fried chicken this good," Trae said, licking his fingers. "You better watch it. I might get use to this."

"Get use to what?" Karina asked.

"Eating home cooked meals every night. We might not ever go out to eat again," he said, teasing her. Trae knew Karina liked to eat at nice restaurants.

"Whatever," she replied. "After the holidays, we're gonna start eating out again."

After dinner Karina cleaned up the kitchen, then joined Trae in the family room. Sitting on the couch, they watched the movie, *Two Can Play That Game* and shared a few laughs. Trae looked down at Karina, who was laying on his lap, and kissed her. He was finally realizing what he'd been missing all his life. Someone to share all the things he'd accomplished in life. Someone to love and someone who loved him. Ever since his grandmother had passed, there hadn't been anyone to fill that role.

Suddenly, Trae's first night with Karina and fairytale lifestyle was

DEEP

interrupted by the phone ringing.

"Yo', what's up? You know you ain't suppose to call my damn house," Trae yelled.

"I know T, but this is important. I need to see you," the voice on the other end replied.

"Shorty, this better be good. I was in the middle of somethin'," Trae said, before hanging up the phone.

Before Karina had a chance to say anything, he ran upstairs, threw on a pair of sweats, a t-shirt, and a pair of Nike boots before coming back down to leave. He grabbed his keys off the kitchen counter then gave Karina a kiss.

"Where you going?" she asked.

"I'll be right back. I gotta go take care of somethin'," Trae replied.

"It can't wait until tomorrow?"

"Naw. When duty calls, I gotta go."

Karina let out a huge sigh and her eyes widened. "When duty calls?"

"You see all those clothes in the closet and the cars outside," Trae asked Karina. He waited for a response, but didn't get one. "In order to pay for those things, I gotta work for them. So when duty calls, I gotta go."

With her heart beating fast, she said, "I understand. I just thought we were gonna spend the rest of the night together."

"We will when I get back," Trae said, as he walked out the door.

It was finally sinking in that business would always be first and foremost to Trae. *Oh well, I can live with him working a few late nights if it means I can have all this.* She thought about the new clothes in her closet and the Jag that sat in the driveway. She also thought about calling her mother since Trae wasn't around. She tried not to talk about her mother much, since she knew that Trae had no one to call mom. But all of a sudden she decided against it, and thought about her new love.

"She can wait," Karina said out loud. "Right now, my man needs me more."

A NOVEL BY DANETTE MAJETTE

DEEP

ANOTHER ONE BITES THE DUST

The parking deck Trae drove into was dark and empty. He always tried to find places like that when he conducted business. He got out his car, and looked out over the parking structure at the city, which was quiet for a change. He wondered if he should just give up the life he'd become so accustomed to. It was the first time he'd ever questioned if everything was worth it. Maybe the attempts on his life was a sign to get out while he had a chance. He had nothing to gain, but everything to lose. Especially his two million dollars in offshore accounts, his soul mate Karina, and most of all, his life.

Trae's thoughts were interrupted by the loud sounds of go-go music. Seconds later, a dark gray BMW pulled up and Monty, one of Trae's many associates hopped out doing a little dance. However, Trae wasn't in the mood to be entertained.

Monty was a two bit hustler from Baltimore, who copped his drugs from Trae and loved to show off. He'd only been hustling for a short time, and every other week he had an excuse for not having Trae's money. Little did he know this time would be his last. He'd just struck out.

"No disrespect, man, but put yo' piece on the hood of the car," Trae ordered. Not wanting any trouble, Monty followed Trae's request. "Now, what's so important that you had to drag me away from my girl?"

"I know I was supposed to see you this week, but I got robbed," Monty said, scared out of his wits.

Trae looked at him like he had two heads. "Nigga, do you think I'm stupid?" He walked over toward Monty. "I heard you bought this car yesterday. What is it, a 550i?" Trae asked, walking around the brand new car.

Monty shook his head. "Naw, this is my man's car. I just borrowed it."

"Oh really," Trae said laughing. He couldn't believe Monty could lie right in his face. What his dumb ass didn't know was that the guy he'd bought the car from was on Trae's payroll as well. As soon as Monty left the lot the salesman called Trae and told him.

"Anyway, I'ma have to see you at the end of the month," Monty said, with a cocky tone.

Trae pulled out his gun and fired a shot into Monty's right leg. Disoriented, Monty quickly tried to escape by limping away.

Where is this fool going? Trae thought. After Monty realized he had nowhere to go, he looked over the wall of the parking garage and considered jumping. That's when Trae fired another shot up close and personal. When Monty's body dropped, he kicked him with his boots and then knelt down beside him.

"I don't think so. You gon' see me now muthafucka," Trae said, as he took Monty's car keys out his pocket.

Trae quickly walked over to the old pickup truck that was parked nearby and opened the door. "Y'all get rid of his body," he said to Big Paul and Ice Man, who were hiding down in the seats.

"Follow me to the chop shop," Trae demanded, as he threw Monty's keys to Kevin, who was getting out the back seat of the pick-up.

Minutes later, they arrived at another one of Trae's investments. The area around the chop shop was as secure as Fort Knox. There were security and guard dogs everywhere. As soon as they saw Trae's car, they scurried to unlock the gates.

Once Trae was inside, he gave the workers instructions to change the car's Vehicle Identification Number, the tags, and then repaint it.

After delegating a few more orders, Trae and Kevin hopped back into Trae's car and drove off. After they rode in silence for a few minutes, Trae couldn't help but think how Kevin might be slipping.

"Yo', Kev you supposed to be my eyes and ears on the streets, man. Why is it that my man down at the dealership knew that nigga bought a new car wit' my money and you didn't!" Trae yelled.

"Cuz I can't watch every damn body at the same time. That's why?" Kevin replied, turning the music up.

Trae looked at the top member of his crew and turned the radio back down. "So now you can't do your job?"

"Man, fuck you," Kevin snapped. He was the only one who could get away with talking to Trae like that.

"No, fuck you, nigga!"

The two sat in silence for a couple of minutes before Trae finally broke the ice. "A'ight, shorty, maybe shit has been gettin' too hectic for one person. Plus, I know I'm not out in the street everyday like you, but why didn't you say somethin' before?"

Kevin didn't respond.

"Stop actin' like a bitch. I'll get you some help," Trae continued.

Kevin knew exactly who Trae had in mind. "Look, I don't know about that, man," he said.

"Oh, so now you talkin' to me?" Trae asked. He looked over at Kevin. "Look, I had her checked out."

Kevin was dead set against the whole idea. "Trae, this chick just showed up out of nowhere and now you want to bring her on board. You not thinkin', man. Don't let pussy be your downfall. It's bad enough you got that girl living wit' you now."

"What the fuck are you talkin' about? This doesn't have anythin' to do with Karina. This is about business." Taking his cell phone out of the holder, he scrolled through his list of contacts. "Let me see what they found out." He quickly dialed the number to his man, who was a private investigator. "What's the word?" Trae asked.

The investigator inhaled then exhaled, "Well, it seems like our friend has a rap sheet as long as the Nile River. Everything from driving under the influence to assault with a deadly weapon. They were also trying to get her on a conspiracy charge, but all the witnesses ended up dead. Makes you wonder, huh?"

"Not really," Trae replied.

"She actually just got out of a maximum security jail in Georgia. Word is as soon as she walked out, she hopped a plane to Jamaica. I guess she decided to lay low for a while before she came back to the states," the investigator stated.

Carmen was just what Trae needed in his organization, an unruly chick that would do anything at the drop of a dime. Not to mention, no one would suspect a beautiful woman of doing some of the things she would have to do. That settled it, first thing in the morning he was going to offer Carmen a job, with or without Kevin's approval.

After Trae dropped Kevin off at Pleasures, he headed back home. The drive seemed like an eternity. All he could think about was getting home to Karina and finishing what they had started...a peaceful evening alone.

A NOVEL BY DANETTE MAJETTE

DEEP

SHIT HITS THE FAN

The next morning, Karina was tempted to call in sick, but decided against it. Instead she made breakfast, showered and got dressed.

"If you don't want to go to work you don't have to," Trae said, kissing her on the neck as she tried to apply her makeup.

"Trae, we already discussed this. Besides, I love what I do."

Karina was upset that Trae wanted her to quit her job after she'd worked so hard to get a promotion.

"I know, but I don't like the fact that my lady is around men all day," he said, sitting on the bed.

"Don't worry, they can't hold a candle to you, baby."

Trae wasn't trying to hear that. What he wanted to hear was that she was going to quit, but he didn't want to make an issue of it just yet. He figured she would come around soon enough, especially if he had anything to do with it.

Karina looked at herself in her black Marc Jacobs Patchwork dress that showed just a little cleavage in the mirror one last time. The new wardrobe Trae had hooked her up with was working out perfectly. Before she left, she gave Trae a kiss, handed him the remote, grabbed her metallic Chanel purse, and then dashed out the door.

Fumbling through the channels, Trae stopped when he saw a news flash that was alarming. His heart skipped a beat as he called Kevin and summoned him to his house. Thirty minutes later, Kevin arrived.

"Yo', that nigga, Monty was a undercover," Trae said, as soon as Kevin walked through the door. Trae began to pace back and forth.

"I know. Word done spread all over the city. What we gon' do?" Kevin replied. Trae was silent. "Yo', Trae, what we gon' do?" he repeated.

A NOVEL BY DANETTE MAJETTE

Still silent, Trae stared at the walls. "Damn, we should'a chopped that nigga up."

"Man, you been watchin' too many fuckin' mafia movies," Kevin said, turning up the television.

"I told Big Paul and Ice to get rid of the body, and the shit was already found, Kev," Trae said, still pacing. "What the fuck did they do, put the body in front of the fuckin' White House?"

Trae's ranting was interrupted by another news anchor, so he directed his attention toward the TV.

Thank you Ted back to our story of the day. Officer Montel Delroy's body was found shot to death in Rock Creek Park . A man noticed the officer's body as he was walking his dog early this morning. So far the police have been tight lipped about Delroy's position in the department. The chief of police said they have no suspects and no motive at this time.

"Dammit!' Trae yelled. He stood up and turned the television off. "What the fuck am I payin' those niggas down in Fourth District for? They were supposed to keep me informed about shit like this!"

Kevin shook his head. "So, what are we gonna do?"

"We need to get out of town 'til this shit blows over."

Kevin wanted to disagree, but he knew it would be a losing battle getting him to change his mind. So he called a travel agent and told her to make the arrangements. After getting a confirmation number, he went home to pack.

Trae pulled out his cell phone and dialed a number that wasn't familiar to him yet. When the woman answered, his face lit up like a Christmas tree. "What's up Carmen?"

"Nothin' much, Trae. What's up with you?" she asked.

"Remember when I offered you that position?"

Carmen tried to hold her composure because she knew what he was getting at. "Yeah," she said.

"Well, I wanted to see if you were still interested because I could use you."

"Of course I'm still interested."

"Good. I wanna talk to you in person, but I gotta make a quick move, and can't do it now. I'll have one of my men give you a call so we can hook somethin' up," Trae replied. "I'll talk to you soon."

"Cool," Carmen said. When she hung up the phone, she immediately started jumping up and down. *Everything is falling into place.*

DEEP

Karina came home later that night to find an overnight bag packed and sitting by the front door.

"Baby, you going somewhere?" she asked in a loud tone. She brushed her hand across the Louis Vuitton luggage sitting on the floor.

"Yeah, I gotta go out of town for a minute, but I wanted to wait until you got here before I left," Trae yelled from the family room.

Karina was confused. Trae hadn't mentioned anything to her about going out of town before she went to work that morning. She walked into the family room and found Trae sitting on the couch, throwing back a beer.

"What's going on?" she asked. "I'm worried about you."

Instantly Trae snapped, throwing his beer bottle across the room and cursing at the top of his lungs. He then pushed over his thousand dollar antique glass coffee table and stood up.

Karina jumped out of the way, so she wouldn't get hit. "Calm down, I just asked a question," she said, with her hands on her hips. "Are you drunk or something?"

Trae wasn't upset that she'd asked him where he was going. He was upset that he had to leave her. Lately their relationship had been the one bright spot in his life.

"I'm sorry. I just got a lot of shit on my mind right now," he said, pulling her closer to him.

I hope this nigga don't need Prozac. "Well, don't take the shit out on me!" she replied, pulling away.

After talking to Karina for a few more minutes, he was finally able to calm her down and assure her that everything would be okay.

"So, when are you coming back?" she asked.

"I'm not sure right now. Hopefully it won't be long," Trae responded, blowing beer breath in her face.

Karina wanted to question him a little bit more, but after the first little incident, she decided to leave the situation alone.

An hour later, Trae left the house when Big Paul showed up to take him and Kevin to the airport.

Walking fast and looking at everyone strangely, Trae sat down at a bar inside BWI airport. He knew his paranoid behavior was starting to get on Kevin's nerves, but he didn't care. All he could think about was the police showing up to arrest him right before he boarded the plane.

Trae nervously watched the television monitor, hoping to get some more information about Monty's death as he sipped on another beer.

He turned to Kevin and asked, "You think they know it was me?"

Kevin sat back in his chair and thought for a minute. "If they did, they ain't sayin' nothin' about it or you wouldn't be sittin' here. Yo' ass would be sharin' a cell with some big black muthafucka."

Trae almost flipped out. "Nigga, that shit ain't funny!"

"Stop trippin'. I'm just sayin', if they had anythin' they would've bagged yo' ass by now. Me too for that matter. Did you forgot I was there?" Kevin sat back in his seat. "Shorty, if they do have some evidence or a witness, we'll take care of it."

Minutes later, the airport attendant announced that their plane was boarding. "You ready," Kevin asked, passing Trae his ticket."

"Yeah," Trae answered.

They picked up their carry on bags, strolled toward Gate #14, got in line and boarded the plane, with Trae looking over his shoulder the entire time.

The five-hour flight to Vegas was exhausting for Trae. Kevin on the other hand, enjoyed sipping on the complimentary alcohol offered in first class. By the time they got off the plane, Kevin was wasted.

Once they checked into their room at the Wynn Hotel, Trae called Karina. When she heard his voice, she was convinced something heavy was going down.

"Baby, talk to me," she insisted.

"We'll talk when I get back. Just know that I love you and I'm never gonna leave you again," Trae said, trying to reassure her.

"You promise."

"I promise," he answered, before hanging up.

Trae made a few more calls then went to meet Kevin in the casino. By the time he got there, Kevin had already lost three G's. That was something new, considering he was normally good at gambling.

"Man, you never lose at craps. What's goin' on?" Trae asked.

"Shorty, I'm so fucked up, I don't know what I'm doin'," Kevin replied.

"A'ight, let's go before you lose your life savings at this table."

DEEP

When Trae left and walked toward the elevators, Kevin was just about to follow him when he heard one of the Pit Bosses mumble something. Kevin turned around and looked at the heavyset white man. "What'chu say?" he asked. "Did I just hear you say good riddens or some shit?"

The Pit Boss' eyes grew wider. It was as if he knew some type of drama was about to go down. Straightening his tie he looked at Kevin and replied, "No, I didn't say anything like that."

"Yes you did, muthafucka!" Kevin yelled.

Suddenly, Trae heard Kevin yelling, so he quickly turned around and walked back toward the crap table to see what was going on. However, by the time he got there things had escalated. Trae knew it was only a matter of time before security was called. Casinos didn't play around with unruly people, and the eyes in the sky were probably zooming in on them at that very moment.

"What's goin' on?" Trae asked, trying to calm Kevin down.

"This fool said some slick shit when I was leavin'."

"Sir, I didn't say anything to you, so please lower your voice, and stop using profanity."

"Yes you did, fat ass," Kevin replied, trying to grab the guy by his jacket.

Trae tried to calm Kevin down and get him out of the casino before security came, but it was too late. They were already on the scene. Trae assured the security officers that everything was cool, but they weren't having it.

"You can stay, but he has to go!" one of the officers yelled.

"We'll both leave, a'ight. Shorty, let's roll," Trae said, pulling Kevin by the arm.

Before they left the casino, Kevin stepped closer to the Pit Boss and whispered, "I'm gonna get yo' fat ass."

The Pit Boss wasn't fazed by Kevin's threat at all. Instead, he straightened his suit and ordered security to ban both of them from the entire casino.

When Trae and Kevin returned to their huge tower suite, Trae was in need of some major relaxation. He was already stressed out about Monty and Kevin's outrageous scene at the crap table had just made things worse. He walked into the bathroom, shut the door and immediately began peeling off all his clothes. Trae turned on the hot water and stepped into the large marble shower.

"Yes, this is exactly what I needed," he said.

The heat, mixed with Trae's aromatherapy shower gel took him to another place. All he could think about was how good the water felt running down his back as he placed the gel over his body. After standing under the huge rainfall of water for several minutes, he finally got out and dried himself off.

Wearing a pair of sweatpants and a wife beater, Trae walked in the room and was quite surprised to find Kevin stretched out on his bed. *After all that shit he just caused, now his drunk ass got a nerve to be sleep.* Trae shook his head as he walked over to the huge floor to ceiling window and stared out onto the Vegas strip. After just committing a murder in D.C., the last thing they needed was to cause a scene on the other side of the country, so Kevin was going to have to chill out.

Although he was tired and ready to go to sleep, Trae stayed up and called Big Paul to see what the word was back at home. When Big Paul told Trae he found out the police had arrested Fats, another big time drug lord from Virginia, for Monty's murder, Trae was ecstatic. *At least something good happened today*, he thought.

Trae got up early the next morning to tell Kevin the good news.

"Wake up, man. You ain't gonna believe this shit," Trae said, trying to wake up his friend.

"Whhhaaatttt? I'm tryin' to sleep."

"Get yo' ass up and listen to me," Trae demanded.

Reluctantly, Kevin rolled over and looked at Trae with disgust. "Damn, man, I can't get any sleep at home, and now you won't let me get no sleep out here either."

"Stop cryin'. I didn't know you needed your fuckin' beauty rest," Trae replied.

Kevin shot Trae an evil look. "Shut up, nigga."

As Trae began to give him the whole story, he noticed Kevin giving him another crazy look. Before he knew it, Kevin had thrown a pillow at him. "You mean to tell me I came all the way out here for nothin'?"

"Well, it's not a total loss. Maybe we can go shoppin' or some shit. It'll be on me," Trae said, feeling bad for putting his friend through hell.

"Oh, that's what's up," Kevin replied immediately forgiving Trae. He quickly jumped out the bed and walked into the bathroom.

So now the nigga wants to get up? Trae thought to himself.

DEEP

Trae and Kevin's first stop was the Forum at Caesar's Palace. Trae knew how much Karina loved Versace, so he bought damn near everything in the store. Kevin was a Gucci man, so Trae bought him a shirt and two pairs of shoes.

"Yo', Trae, how we gon' get all this shit back to D.C?" Kevin asked, struggling with all Karina's bags.

"When we get back to the hotel, we can have them ship all this stuff back home," Trae said, exhausted from all the shopping.

"Cool, let's go get something to eat. I'm hungry as hell!" Kevin said.

They jumped in a cab to go drop all the shopping bags off at the hotel, and twenty minutes later, they were on their way to Delminico Steakhouse, a nice restaurant located inside the Venetian Hotel.

When they arrived, Kevin immediately started making small talk with two busty ladies who were seated at the table beside them. Trae however, wasn't in the mood. All he could think about was Karina, and wondered what she was doing at that very moment.

"Hey yo' Trae, I think they tryin' to hit us off," Kevin whispered, after the waiter took their order. By that time, Kevin was already on his second shot of Patron.

"Shorty, I ain't fuckin' with those broads, man. They just tryin' to get in a niggas pockets. If you were sober you would see that," Trae said.

"Man, I'm far from being drunk. I'm just tryin' to have a good time."

"Okay, go ahead, that doesn't mean I have to be involved," Trae responded. "Don't let me spoil your fun."

Throughout dinner, Kevin continued to talk to the two women as Trae quietly ate his ribeye and gulf shrimp. Every few minutes, Kevin would look at him like he was crazy, but Trae just ignored his strange stares. To Trae, these girls were nothing but trouble, and he refused to travel down that road.

"You ready to roll?" Trae asked Kevin as he took his last bite.

"Not really. I'm havin' a nice conversation with these two beautiful women," Kevin replied, picking up one of the ladies hands. She let out a high pitched giggle.

"A'igh't, well I'm out. I'll see you back at the hotel." Trae stood up, went in his pocket and pulled out a huge roll of money, before placing five hundred dollars on the table. "That should cover our bill and your two friends." When he looked at the two women, they were staring at him with huge smiles.

"Why don't we go somewhere to get to know each other a little better?" one of the women suggested. She never took her eyes off Trae or the bulge in his pocket.

"I'm sorry, ladies, I have to go. But my man will take of you," he responded, pointing at Kevin. "Y'all have fun."

They watched as Trae walked out the restaurant. "Don't worry ladies, I promise to show you all a good time," Kevin said, with a wide grin.

As soon as Trae got back to his room, he called Karina. As much as he hated to admit it, she had his nose wide open, which felt weird. Normally, he didn't even allow women to get this close to him, but Karina was the first thing he thought about in the morning and the last thing he thought about at night. She brought some sanity to his crazy life. He wouldn't dare say this to Kevin, but for the first time in his life he was in love.

The first time he called Karina there was no answer. So after a few minutes, he called again. This time she answered on the first ring.

"Hey baby," Karina said, glad to hear Trae's voice.

"Hey. Where were you?" he asked, with a slight hint of anger.

"I was in the shower. I was hoping that would help me feel a little better."

Trae was concerned. "Why, what's wrong?" he asked.

Trying not to alarm him, Karina told him they could discuss it when he came home. But Trae wasn't letting up. He wanted to know what was wrong and demanded an answer.

After pausing for a few more seconds, she finally answered. "I think you're gonna be a daddy," she blurted out. Silence fell over the phone for what seemed like an eternity. "Trae, did you hear what I just said?" Karina didn't understand why he was so surprised about her possibly being pregnant. Especially since they always had unprotected sex.

"Yeah, I heard you," he said, in a frail tone. "So, why did you say you think I'm gonna be a daddy?"

"Because I just took a home pregnancy test to confirm the results, but I'm almost certain that we're gonna have a baby."

Again, there was a long period of silence.

"Well...are you gonna say anything?" Karina asked, feeling like Trae wasn't excited about the news.

DEEP

"I mean, what is there to say? If you pregnant, you pregnant," he answered in a nonchalant tone.

Karina's mouth fell open as a single tear strolled down her cheek. "I knew you weren't gonna be happy about this," she said.

"Baby, what are you talkin' 'bout'? I mean, I'm shocked that's all. I thought you were takin' somethin'," Trae responded. He took a deep breath. "Trust me, I'm happy. How could I not be happy?"

Karina could sense Trae wasn't telling the truth, but decided to let it go for the moment. "When are you coming home," she asked.

"I'll be back tomorrow," Trae replied. He could tell she was still upset.

"I'll see you then, I gotta run to the bathroom." She hung up before he had a chance to respond and held her stomach, thinking about her situation. *Maybe Ashley was right about him,* she thought.

It was 6:18 p.m. when the plane touched down on the runway of BWI Airport the next day. As soon as the plane cruised into the gate and the seatbelt sign disappeared, Trae and Kevin gathered their baggage from the overhead compartments and waited patiently to depart.

Big Paul and Carmen were waiting for them like Secret Service agents at the front entrance as soon as they walked out.

"What's up wit y'all niggas? Off runnin' around and shit while we got business to tend too," Big Paul said laughing, as he threw the bags in the back of his Navigator.

Trae could sense the uneasiness in the way Kevin looked at Carmen and kept mumbling something under his breath. But he didn't care, this was business, so Kevin's personal feelings would have to be put aside.

"It couldn't be helped, we had to roll out," Trae said, as they all hopped in the truck. "So what's the word on that thing?" he asked.

Big Paul looked in the back seat then back at Trae, "Everythin's everythin'. We have nothin' to worry 'bout," he said, whispering.

Thank God Big Paul had enough sense not to say nothing. What the fuck is Trae thinking talkin' 'bout business in front of this bitch? Kevin thought to himself.

About two miles from D.C., Trae asked Big Paul to pull over on the side of the road. The moment Carmen heard Trae's words her heart raced. *Oh shit,* she thought. *Does he know about me?*

When Big Paul stopped the truck, Trae told Kevin to switch seats with him.

Carmen's heart pounded as she watched Trae get in the back and sit beside her.

Trae knew what he was about to say was going cause a problem between him and Kevin, but he didn't care. They needed more man power, and Carmen was a perfect fit.

"So, are you sure that you wanna do this?" he asked looking at Carmen. "Because once you in...you in."

"What the fuck you mean she in?" Kevin snapped from the front seat.

Trae gave him a dirty look. "Shorty, we'll discuss this later. Look, have I ever steered us wrong before?"

Kevin turned around and rocked back and forth in his seat. "You makin' a big mistake," he mumbled.

Carmen ignored Kevin's temper tantrum and asked, "When do I start?"

Trae looked in the front of the truck at Kevin, who was so pissed he considered walking home. "I'll call you in a couple of days," he said.

"Cool."

Trae looked down at his diamond bezel Rolex watch. "Big P. drop me off at the club," Trae commanded. "I need to check on things before I head home."

"How you gonna get there?" Big Paul asked.

"One of my hoopties is there. I'll drive that."

Just as the foursome pulled up in front of the club, Trae's phone rang. When he looked at the screen, he took a deep breath.

"The test was positive...I'm pregnant," Karina said, as soon as Trae answered.

"Are you sure?" Trae asked.

Karina paused before answering. She couldn't believe he was asking her that. "Of course I'm sure."

Trae and Karina talked for a few more minutes before he hung up. His face went cold as stone as he ended the call.

"Yo', what's going on?" Kevin asked. He could tell from the tone of Trae's voice that something was wrong.

"Nothin', Trae said irritated. Trae refused to talk about it. Instead, he got out the truck and headed inside the club.

Trae's friends knew he was going through it with the business, but they had no idea how he was going through it personally. Trae tried

DEEP

hard to keep his personal life private, but he knew things were about to come to a head.

Once Trae made his rounds, he walked down the hall toward his office, and the first person he bumped into was Sommone. The sexy schoolgirl uniform she wore had him wanting to be a teacher instantly.

"Hey beautiful. How about' havin' a night cap with me," Trae said, jingling his keys in his hands.

"Ah, sure," Sommone said, not knowing exactly why she was being asked. "I'm free, I just finished my set."

Once Trae was sure no one saw him and Sommone enter the office, he put his *Do Not Disturb* sign on the door and locked it. He walked over to his desk and placed his keys on top before going the small bar he kept in his office and fixed two Hennessy and Cokes.

"Here you go," Trae said, handing Sommone a glass. He sat down on his plush red leather coach and patted the seat. "Come sit next to me."

I don't even drink this shit, she thought. "Thanks, I needed a drink. I had a rough day," Sommone replied, as she sat down. Even though she was a little nervous, she had to play it off.

"Join the crowd. I'm always having rough days." He looked at Sommone's sexy costume and licked his lips.

Trae's intense stare made her feel uncomfortable. "Umm...so I haven't seen you around in a few days. Is everything okay?" she asked.

Trae took a sip of his drink. "Yeah, everything's good, but thanks for askin'."

After talking for at least an hour, Trae didn't realize how tired he was and began drifting in and out of the conversation. Minutes later, Sommone's face was the last thing he saw before he fell asleep.

After watching Trae sleep for a few minutes, Sommone knew what she was about to do was extremely risky, but she had to take care of business. She quietly made her way to Trae's desk and went through his stuff for a few seconds before finding what she was looking for. She lifted up her short pleaded skirt and placed the item inside her panties just in case Trae woke up.

After completing her mission, she looked at Trae, who was snoring by that point and quietly whispered, "I got you know now."

A NOVEL BY DANETTE MAJETTE

That same night, Carmen took a shower, put on her pajamas, then called to check in.

"I'm in," she said.

"Good. When do you start?" Willie asked.

"I don't know. He said he'd call me in a couple of days."

Willie had already explained to Carmen how dangerous this assignment was, but he felt he needed to remind her again. He knew that if anything ever happened to her, he would never be able to forgive himself. She was not only his employee, she and her husband were good friends of his. Willie wanted Trae locked down more than any other criminal, but he didn't want to lose Carmen in the process.

"By the way, Sommone is in too," he uttered. She got really close to him tonight. So close, she could've killed his bitch ass while he was sleep," he joked.

DEEP

A COSTLY AFFAIR

The next morning, Trae woke up to the sounds of beer bottles being tossed in the trash. When he looked around at the Stacy Dash Playboy pictures that were on his wall, he realized that he'd fallen asleep in his office. *Damn, I must've been tired,* he thought, as he looked at his watch that read 8:09 a.m.

"Well my clothes are still on, so I guess Sommone didn't seduce me last night," he said aloud, followed by a laugh. He stood up and stretched before walking over to his desk to get his keys. When he couldn't find them, he began to rub his bald head.

"Damn, I thought I put 'em on the desk," he said, to himself.

When he glanced back at the clock, he knew he had to get home, so he went to his safe, punched in the code, and pulled out a spare set before quickly walking out the door.

After giving some of his Spanish workers a few orders, he hopped in his hooptie and headed to Bethesda. Even though it was the last thing he wanted to do after hearing the news that he was going to be a daddy. He loved Karina, but fatherhood was not on his mind. Besides, they hadn't even been seeing each other long enough to have a child yet. Trae had a problem that he hoped would eventually go away, but it did the exact opposite. Now he was trying to figure out how to handle it.

Still lying in bed, Karina opened her eyes when she heard Trae coming into the bedroom. He walked over to the nightstand and tossed his keys on the dark colored wood.

"Where have you been? I thought you were coming back yesterday?" she asked, sitting up in the bed.

Trae couldn't concentrate on what she said, after seeing her glowing skin in a black baby doll lingerie set.

"Did you hear me?" Karina yelled. "Where were you?"

A NOVEL BY DANETTE MAJETTE

"Karina, I had some business to take care of at the club last night. By the time I finished, I was too tired to drive, so I just slept on the couch in my office," Trae said.

"Did you sleep by yourself?" she asked, on the brink of tears.

"What?"

"You heard me!"

Trae was too tired to even argue. Instead, he stood by the closet door and took off his shirt. It was obvious that her attitude had changed drastically. "I think this baby thing is getting to you already!" he yelled.

"Don't try to put this on my hormones. Answer the question," Karina snapped.

Trae walked over and sat on the edge of the bed. Looking Karina in her eyes he answered, "Baby, I didn't sleep with anybody last night or any other night for that matter. I wouldn't do that to you."

Karina's tears began to flow heavily. "I don't know what to do. I thought the baby would bring us closer, but I can tell you don't even want it!"

"I never said that I didn't want the baby."

"Oh yeah. Well, you didn't say you wanted it either. I don't even think you want to be with me anymore. Especially when you got all these skeezers after you!" she yelled, changing gears.

"I don't want those bitches!"

"Yeah right!" Karina yelled, getting out of bed. "You think I don't know what you out there doing. People talk, Trae. I know about all of them! You just remember something, I'ma be the one there when your ass get locked up!" she screamed.

The writing was on the wall. Trae jumped up, and just as he was about to grab Karina by the throat, his grandmother's face flashed in front of him. *Don't you dare! You know you should never put your hands on a woman. What would your mother say if she saw this?* Instead, he slammed the cordless phone that was on the dresser against the wall. Karina's eyes followed the phone as it slid down the wall and onto the floor.

She turned back to Trae.

"Get out!" she yelled. "Get out!"

"This is my damn house. I ain't goin' nowhere."

"Oh, you will once I call the cops and tell them you're a fuckin' drug dealer!"

Trae instantly snapped and clutched Karina's throat tightly, slamming her against the wall with force. Karina was too afraid to cry. Her

DEEP

back was in pain from hitting the wall, but she didn't say a word.

Coming to his senses, Trae finally let go. He grabbed his keys, along with his shirt and walked out the door.

Karina yelled and cursed at Trae as he walked down the steps. She couldn't believe what he'd done. When he got to the front door, he slammed it so hard, a picture of his mother fell off the wall and onto the floor. He never looked back as he quickly drove off, leaving Karina in the doorway.

"Fuck you!" she yelled, as she picked up a rock and threw it at his car.

For a brief moment Trae was tempted to drive back and smack Karina in her face when he heard the rock graze his truck. *Oh, this bitch must be crazy. Don't nobody fuck wit' my car.*

Later that evening, after napping the day away, Karina got up and went into the kitchen for a snack. Standing at the kitchen counter, she made a turkey and cheese sandwich. After adding two pickles and chips on the side, she sat down at the dining room table and began to eat. When she finished, she cleaned up, and got back into bed. *Damn, why did our first fight have to end like this? I hope this is not a sign of how this relationship is gonna be. He better not ever put his hands on me again because I'll leave all this shit behind!*

She continued to think about her life with Trae until she was almost asleep, when suddenly a sharp pain jolted across her stomach. "Ahhh…ahh!" she screamed in agony. The pain subsided for a few minutes, but then returned. "Aww…!"

Convinced something was definitely wrong, she looked around on the bed for the phone to call Trae. "Damn," she said, remembering he'd thrown the phone across the room.

Just as she attempted to get out of bed, she was hit with another pain that sent her falling back onto the bed. Laying still and taking deep breaths, Karina prayed for the strength to get up. She waited for a few minutes then tried to get up again. She was almost on her feet, when she collapsed.

She'd been laying on the floor in a fetal position holding her stomach, for what seemed like eternity, when she heard Trae come in the bedroom.

"Karina!" he yelled, as he rushed to her side. "Karina, come on baby get up!" She didn't budge. Trae looked at the oversized light blue shirt she wore, and noticed a huge spot of blood.

Karina finally opened her eyes and looked at Trae. "You don't have to worry about the baby anymore," she said, with a dazed glare in her eyes. "It's gone."

Trae's mind went blank for a minute. Then he reached into his pocket, pulled out his cell phone and dialed 911.

When the ambulance arrived, Trae ran down and let them in.

"My girlfriend is in the bathroom. I think she just had a miscarriage," he said sadly.

The paramedics quickly walked to the bedroom, where Karina was laying on the floor, and immediately started to work on her.

"We need to take her to the hospital. She's lost a lot of blood, but she'll be alright," one of the paramedics said, patting Trae on the back.

Trae felt like shit. *If only I hadn't left her. She wouldn't have lost the baby,* he thought.

In a cold and dark hospital room, Karina laid in the bed and cried until her tear ducts were empty. Not only had she lost her baby, but she felt like she'd lost Trae as well. As far as she was concerned the relationship was definitely over. In her mind, he was the one responsible for the loss of their child.

Sitting in the waiting room, Trae saw his grandmother's face. *What's wrong with you, son? Why would you do something like that? She was the mother of your child. Don't you know that girl loves you? Now you may have lost her.*

Trae wiped the tears from his face and walked down the hall to Karina's room. Before he entered, he took a deep breath and prayed she would forgive him. When he opened the door and saw her lying there defeated with grief, he felt like the animal people said he was.

A distraught Karina ripped the IV's out of her arms, trying to get out of the bed when she saw Trae's face. Once she pulled out the last needle, she ran toward him like a deranged lunatic.

"You bastard!" she yelled, hitting him repeatedly. "This is all your fault!"

Ignoring the alarms that went off from the monitors, she continued to lash out at Trae. He tried to calm her down, but she wasn't having it. She started throwing everything in sight, until a nurse came in and asked Trae to leave.

DEEP

"I don't want to leave. I need to be here wit' my girl," he responded.

"Sir, can't you see she doesn't want you here? Come back when she calms down," the nurse said, trying to hold Karina back.

"You did this," Karina said, pointing at Trae.

He shook his head, then turned around and left the room. He knew Karina would be upset, but he had no idea she would act like that. It amazed him how she had the strength to do that after a miscarriage.

When he got in his car, he couldn't bear to go home, so he sped off in route to Pleasures. Thinking about Karina constantly, his mind was all over the place, causing him to almost cause a few accidents. He silently cursed at himself for not wanting the baby in the first place, but putting his hands on a woman was dead wrong considering what happened to his mother. He figured he would have children with Karina one day, but he thought it would be once their future was secure. *Damn, it is my fault.*

Trae arrived at the club a few minutes later, and walked straight to the bar.

"Yo', give me a Hennessy and Coke," he said to Sam, one of his bartenders. As he waited, he looked to his right and caught a glimpse of a familiar face. The girl was talking to her friend, but staring back at Trae.

After exchanging a few more glances, she strutted over with confidence and stood behind him. He turned around, looked her up and down, and smiled.

"You remember me?" the woman asked.

"Of course I remember you. Why did you front on my girl like that?" Trae asked. "I mean, you were gettin' ready to fight in your Cheesecake Factory uniform and everythin'."

Courtney laughed. "Well, when I see something I want, I go for it. I don't give a shit if you got a girl."

Trae laughed. "Damn, you bold."

"So, why did you take my number at the park that day, if you were never gonna call me?"

"Oh, I'm sorry. I've just been busy," he replied.

"Damn, I look that bad."

"Naw. It's nothin' like that."

Courtney got closer to Trae. "Then make it up to me and buy me a drink."

"A'ight," Trae responded.

As he ordered Courtney an Amarillo Sour, he looked at the tight jeans she wore that hugged her in all the right places. "Can I ask you a question?"

"Sure."

"What are you doing at a strip club? You're not gay, are you?" Trae asked. "Or are you looking for a job?"

Courtney smiled and placed her long manicured nails over her mouth. "Honestly, me and my friend come here to meet guys."

"Are you serious?" he asked.

"Yeah. All the dudes that be up in here lookin' at pussy. I'm bound to find somebody. Shoot, I found you up in here," she said.

When Sam handed Trae the drink, he passed it to Courtney. "Actually, I'm in here almost every night, but not because I want to look at pussy, it's because I own the place."

Courtney looked surprised. "Really, I had no idea you owned this spot. Well, you got a nice lil' titty bar here."

They both cracked up. "Hey, why don't you come go wit' me to my office? We can have a little more privacy there," Trae suggested.

"Alright. Let me just say bye to my friend, she's about to leave," Courtney said.

She went back over to where her friend was sitting. Smiling from ear to ear, she told her friend that Trae owned the club, and that he wanted to take her to his office.

"So, I guess your plan is working," her friend said.

"I guess so," Courtney responded before walking back in Trae's direction.

Trae and Courtney drank, laughed and talked until the wee hours of the morning. For a moment, he had forgotten all about his troubles with Karina.

"You look like you're upset about somethin'," Courtney said, as she sipped on her fifth glass of champagne.

"Yeah, my problem is that I want you," Trae revealed, pulling her close to him on the couch.

Her perky D-cup breasts sent shockwaves through his body. Trae could tell by her response that she was the type of woman who went after what she wanted. She stood in front of him guiding his hands between her thighs. Not wasting time, Courtney pulled her designer t-shirt over her head. Her breasts bulged out of her silky Victoria Secret

DEEP

bra, which was rapidly removed.

Although Trae was horny, he tried to act cool as he got undressed. But that went out the window when Courtney pulled down her jeans, exposing her shapely thighs and huge round ass. He got in on the action, by helping her out of her panties, and slowly pulled them down her legs. Her body was a work of art.

Excited, he quickly took off all his clothes and stood in front of her with his dick at attention.

Courtney smiled. "That's an old place for a scar," she said, pointing to Trae's dick.

"It's a birth mark," Trae replied. "Now, can we get on to business?"

"Oh, absolutely."

As Courtney's wet tongue licked and stroked every inch of his body, his shaft began to pulse uncontrollably. He thought he was going to lose his mind when she took her tongue and slid it down the crack of his ass.

"I see you like that," Courtney said seductively. "Well, let's see if you like the way I play with this python," she said, placing her hand around his dick. Her tongue began exploring the head, circling the ridge like an expert. Carefully covering every inch of skin with saliva, she licked it like a pro.

"Yeah, that's it, baby!" Trae said, enjoying her stiff oral grip. His dick throbbed with enjoyment as her lips slid deeper down his manhood.

Trae's breathing got heavy as he grabbed her head and guided her strokes. From the way his hips jerked against her face, she knew he was about to blow. Instantly, she pulled his dick out of her mouth, not wanting him to cum yet.

"Okay, let's see if you're ready for what I got," Courtney said, kissing his stomach.

She stood up and positioned herself over the couch, so Trae could hit it from the back. As soon as he entered her, she started moaning at the feel of Trae's large dick inside her walls.

"Damn girl," Trae said, grabbing a fistful of Courtney's long hair.

"Oh, I'm just getting started," she said, shaking her ass back and forth.

Turned on by Courtney's animalistic behavior, Trae smacked her on the ass.

"Yeah, that's it, baby," Courtney muffled, as she moaned and wiggled her ass. "C'mon, fuck me harder," she commanded.

A NOVEL BY DANETTE MAJETTE

Trae started slamming his thick post deeper inside her. "Oh you like it like that, huh," he said, feeling her body tremble.

"Yeah, just like that," she mumbled, like her mouth was stuffed with something.

It wasn't long before electric shivers ran through Courtney's body. Slowly, she started to float back to earth. Then without notice, all Trae's built up tension shot down his shaft. Exploding and howling like a coyote, he shot a sticky load of sperm right into Courtney then began to gradually wilt inside her.

Soon, the two sat on the couch sweating, panting, and gathering their senses.

"Damn that shit was good!" Trae yelled. "Are you on somethin'?

"What do you mean am I on somethin'?" Courtney asked.

"I mean like birth control. I forgot to strap up."

"Oh, don't worry, I'm on the pill," she said, massaging his chest.

Wow, he thought. *I gotta keep her around, she's good. Damn good!*

It was eight-thirty the next morning when Trae's phone rung, waking him and Courtney. When he saw it was the hospital, he panicked.

"Oh shit, I gotta go. Get dressed," he said, damn near throwing Courtney's clothes at her."

"Is everything okay?" Courtney asked.

"No, it's not. I need for you to get out of here."

"Well, am I gonna see you later?" she asked.

Trae sighed. "No, I got a girl, so I don't think so. As a matter of fact, my girl is in the hospital and needs me right now, so hurry up wit' your shit," Trae replied.

Courtney was heated. "Does your girlfriend know that you cheat on her?"

Trae gave her a deadly stare. "Don't concern yourself wit' my girl. Your pussy was good, but not good enough to throw threats around. Get dressed and get the fuck out!"

Courtney did just that, while keeping a mental note of how Trae treated her in the back of her mind. As soon as she walked out of his office Trae knew he hadn't seen the last of her. She left civilized, but the vindictive look on her face told him otherwise.

Picking up his cell phone, he called the hospital back. When he talked to one of the nurses on duty, she told Trae that Karina had

DEEP

agreed to see him. *I guess she wants to tell me it's over,* he thought. *I deserve it. I've cheated on her and caused her to lose our baby. Why would she want to stay with me?*

Trae quickly got dressed, and went in the bathroom to splash some water on his face. Before he walked out the door, he looked back at his leather couch. *If Karina ever finds out about last night, I'm fucked,* he thought.

He walked out into the parking lot, jumped in his car and drove toward Bethesda. Sitting at a light that seemed to take forever, Trae's mind wondered. A few seconds later, a driver behind him honked angrily, bringing him back to reality.

"Keep your pants on!" Trae yelled at the car, who quickly went around him. "I hate fuckin' aggressive drivers," he said, as his thoughts went back to Karina.

Minutes later, Trae was walking down the hospital corridor, headed for the gift shop. After making a few selections, he went to the counter. "I'll take these and this," Trae said, digging in his pocket.

"Must be a very special lady," the clerk said, smiling.

Trae nodded his head. "Yeah, she is."

Outside Karina's door, his heart raced as he tightly held the dozen red roses and a teddy bear that said *I Love You* in his hand. The thought of Karina leaving him had Trae nervous. *You know you're on the chopping block, right. You better do some serious sucking up,* he heard his grandmother say in the back of his mind.

He stuck his head in the room first, to make sure the coast was clear before entering. Besides, he didn't want everybody in his business if Karina was about to go off again. Taking a seat beside Karina's bed, he looked at her hands as they shook uncontrollably.

"Are you a'ight?" he asked.

She nodded.

He handed her the roses and the bear.

Karina smiled slightly. "They're beautiful," she said, smelling the flowers.

"You sure you alright?" he asked again.

When she looked down at her hands, she saw why he'd asked. Her beautifully manicured nails were now broken remnants from the night before. They both started to speak at the same time.

"Wait, let me talk first," Trae said, holding Karina's hand. "I know I haven't been the ideal man lately. And then to top it off, we have our first and last fight, then lose our baby. I know all of this shit is enough to make any woman leave, but I'm begging you, give me another chance. I know we can make this work." Tears wailed in his eyes. "Please."

Trae's tears surprised Karina. She sat up in her bed. "It's funny how you want to make this work now. Even though we haven't been dealing with each other long, it doesn't seem like I'm your first priority," Karina said.

"I know, I know," he said, squirming in the chair. He looked up toward the ceiling. "I promise I'll have more time for you now. I just hired a girl named Carmen, and she's helping Kevin take a lot of shit off my plate."

"A girl?" Karina asked.

"Yeah, but it's not what you think. She's a Bonnie and Clyde meets ride or die kinda chick."

"I don't want someone to take things off your plate. I want us to move and start a normal life. A honest life," Karina said.

Even though he still hadn't told her anything, she knew from the start what Trae did for a living, but she always hoped he would give it up. For Trae, that was easier said than done. He was in too deep.

"Baby, I promise we will live a honest life after this last big job. I'm telling you, it's gonna have us set for life."

Trae's plea seemed sincere, but Karina was unsure.

"I don't know. I just need some time to think about this, so I'm gonna go stay with Ashley for a while," she replied. She waited for Trae to flip out, but he didn't. Instead, he told her she could go home and he would go stay at Kevin's place for a few days. Karina agreed.

DEEP

ON THE GRIND

With Karina needing some time away from Trae, it gave him the time he needed to completely focus on business, so he called a meeting.

At the head of the table, Trae peered at Carmen and asked her if she was ready for her first big assignment. When she said she was, Trae looked at Kevin, who was frowning. He was obviously pissed. Kevin had made it very clear that he was leery of Carmen even being in the organization, let alone a part of their most outrageous scheme to date. Kevin would put his life and freedom on the line for Trae, Big Paul or Ice Man any day, but a new cat on the block was a major problem for him.

"Big P., are we set up with the armory?" Trae asked.

"Yeah. We should hit in a few months while the MP's are doin' a night exercise," Big Paul responded.

"Kev, what about the Dominicans? They money right?" Trae asked.

"I gotta check, but they should be ready when we are," Kevin replied, leaning back in his chair. He inhaled smoke from his blunt.

"I guess we set then," Trae informed them.

"What about me?" Carmen asked, looking at Trae.

"What about you?" Kevin asked laughing.

Carmen gave him a smirk. She knew Kevin was intimidated by her presence, so she went in for the kill. "Well, I guess I'll be wherever you are Trae. You might need someone to watch your back."

"What the fuck is that suppose to mean?" Kevin asked, raising up in his chair.

"I think we both know what it means," Carmen answered, with a sneaky smile. "You hating on me 'cuz I'm a woman. Yet, I'm the same woman that saved yo' boy's ass when you couldn't."

Trae could feel the tension in the room. And even though Kevin was his boy, Carmen had a point. There had been two attempts on his life, and Kevin was with him both times and didn't pull his weight.

"Look, we didn't come here for all that. We got business to do. If we don't do this just right, we all gonna be doin' twenty to life in the pen. So let's make sure we cross all our T's and dot our I's," Trae said.

Carmen listened attentively as Trae ran down the plan to rob the Armory on the 8th and I Marine Corps Base in Southeast D.C. Big Paul's cousin, Richard, was a private at the command, and told him how it could be done with him on the inside. They were going to steal some major firepower, then sell it to the Dominicans for five million. And in return, all it was going to cost them was three hundred thousand, which was Richard's fee.

Trae pointed to the blueprint and said, "Carmen, Richard said the Armory is located next to the mess hall where the soldiers eat. They get deliveries on the base every morning, so I bought a white van, and I'm gonna disguise it as a contractor as the get away car."

"Let me get this right, y'all gonna hit an armory on a base?" Carmen asked confused.

"Yes, we're gonna overpower Richard, steal the goods and be out," Big Paul said.

"Don't you think the Feds are gonna be all over your cousin?" Carmen asked.

"Why you gotta bring up the Feds? Do you know something that we don't?" Kevin asked suspiciously.

Carmen and Kevin stared at each other for a few minutes before Trae spoke up. "Kev, let Big Paul finish."

Big Paul explained to them that if and when the military came looking for his cousin, they wouldn't be able to find him because that wasn't his real name. He went on to explain how his cousin had committed identity theft, and the real Richard Daniels was a dorky white dude who lived in England.

"Oh," Carmen replied in shock. She knew Trae was a big time drug dealer, but she had no idea he was into other illegal activities.

"After that 9/11 shit, they've been trying to recruit any and everybody. So when my cousin walked in looking sharp with all of Richard's credentials...his degree from Penn State, his birth certificate, and social security card, saying he wanted to join, they hopped on him," Big Paul said laughing. "Them army niggas green as hell, cause my cousin's real name is Greg."

DEEP

Carmen wanted to ask what Greg's last name was, but didn't want to bring about any added suspicion. Kevin was already on her heels.

"As you can see, we've had this planned for months. Greg had to go through boot camp and all that shit, but it's gonna be worth it. He was on a 'get rich or die tryin mission'. Not a save 'George Bush's oil empire mission and die for free'," Trae said, with a serious look on his face.

After they went over the last minute details of the heist, they played cards. *We have totally underestimated these fools,* Carmen thought to herself, as she laid down her two of spade, cutting Kevin's king of hearts.

DEEP

INDUCTION INTO THE FAMILY

Later that night, it was time for Carmen's initiation. She just wasn't aware of it at the time. The crew drove to a house at the end of a deserted street in Northeast D.C. No one was outside, but Carmen could hear music coming from the basement. As they got out the car, Big Paul went through the door of the crack house first. They led Carmen to a small room, where a group of guys were sitting around playing craps.

"Yo', what's the deal? That nigga Rico get here yet?" Trae asked, a scruffy bearded guy, who was sitting in the corner.

"Naw. He said he on his way though," he replied.

Kevin went and sat down at the table and watched the men as they rolled the dice and talked shit to each other. Sipping on a beer, he grabbed from the refrigerator, he stared at Carmen with contempt.

"What's up with that?" Ice Man whispered.

"Man, I don't know. Her pussy and good looks done swindled her way into the fam, but I don't trust that bitch. It's somethin in her eyes," Kevin said, quietly in Ice Man's ear.

"Well, we'll see what she's about in a few minutes." Ice Man replied. "When Rico gets here, it's show time."

Ten minutes later when Rico arrived, it looked like he was about to jump out his skin when he opened the door and saw Trae.

"Check him for a piece, Carm," Trae ordered, sitting in a chair nearby.

Carmen quickly jumped out her chair and searched Rico. "He's clean," she said.

"Shorty, you got my dough?"Trae asked acting like a true mobster.

Rico looked terrified. "I only have half right now. I need a couple of days to get the rest. I needed to pay some bills for my girl."

"What? We ain't got bills to pay?" Trae asked. "Nigga, you been

A NOVEL BY DANETTE MAJETTE

fuckin' wit' my money for a while."

"Come on Trae, man, I'm good for it," Rico pleaded.

"So what, I'm suppose to forget you owe me?" Trae asked, in disbelief. He scratched his head. "If I do that, word would get around that I'm some kind of bitch. Then what? I'll probably be out of business," he said. Trae pulled his Glock out and pointed it at Rico, who looked as if he was about to faint.

"Hey, Carm, you want to do the honors?" Trae asked.

Carmen's heart pounded rapidly, but she knew that if she didn't do what Trae asked, her cover would be blown. "No doubt," she answered with a frown. She walked over to where he was sitting and grabbed the gun from his hand. Turning around to Rico, she prayed. Holding the gun up to Rico's heart, she slowly placed her finger on the trigger and pulled it.

Luckily the chamber was empty. She clicked it a second time, but again nothing. Carmen paused for a moment, then lowered the gun and looked at Trae.

Rico yelled, "Wait!" He broke into a cold sweat. "I can go get your money right now from my place."

"Now you're talkin'!" Trae said, shaking his head. "Ice Man, go wit' him. You know what to do if his ass doesn't come correct."

When the two left for Rico's apartment, Trae, Carmen, Big Paul and Kevin sat back and had a good laugh as all the other guys in the room looked terrified.

"I guess I underestimated you," Kevin said, shaking Carmen's hand. "Welcome to the family."

Carmen was relieved. Not only had she gotten out of shooting a man, she finally had Kevin's trust.

Sitting on the edge of her hospital bed, Karina waited anxiously for the nurse to return with her release forms. Moments later, a short bald man wearing a white coat came into the room.

"Hello. I'm Doctor Roper. How are you feeling today?" he asked, checking her pulse.

"I'm fine, but I'll be even better once I get out of here," Karina replied.

"Well, I know the nurse gave you your after care instructions, but I just wanted to see if you had any last minute questions."

Karina shook her head and said, "No, I don't."

DEEP

After writing a few notes on his clipboard, he wished Karina good health and left.

A few minutes later, the nurse returned. "Just sign in these two places, and then you can be on your way," the burly nurse said.

Karina signed the papers and handed them back. "You're all set," the nurse said, grabbing the wheelchair that was positioned in the corner of the room.

"I don't need that," Karina said, pushing the wheelchair away from her.

"I have to wheel you out. It's standard procedure," the nurse responded.

Karina cursed the nurse under her breath. "Whatever it takes to get me out of here," she mumbled, as she sat down in the chair.

Ashley was waiting at the hospital's entrance when Karina exited the electric double doors. The nurse stopped and locked the wheels, then helped Karina into Ashley's car. As the nurse waived goodbye, Karina reclined the passenger's seat, and placed her Gucci glasses snuggly over her eyes to block the sun.

"You're gonna be Hollywood to the end," Ashley teased, trying to lift Karina's spirits as she pulled off.

"I'm not trying to be Hollywood, I'm trying to see. I've been in that dark ass hospital room for two days. Hell, I almost forgot the sun existed until I got to the door," she said laughing. Soon the laughter turned into tears.

Ashley immediately pulled over and comforted her friend with a huge hug. "I know it hurts, but you're gonna get through it. And I'm gonna be there with you every step of the way," she said.

Ashley's kind words made Karina feel even worse. Since moving in with Trae, she rarely had time for Ashley, except when they were at work. After sitting on the side of the road for a few more minutes, Ashley pulled back into traffic.

When they pulled up in the circular driveway of Trae's house, Ashley turned off the ignition, and jumped out. When she saw Karina struggling to get out, she quickly ran over to her side of the car.

"Would you wait a second? You need to take it easy!" she yelled.

"I'm not disabled or some shit," Karina said, as she walked up to the door with Ashley at her side. Once inside, she sat on the couch and watched Ashley's strange stares.

"Damn," Ashley said. "You over here living good." It was her first time at Trae's house, so Karina told her she could take a look around.

Ashley was actually a little jealous of the way Karina was living. She felt like Karina didn't have a care in the world, while she was having a hard time making ends meet ever since Karina moved out and left her paying all the rent.

Ashley strolled back into the living room, and found Karina laying on the couch. "Why don't you go up and take a long hot bath? I'll make you some lunch," Ashley suggested.

"Thanks. And I don't mean just for offering to make me lunch. Thanks for everything," Karina said.

"You're more than welcome," Ashley replied, heading off to the kitchen.

Tears formed in the corner of Karina's eyes as soon as she walked in the bedroom and saw the partially cleaned blood stain on the floor. She wiped her eyes, pulled herself together, and walked into the bathroom to run her bath water.

Minutes later, she was settled in the tub surrounded by scented candles, and reminisced about the night she lost her baby along with the events that led up to it. *Why did this happen? How did this happen?* Eventually all her thoughts led back to Trae.

The bath soothed Karina and allowed her to let her worries go. She dried off, threw on her favorite pajamas, and then went down to the kitchen.

"Hey, you feel a little better?" Ashley asked, fixing their plates.

"I don't know about better, but I sure feel a whole lot cleaner." The two friends laughed.

"I whipped up these BLT sandwiches. Bacon was all I could find in the refrigerator. How can you and Trae be living so fly, with no food?"

Karina laughed. "You're so crazy. Let's eat this outside. It's a nice day."

Sitting out on the patio, Karina and Ashley laughed about old times. But suddenly Karina got serious.

"So why haven't you said you told me so?" The question totally caught Ashley off guard. "I know you probably think I brought all this misery on myself."

Ashley put her sandwich down and grabbed her friend's hand. "I would never think that."

Karina looked dazed and confused. "Sometimes I wonder if this relationship is worth it."

"What are you talking bout?"

"Is all the pain and misery worth it?"

"Worth what?" Ashley asked.

DEEP

"You know, having the finest cars, shopping for clothes whenever I want, eating in fancy restaurants, and living in this big ass house."

"Karina, only you can answer that question. You know so many women get caught up in the material things, they don't realize that they're paying a price for it. Women always pay a price for it emotionally, but sometimes it can be physically. Trust me, I know."

Karina looked at Ashley, sensing she had a story to tell. "How do you know? You never get involved with bad boys."

"That's because a bad boy almost got me killed. I never told you this, but I used to date this guy named, Red who was a big time dealer from Barry Farms. One night I heard a noise downstairs in the kitchen, so I called out to him, but he didn't answer. I thought he was playing a trick on me, so I got back in bed and waited for him to come running in the room. Oh girl, I was actin' up, yelling down the stairs, telling him to hurry up so I could suck his dick 'till his toes curled up."

Karina giggled. "Then what happened!" she asked.

"The worse thing that could ever happen to a woman."

Karina was really confused when Ashley started to tear up.

"A few minutes later, three guys ran in. Girl, I jumped up scared as hell, screaming like a maniac. I was about to smash one of them over the head with a lamp, when the smaller guy pulled out a gun and hit me across the face with it. But that didn't stop me! I kicked, screamed and punched him until one of the bigger guys grabbed me and threw me down on the floor."

"What! Oh my God, Ashley, you never told me that. Who were they?"

Ashley tried to hold back tears as she continued to tell her story. "The one guy had me pinned down, while the other two groped and felt on me. Then they ripped off my clothes and told me to tell Red this is what he gets for fucking up their money. That's when they each took turns raping me."

Karina was so dumbfounded, she didn't even know what to say. She knew Ashley had a dislike for thug type dudes, but she assumed it was because one had treated her wrong. She had no idea it was this bad.

Ashley walked over to the pool that was covered for the season. "Those bastards did some of the most disgusting things to me. They tore my insides up so bad that I'll never be able to have children. And for what!" she screamed. She turned to Karina. "All because the guy I was with fucked them over, not because of anything I did."

After seeing the expression on Karina's face, Ashley apologized.

"You don't have to apologize," Karina said, holding her friend in her arms. "You have nothing to apologize for."

"I didn't mean to lay all this on you. You have your own problems to deal with. I just want you to understand that this gangsta shit ain't no joke. These guys don't care out here. If they can't hurt Trae, they'll try to hurt you." Ashley then made a startling confession to Karina. "Do you know that after everything I went through I stayed with Red?"

"Are you kidding me?" Karina asked in shock.

"Nope. Two weeks after I was released from the hospital, he bought me a condo and my car. I guess you can say all was forgiven after that."

Karina shook her head. "Why?"

"Well, I wasn't smart enough to save any of the money he gave me. If I had left, I would've had to go live with my mother in the projects, and face the bitches I once looked down on. I wasn't having that back then. I was only nineteen, but I woke up one day."

"Ashley, I hear what you're saying and if it was just about the material things then I would leave, but I love Trae. I don't know what I would do without him," Karina said.

"Karina, you don't need a man in your life to make you complete. Take care of yourself first. Let that nigga compliment you."

After talking for a few more minutes, Karina gave Ashley a big hug then walked her to the door.

Later that night, Karina was spooked by any little noise she heard downstairs. *Damn! I never thought I would be scared to sleep in my own bed.* Seconds later, the sound of her cell phone ringing nearly sent her through the roof. When she looked at the caller ID, her face frowned. *I thought I told him not to call me,* she thought, as she clicked the talk button.

"Hello," she answered.

"Hey, I know you told me not to call you," Trae said.

Well, evidently you didn't listen, Karina thought, as she rolled her eyes at the sound of his voice.

"I just wanted to make sure you were alright. Did you set the alarm?"

"Yeah, why?"

"No reason, I was just checkin'. Umm…I'ma be at the Grand Hyatt

DEEP

Hotel downtown if you need me," he said.

"I thought you were gonna stay with Kevin?" Karina asked suspiciously.

"I was, but I told him I needed some peace and quiet. Even though he said I would have some, I know Kevin's idea of peace and quiet. It's a small party of about fifty," he said laughing, trying to lighten the mood. When Karina didn't respond he continued. "Anyway, if you need me, that's where I'll be. I haven't checked in yet, but I'll inform the front desk to give you my room number if you need it."

Karina felt a little better knowing Trae was willing to tell her where he would be staying and the room number. *He wouldn't dare invite another chick to his room now that I know where he is.*

"Well, I'm a little tired. I'm gonna go to sleep now," she said.

"Okay. Karina, I know this don't mean shit right now, but I do love you." Trae waited for a response, but there wasn't one. Instead, he heard the sound of a dead phone line.

Hearing Trae say he loved her made Karina's heart ache. She knew she would either have to put the past behind her or move on with her life. It wasn't going to be an easy decision. Nevertheless, it was a decision she would have to make eventually. She knew it was only going to be a matter of time before Trae would get fed up and make his own choice.

A NOVEL BY DANETTE MAJETTE

DEEP

SLIPPIN

A few days later, Carmen checked in with Willie at the clothing store on M Street that was the FBI's front. Draped in more baggy urban gear, she strolled with a street savvy swagger over to the register and asked for Monster.

"Who are you?" the store clerk asked.

"Tell him Cee's here," she said, inspecting the guy.

"Follow me," the guy said, picking out a few outfits before escorting Carmen into a dressing room that led to a lengthy hallway.

Once Carmen was halfway down the narrow space, the guy locked the door behind her and went back to the front of the store. At the end of the hallway Carmen saw a door marked *'private'*. When she knocked, there was no answer. Then out of nowhere Willie appeared.

"Damn! You scared the shit out of me!" Carmen yelled, wiping the beads of sweat from her forehead. Willie let out a hearty laugh then led her into a small room for a quick meeting.

"What's hanging homegirl?" one of the white agents said, mocking Carmen.

"This shit ain't a game. I had a really close call the other night," Carmen replied, throwing her baseball hat across the table before sitting down.

The room grew silent as the agents looked around the room at one another. Willie broke the awkwardness by asking Carmen how she was doing. Without any cut cards, she let Willie know that some serious shit was about to go down.

"Well, first tell me about the other night?" Willie asked with concern.

"That crazy ass nigga, Trae, wanted me to take this kid out because he owed him money and wouldn't pay. Luckily, there wasn't anything in the chamber," Carmen responded, shaking her head.

A NOVEL BY DANETTE MAJETTE

"You were actually going to shoot him?" one of the agents asked.

Carmen shot the agent a dirty look. "What the hell was I suppose to do?" She looked over at Willie. "I was gonna shoot him, but I wasn't gonna kill him. At least that would've kept them off my ass."

Willie sat down beside Carmen. "Hey, you used your best judgment. Remember, whatever it takes."

She looked at him as if to say, "That's easy for you to say."

"So, what else have you found out so far?" Willie asked. Even though he felt bad that Carmen was put in this situation, he was happy that she'd been able to get close to Trae.

"Their next move is the 8th and I, Marine Corps Armory," Carmen informed them.

"You can't be serious," Willie said, laughing so hard he was bent over in his seat. He looked over at Carmen, and saw the look on her face. "You're not kidding, are you?"

"I'm serious as a heart attack," she replied. "They plan on hitting the Armory with help from a guy on the inside."

"How did they get someone on the inside of the armory?" another one of the white agents asked.

Carmen laid out Trae's plan in great detail as everyone sat in amazement.

"Did you see any evidence?" Willie asked.

"Yeah, he has blueprints of the base in his office."

"He definitely has been keeping this shit a secret.This is one crazy son of a bitch. You know that!" Willie yelled, while banging on the desk.

"Hell, you ain't got to tell me that. Remember, I'm working for him now. Now the question is, how are we going to stop him?" Carmen asked looking around the room.

Willie stood up and walked over to another bulletin board that displayed Trae's picture. Thinking about how they could use this to their advantage, he said, "We're not!"

Carmen's eyes grew big. "What do you mean we're not going to stop him?"

"Go along with the plan, just keep us in the loop," Willie responded.

"Willie you're not making any sense," Carmen said, walking over to the board. "Did you hear what I said? They're gonna hit an Armory on a military base!"

"I heard you," Willie responded, not making eye contact with her.

"So what, we're just gonna let them get away with it?" Carmen

DEEP

was confused. She knew Willie wanted Trae, but this was a bad idea.

"I didn't say we're going to let them get away with it. I just said we're not going to stop them. Do you understand?" he asked.

"Yes, I understand. I understand that you're about to do something crazy," Carmen replied, as she shook her head back and forth.

She'd been around Willie a long time and understood his dedication to his job, even though she didn't agree with some of his tactics. They'd worked on many cases together, so she knew how he operated. From the look on his face, Carmen could tell he was definitely up to no good again, and way over his head Truth be told, she was just as dedicated, just in a different way.

Willie had a by any means necessary mentality that got him into a lot of trouble with the big wigs. That's until he got the bad guys off the streets.Then, as far as they were concerned, all was forgotten.

Carmen stood up, grabbed the clothing she bought with her to supposedly try on and marched to the front of the store. After throwing the clothes up on the counter, she walked out. Rummaging through her pockets, she pulled out her cell phone to see if she had any messages. Suddenly, she quickly looked up after hearing the sound of a familiar voice. When she turned around, her heart dropped. It was Trae.

Damn! Carmen thought.

"Yo', what's up? What you doin' over here?" Trae asked, walking up to Carmen.

"What's up?" Carmen said, nervously hoping like hell she hadn't blown her cover.

Just as she was about to come up with a bogus excuse the clerk ran to the door with a bag full of clothes. "Hey, cutie, you forgot your bags!"

"Thanks." Carmen looked at Trae with a worried expression. "I did a little shoppin'. You how women love to shop," she said, grabbing the bags.

Trae laughed. "You must not like to shop too much. Forgettin' yo' bags and shit." He watched as the clerk turned around and walked back to the store.

"I got sidetracked talkin' on the phone with this dude I met last night," Carmen said, holding her cell phone up. "I'm glad you're so concerned about me," she said sarcastically. "So, what you doin' over here?"

"I was just ridin' by, and I spotted that bangin' ass jacket in the

A NOVEL BY DANETTE MAJETTE

window, so I decided to come and check it out," Trae said.

"Oh yeah, it is hot," Carmen said, turning toward the window where the jacket was. "Umm...can't wait to see you in it." There was a temporary awkwardness between them. "Anyway, I'ma holla at you later," she said.

"A'ight. Stop by the club tonight. I got this new chick named Sommone. She got the niggas goin' crazy with her moves."

Yeah, I can' wait to see her put your ass in handcuffs. "Why are you tellin' me that shit? I'm not a lesbo. I'm strictly dickly, baby," Carmen responded. She tried her best to act offended.

Trae smiled. "My bad. I guess I got the wrong impression. It's just that you dress like a dude all the time," he replied. "Well, if you get a chance stop by anyway."

Damn, maybe I shouldn't dress like this. "Bet. Oh well, I gotta go. Talk to you later."

After taking a glance back to make sure Trae wasn't watching her, Carmen broke down the street in a nervous sweat headed for the Metro station. Safely on the blue line train headed to her car, she took a seat so her heart could catch up with her chest. *That was close,* she thought. *I've got to shape up on my skills, otherwise this whole operation might be jeopardized.*

DEEP

EMOTIONS RUN DEEP

It was 11:30 a.m. before Karina woke up. She didn't have any plans, so she washed her face, brewed a pot of coffee, and curled up on the couch with a novel she was eager to finish. The dead silence of an empty house made her drift off, sometimes thinking about the loss of her baby and her disastrous relationship with Trae.

She had just turned the page to start chapter seven, when she heard the doorbell ring. Pulling back the curtain, she looked through the bay window and saw a geeky delivery guy holding a dozen of long stem roses.

"Hi, can I help you?" Karina asked, cracking the door open slightly.

"Yes, I have a delivery for Mrs. Keal," he said.

"Mrs. Keal?"

"Yes Ma'am, Mrs. Keal." Karina knew the roses were from Trae, so she opened the door all the way. "Thanks," she said, taking the flowers.

When Karina closed the door, she smelled the roses, then opened the card. *Just wanted to show you how much I love you!* The card and flowers brought a slight smile to her face. Trae had a way of doing that. She sat down on the couch and grabbed her cell phone.

"No, I'm not gonna call him," she said out loud.

Karina laid the phone down and picked her book back up, but her mind kept drifting. Every time she looked at the roses, she was reminded of happier days with Trae. At that point, she was so confused. On one hand, she missed him and wished he was there. On the other hand, she wanted him to stay away, so she could concentrate on what her next move was gonna be without emotions getting involved.

Karina was at the height of the book when she suddenly heard the front door open. When Trae walked into the living room, she noticed

A NOVEL BY DANETTE MAJETTE

how good he looked in his Diesel jeans and Hugo Boss shirt. When he walked in the living room and saw Karina on the couch, he let out a huge smile.

"Hello," he said, but she didn't respond. "I said hi," he repeated.

"I heard you," she replied.

Trae could tell she still had an attitude and didn't want to be bothered so he went into the kitchen. Sitting at the table, he started going through the mail he'd picked up on the way in. Once he was finished reading all the mail, he went to the fridge, got a bottle of water and opened it.

Trae ran up the stairs to their bedroom and grabbed a few items. After packing up some more of his clothes, he walked back down the stairs and sat his bag by the door.

"You feelin' a'ight," he said, not sure what else to say.

"I guess."

He sat down beside Karina on the couch. She was just about to get up and move to the loveseat, when Trae moved closer and took her hands into his.

"Karina look, what's done is done. We can't turn back the hands of time, nor can we bring our baby back. But I would like to try and make it up to you. Tears fell down Karina's cheek. "We can't let something like this come between us. We gotta decide what we're gonna do."

As tempted as she was to jump in Trae's arms, she was reluctant. Instead, she turned away from him. "I need some more time," she replied.

At that point, it was a wrap for Trae. He had just poured out his heart and she'd shot him down once again. It was time for him to move on. He really didn't want it that way, but felt he had no other choice.

He finished his water, picked up his bag and left slamming the door behind him. Anger flashed across his face as he turned and looked back at Karina's face through the living room window.

"Fuck this shit!" he yelled, as he got into his car. "I'ma give her ass a few more days then she gotta bounce."

Karina was afraid of what Trae's reaction meant. She was in deep need of someone to talk to. *I've got to get out of his house,* she thought. *Maybe Ashley can cheer me up.* She quickly got dressed and headed to Nordstrom's.

DEEP

The store looked so different. It was going through a major renovation, and from the looks of things, their store was going to be the spot to shop at. As soon as Karina walked in, Ashley grabbed her by the arm scaring her half to death.

"What you doing here?" Ashley asked, hugging her friend.

"I came to see you. Can you go on your break now?"

"Hell yeah, especially if you're treating."

"Of course," Karina said laughing. Ashley was always broke.

After Ashley got her purse, the two got on the escalator and went down to the first floor. As they were stepping off they ran into a beautiful woman who was walking around telling everybody what to do. From the look of her strut, you knew she was in charge. She was giving instructions to one of the construction workers, who didn't look too happy about it either.

"Who was that?" Karina asked as she and Ashley walked out into the mall.

"That would be our new store manager."

"She's our new store manager?" Karina said, doing a double take.

"Yep."

"Oh, you know she slept her way up the ladder," Karina said, staring at her amazing athletic shape.The two laughed.

"You ain't never lied. Don't get it twisted though, she knows her shit. She running this camp like it's the army," Ashley replied, with a serious look.

"Well, she looks like she's really nice."

"Nice. Girl, that bitch is the devil in a St. John suit." The two laughed again.

The walk to the food court was a little exhausting for Karina and Ashley could tell by the way she kept slowing down and holding her stomach.

"You sure you should be out?" Ashley asked.

"I'm fine. I'm just cramping a little."

Panda Express was Ashley's choice, while Karina over did it on Johnny Rockets. They grabbed a table, sat down and dug in.

"So, you heard from Trae?" Ashley asked, putting a fork full of rice in her mouth.

"He stopped by this afternoon to pick up a few things...so he said," Karina replied.

"Why do you think he came by?"

Karina swallowed her food, and took a sip of her iced tea before-answering. She was taking too long, so Ashley decided to say it for her. "He only came to see you. I know I didn't care for him too much in the beginning, but after seeing you two together, I can honestly say he loves you," Ashley admitted.

"I know he does, but this situation just makes me wonder sometimes."

"Well, while you're wondering, some other chick is gonna be keepin' him company at night. You sure he ain't already got somebody at that hotel with him?"

"Ashhh!"

"What? I'm telling you the truth. Trae has an image to uphold. He ain't gonna keep lettin' you make a fool out of him. Besides, it's his house. You're gonna have to make a decision soon. But wait too long, and some good lookin' chick will be stroking your man, and living in that big ass crib."

"You're sick, you know that."

"I know. You are too. The only difference is you're lovesick. Call that man, girl."

Karina knew her friend was right. She couldn't keep stringing Trae along and expect him to be there once her decision was made.

Once they were finished eating, Karina and Ashley headed back to the store.

"Girl, I'm so stuffed I can barely stand up," Karina said, rubbing her stomach.

"I know. I don't know how I'ma make it through the rest of the day," Ashley agreed.

Walking quickly so Ashley wouldn't be late getting back from lunch, Karina made an abrupt stop when she looked through the Victoria's Secret window.

"Girl, come on, I gotta go!" Ashley yelled. But Karina didn't budge. "What's wrong?" Ashley asked, walking back and looking through the store's window. She turned back to Karina, who was about to lose it after spotting Trae and Sommone.

"I knew something was goin' on between them," Karina said, on the brink of tears.

"Oh shit, it's about to be on. Fuck being late now," Ashley said. "Okay, let's just calm down, maybe there's a good reason they're together."

"What fuckin' reason could he have for being with a stripper in Victoria's Secret?"

Ashley didn't have an answer, so Karina went to find out for her-

DEEP

self. Pushing people out of her way like she was about to do a sequel to *Set It Off,* Karina walked up to Sommone and snatched the white thong she was holding out of her hands. Sommone and Trae were surprisingly shocked. Especially Trae. Not even three hours ago, Karina acted like she wanted him out of her life.

A customer who was yelling and cursing at the employees for not moving the line fast enough, suddenly stopped talking and got out of the line, when she saw what was going on. She wanted to get a front row view of the action. "Oh, I can tell this is gonna be good," the woman remarked.

"I knew you were after my man, you nasty bitch!" Karina yelled.

"Whoa, what are you talkin bout?" Sommone asked, throwing up her hands.

The manager swiftly walked over to Karina and Sommone. "Excuse me."

Karina ignored the woman. "Don't play the fuckin' innocent role. You know exactly what I'm talkin' 'bout, bitch! You've been after Trae since day one, but it ain't goin down like that. Stay the fuck away from my man, and I'm not gonna tell you again."

"I can't believe I'm standing here listening to this." Sommone made an attempt to leave, but Karina stood in her path. "Look, I'm tired of this shit! You wanna do something?" Sommone asked, placing her handbag on the floor. All her professionalism had gone out the door.

"Do you, bitch?" Karina asked, throwing her bag on the floor as well. Ashley ready to throw down too, stood behind Sommone. When the manager ran behind the counter and picked up the phone, Trae pleaded with her. "I'll take care of this," he assured.

"Okay, well do it now!" the manager snapped as she finally gave in to Trae's request.

He walked over and pulled Karina by the arm and escorted her outside the store. "Karina, what's wrong wit' you? One minute you act like you can't stand the sight of me, then the next minute you're ready to fight a woman in public over me. You got issues," Trae replied.

"I got issues? We just lost our baby because of you and now you're at the mall with that slut takin' her shopping for fuckin' underwear."

Just as Trae was about explain, Kevin walked up. "Hey yo', what's up? Where's Sommone?" Kevin asked, not even acknowledging Karina.

"She's still in the store," Trae responded.

"Well, she gotta hurry up or she's gonna miss her set," Kevin said. "Did they have that angel costume she wanted?"

Before Trae could answer, Kevin walked past the pair and went in the store. Karina embarrassed by her behavior, walked away leaving Ashley behind. Trae just stared and shook his head as he watched Karina quickly disappear.

"Girl wait up!" Why you leave? I was ready to beat dat bitch dooownn!" Ashley said, punching her hands. She had to do a light jog in order to catch up.

"I can't believe this shit," Karina yelled.

"You can't believe what? The fact that Trae has moved on, or that you still love him?"

Karina took a seat on a bench in the center of the mall. She watched as young mothers dragged their children in and out of stores looking for club outfits. It was a couple of days before Ne-Yo was performing at the Platinum Club, so everybody was trying to get dolled up.

"Ash, I don't know what's wrong with me," she said.

"I do. You're in love with Trae. Admit it. Only women who truly love their men are willing to fight for them."

Karina was starting to think that Ashley was right. Although she was still hurt and angry, she did love Trae. Her pride just wouldn't allow her to see it.

Ashley glanced down at her watch. "Oh shit, I'm late. I gotta go."

The two hurried through the mall, almost knocking down a few people in the process. Once they were back at the store, Karina took the escalator up to the third floor to human resources to let them know she would be back at work in a couple of days. They were happy. Karina was one of the top sellers in the store.

On the drive home, Karina tried to call Trae, but he didn't pick up. This made her mind wonder. *Why isn't he picking up his phone? Is he with that bitch? Is he mad at me?* As she continued to drive, all the questions floating around in her head, caused her to lose focus and she drifted into another lane.

"Oh shit!" she screamed, as the driver of the other car honked the horn a few times. "I'm sorry! I'm sorry!" she screamed over and over as tears began to roll down her face.

Pulling over onto the median, Karina took several deep breaths. *I have to get myself together.* After she calmed down, she pulled back into traffic, and headed home.

DEEP

Thirty minutes later, Karina threw her keys on the counter, kicked off her stilettos, and headed straight to the bar. Pouring herself a shot of Captain Morgan's, her hands shook like a leaf.

A hot shower and two drinks later, she sat on the couch, wondering where things went wrong. More importantly, how she was going to get them back on track, especially her relationship with Trae. As much as she tried to hide her feelings, she knew living without him wasn't an option.

DEEP

LOSING CONTROL

Sommone examined her new black g-string, with matching diamond bra, in the mirror for a few seconds, before giving herself the sign of approval. After putting the finishing touches on her makeup, she made a quick phone call.

"Hey, I'm about to go on. Are you still coming?" she asked.

"Yes," Willie said.

"Trae sits in the audience and watches me dance just in case the guys get too rowdy. That should buy you some time to look around in his office."

"Good. Remember, I need time, so dance real slow."

Sommone was a little worried. If Trae got wind of what was going on, it was going to get ugly for the both of them. "Be careful," she insisted.

"You too."

Walking through the crowd in true diva mode, Sommone scanned the room for Trae. When she spotted him by the bar chatting with some groupies, she walked over with a sexy strut.

"Hi boss," Sommone said, whispering in Trae's ear. "You ready for the show of your life."

Trae turned around and eyed Sommone up and down. Her body looked good enough to eat. "Yeah, I wouldn't miss it. I want all my money's worth. Especially after buying you all that shit today," he said jokingly. "You want a drink before you go on?"

"Naw, I need to keep a straight head," she replied.

Trae smiled. "I can definitely understand that."

Not wanting to miss a second of the show, Trae made his way up to the stage and took a seat in the corner. When R.Kelly's song *Sex Me* started to play, a single spotlight highlighted Sommone's presence on stage. She captivated every man in the club. Tuning out the music,

A NOVEL BY DANETTE MAJETTE

Trae watched as Sommone moved her hips slowly in a circular motion.

Damn, I need to hit that, he thought.

Wiggling her ass and thrusting her hips, Sommone accomplished her main goal. She kept Trae deliciously entertained long enough for Willie to do what he needed to do in Trae's office.

"Trae, you want a drink?" the waitress asked, but he didn't respond. "Trae, are you okay?"

"What?" he asked, snapping out his trance.

"Do you want something to drink?" the waitress asked again.

"Naw, I'm cool." When he looked at Sommone's half naked body, his dick began to throb. "On second thought, I'll take a Hennessey and Coke," he said, catching the waitress before she left.

Willie knew that it was impossible to get into the club without being spotted, so he slipped in through the back door. The stairway that led up to Trae's office was dark. Wearing all black and a baseball hat, he clung to the side of the wall, making sure no one saw him as he continued to make his way. Once he reached the office door, it was locked, so he used the key Sommone had stolen from Trae the night he fell asleep.

As he worked the lock, he thought he heard a noise inside, so he stopped and listened, but the only thing he could hear was the base from the loud music. He cautiously glanced around before turning the knob, and after seeing that no one was in sight, he pushed the door open.

Quietly, Willie closed the door behind him and stepped into the middle of the room. He placed his hand on his gun, just in case something popped off and slowly moved around the office. In the corner of the room was a door marked, '*Supplies.*'

What kinda supplies does his ass need? When he opened the door, he saw the cameras that monitored all the areas of the club, which included the backdoor and the parking lot.

Shit! He hit the rewind button on the tape marked back door, but didn't see anything. That's when he noticed the time. Apparently the camera had started recording after he was already in the building. He breathed a sigh of relief, wiped the sweat from his forehead then continued rummaging through Trae's office.

He was about to give up any hope of finding anything, until he ran

DEEP

across a safe behind a picture of Stacy Dash on the wall. *Jackpot!*

As Trae continued to watch the show, he looked at his watch and decided to go make a phone call in his office. However, when Sommone saw that he was about to leave, she had to get his attention somehow, so she unbuttoned her shirt and pulled it open. With her diamond bra showing, she ran her hands across her breasts and gave them a gentle tug. She licked her lips and gave Trae a blink with her left eye. For some strange reason, she was starting to enjoy the show that seemed like it was meant just for Trae.

Taking the set to another level, she slid her skirt off and threw it out into the crowd. Turning around to expose her black g-string, she gave her ass a hard smack then dropped down to the floor. Quickly flipping onto her stomach, imitating an exotic doggy style move, she turned to Trae and displayed a devilish grin.

Stimulated by Sommone's sexy performance, Trae's blood rushed immediately from his brain to his dick. He took a sip of his drink. *Damn! I can't take this shit.* When the final note played, Trae got up and headed upstairs to his office.

Willie was still trying to get into the safe when he heard a muffled sound. Someone was in the hallway. For a second he froze. He had to get out of there fast, but didn't know how. Closing the door to the closet and checking to make sure everything was still in place, he stood behind the door and took a deep breath. *Come on Sommone, I need you,* he thought.

Sticking his spare key in his office door, and slowly turning the knob, Trae suddenly heard footsteps behind him. Turning his head, Trae's eyes locked with Sommone's. They stood in silence, only talking with their bodies.

"Why did you leave? You didn't like my performance?" Sommone asked seductively, pressing her body up against his. Trae instantly released the doorknob.

That's a good girl, work that nigga, Willie thought to himself as he listened to his agent.

"Not at all. I liked it too much," Trae said.

"Is that why you left?" Sommone asked, licking his neck. Being so close to Trae was starting to excite her.

Trae shook his head. "You're mad hot, and trust me, the old Trae would've fucked you on the first night. But I'm tryin' get back on track wit' my girl, so I can't do this."

Sommone sighed and appeared disappointed. "I understand. Can you at least have a drink with me? I mean, I didn't see you throwin' no tips on stage." Trae chuckled. "I'm serious," she said.

After some heavy convincing, he agreed, and the two headed back downstairs to the bar.

Get the fuck outta there, Willie, Sommone thought as she led Trae away from the door.

Willie slid down the stairs, jumping the last four steps. Once he was out the back door, he ran down the street and around the corner to a waiting car.

Racing on all four wheels, Damien took 395 North toward Baltimore. "What took you so long?" he asked.

"He came back up to his office," Willie said, still out of breath.

"How the hell did you get out of there?"

He was too out of breath to explain, so all he said was, "Sommone."

After catching his breath, he told Damien about the safe in Trae's office. "We've got to get in there," Willie said. "I'm sure that's where he keeps the blueprints."

"How?" Damien asked. "Going back like that may be a little too risky."

Willie cleared his throat. "I know...because he has cameras, so I might've been seen running out the building." He paused for a moment. "Carmen may have to do it."

Damien hated that fact that his wife was involved in such a dangerous assignment, but it was her job and had to be done. "Send her in."

DEEP

MEETING OF THE MINDS

The next day, Kevin, Big Paul, his cousin, Greg and Ice Man met in Trae's office to go over the plans for the heist. Once everyone was seated, Trae reached in his safe and pulled out the blueprints.

Sitting down in his plush leather executive chair, he thought about how life was going to be after the deal for the weapons was made. It was going to be top of the line all the way...from cars to vacations. His life as he knew it was about to do a three hundred and sixty degree turn. The first thing he planned to do was leave D.C. Maybe live in the Bahamas or some small town in Texas, where no one knew him. The only thing missing was Karina.

He was still staying in a hotel instead of his own home, just so she would have a place to stay and until she felt better, but the arrangements were starting to frustrate him. He was also beginning to even wonder if Karina was worth waiting for.

Carmen tapped on the door before opening it. "Sorry I'm late," she said, locking the door behind her.

"You right on time," Trae responded. "A'ight, let's get started."

Trae opened the blueprints and laid them across his desk. "Big Paul, you, Ice Man and Kevin will be wit' me. Carm, you'll be driving."

"So what's the plan?" Kevin asked.

"Well, remember I have a van being fixed up right now to look like a contractor working on one of the buildings. They're known on the base, so no red flags should go up when we enter. We'll change into camouflage uniforms once we're on the base, so we can blend in with the rest of the soldiers."

Greg stood up. "Me and at least one other marine opens the armory every morning. I'll make sure to unlock the weapons room first, and then y'all can come in as soon as I yell all clear to the other marine."

A NOVEL BY DANETTE MAJETTE

"What do we do if the other nigga starts wildin' out?" Ice man asked.

"We'll tell 'em, he can either get down or lay down," Kevin said, pulling his .45 out.

Greg continued. "Kevin, you lock us in the cage, then tell the marine to give you the code to turn off the Armory's alarm system to the weapons room. Once that's done, y'all only have about fifteen minutes, before other soldiers start to come in, so you have to get in and get out."

"What if he refuses to give me the code?" Kevin asked.

"It's going to be between Private Riviera or Corporal Adams so you have nothin' to worry about. Both of them have a wife and kids. Trust me, they ain't tryna die."

Carmen looked around at all the men, and knew this was serious. She couldn't believe Willie was letting this heist go down, but she figured this was what he had to do to make sure Trae and his crew didn't beat the system again.

"A'ight, but if they don't comply then I'ma bust a cap in they ass," Kevin added.

"Kevin, robbery on a base is one thing, but murder is automatic death. So chill," Big Paul warned.

Trae agreed. He wanted to live long enough to spend his money and also have his freedom.

The men went over the heist from beginning to end several times. They had to make sure everyone was on the same page and ready for the big day.

Carmen, however, was in awe. *Who would've thought a few knuckleheads from the projects would grow up to be such criminal masterminds?*

Their meeting was just about to wind down when someone knocked on the door. Trae quickly balled up the blueprints and tossed them in the safe. He made sure everyone was straight before he opened the door.

"Hey Sommone. Come in," Trae said, moving out the way.

"What's up? I came to see if I could get an advance for next week," Sommone said, looking around the room at all the guys and then at Carmen. *I hope you're getting all the information we need, partner,* she thought. Sommone was also hoping to see some type of evidence when she interrupted the meeting.

"Sure. How much you need?" Trae asked, reaching in his pocket.

She thought for a minute. "Are you in a good mood?"

DEEP

The guys laughed. "Yeah, daddy's in a real good mood," Kevin mimicked.

"Oh well, in that case, I'll take five hundred off your hands."

Trae pulled off five crisp one hundred dollars bills from his stack. "Here you go. I'll see you tonight."

"Thanks," Sommone replied, walking out the room shaking her curvy hips.

Trae couldn't keep his eyes off Sommone's ass as she walked away.

"Shorty, all that subtle flirtin' is gonna come to a head one day," Big Paul said.

Trae knew Big Paul was right. The chemistry he and Sommone shared was definitely starting to heat up. He was trying to be faithful, but was slowly losing the fight when it came to Sommone.

"Shorty, you ain't hit that yet?" Kevin asked.

Trae looked at Kevin with disgust. "Naw Sommone's different. She's a nice girl, I wouldn't fuck around like that with her."

"She looks like she might be able to steal you from Karina," Carmen added.

"Yeah, she looks like the type that would fall in love with you after you smack it, flip it, and rub it down," Ice Man added as well.

Trae laughed, but he took Ice Man's words to heart. He couldn't get caught out there after everything he had done to prove to Karina that he could be trusted. She already thought there was something going on between the two of them. If he slipped, he would be proving her right.

Minutes later, Kevin was the first to leave the meeting. He was on his way to yet another date with a girl he'd met the night before. Ice Man, Greg and Big Paul followed, leaving Trae and Carmen behind.

"Trae, do you think we can really pull this off? I mean, when is this shit goin' down?" Carmen asked.

"I hope so. We have to wait a few more months. The Dominicans need time to get the loot together, and we still need to work a few things out," Trae replied, as he looked over at Carmen. "I'm so tired of lookin' over my shoulder and doing shit I know my grandmother wouldn't approve of. I want out."

For a moment, Carmen forgot about what a monster Trae was and started to empathize with him. "You've had a hard life, huh."

"Hard ain't the word for it."

"Yeah. Me too."

Carmen asked Trae if he wanted to go get a drink. Instead of answering, he reached down in his compact refrigerator and grabbed two Coronas. "I hope you like beer," he said.

"Beer is cool." Carmen thought that if she could get Trae to open up she would have some insight on what made him such a menace to society. Instead of prying, she opened up about herself first. A tactic she learned in the academy.

"When I was five days old, my mom's left me with my aunt," Carmen said.

"Why? She couldn't hack it?" Trae asked, sitting on his couch.

"Naw, word on the street was she took up with some slick cat and moved up North. She would call my aunt sometimes to check on me, but that's about it. I even overheard my aunt saying she had another baby. So I have a brother or sister out there somewhere. A few years later, my aunt came in my room and told me that my mom's had died. Nobody ever talked about her again. I think my aunt knew I was better off without her anyway. The crazy thing is, I never got the chance to get the whole story because my aunt died too."

Carmen's words hit home with Trae. "My mom's died too. She was a prostitute." Carmen seemed a bit uneasy in her chair, letting Trae know she was a little uncomfortable about the information he was telling her. "It's a'ight. Everyone knows. It's not like it was a secret or anythin'. She was well known in D.C., so her death was big news. That was one of the worse days of my life," he said, with his head down.

"Sorry to hear that," Carmen responded.

"It's cool. I went to live with my grandmother after that, but she died when I was in high school. That's when I really lost it." He stood up and walked over to his small bar for something harder. Vodka was his choice as he poured them both a shot. "My grandmother was a remarkable woman. She would always keep me close to her, and told me repeatedly that she didn't want me runnin' with no rift wrath," he said snickering. "She's probably rollin' over in her grave right now."

"Yeah, I'm sure my aunt is doing the same thing. When she found out I was selling drugs for this dude in my neighborhood, she put me out. After that, I started going hard, pushing weight with my boys until I caught a charge." she said, taking the shot of Vodka. "I did a whole bid cause I wouldn't snitch. You think those niggas sent me a dime or even came to see me...hell naw. It was like they were sayin' *fuck that bitch*. And after everything I did for them."

"Hey, let's change the subject before we start to crying up in here,"

DEEP

Trae joked.

"I agree," Carmen responded with a smile.

Talking about everything from politics to sports, Trae and Carmen seemed to click. Getting suspects to trust her was easy. She was laid back, beautiful, and easy to talk to. And when the time came for her to turn them in, it was harder on the suspect. They felt like Carmen was a wife that had cheated on them. However, it didn't faze her at all. As far as she was concerned, it was just a job.

"Oh by the way, I hope I didn't offend you the other day in front of the store," Trae said.

"It's alright. I get that all the time. They see a girl dressed like me, going hard like a nigga, and they just assume I'm gay," she said.

"Hey, there are some pretty gay women out here now," Trae replied, laughing.

"Oh…so you think I'm pretty?"

Trae smiled. "You can say that. As a matter of fact, I think you're gorgeous."

"I guess we have something in common then, because I think you're fine as hell," she said, leaning in and kissing him.

Trae was caught off guard by Carmen's actions, but didn't pull away. As he began to place his hand on her breasts, she suddenly began to wonder if she should let it go any further.

DEEP

A SECOND CHANCE

Making her way through the club's doors, Karina walked over to the bartender and asked for Trae.

"He's in his office," Sam replied.

As soon as she turned around, she bumped into Sommone. "Hi Karina," Sommone said, with a sneaky grin. "Has Don King called you about any boxing matches yet," she joked.

"Fuck you, hoe," Karina snapped. She told Sam thank you and gave Sommone an evil glare. "One of these days slut, it's gonna be you and me," she said.

"One of these days? How about today, bitch?" Sommone yelled. Pissing Karina off was starting to be fun for her.

The two women stood toe to toe, cursing at one another. "Every time you see me, I got to be a slut or a bitch!" Sommone screamed, pointing her finger in Karina's face.

"That's because you are a slut!" Karina yelled back, pointing her finger.

"Your man don't think so. As a matter of fact, he loves himself some Mone'."

Karina clenched her jaw. "Whatever. Trae ain't thinking about your nasty ass."

The two women continued to exchange insults as a bodyguard made his way between them. He knew that if he let them get into a fight on his shift, it would be his last day on the job. He silently prayed that someone would go and get Trae, so he could put out the fire.

After going back and forth with Karina, Sommone decided she wasn't worth losing her job, so she rolled out. Before she left, she turned to Karina, whose eyes were fixed on her and said, "Your day is coming, sweetheart. Believe that." *When Trae falls, I'm gonna make sure I lock that bitch up for conspiracy, even if the charges don't stick.*

A NOVEL BY DANETTE MAJETTE

"Shut the fuck up!" Karina yelled, swinging her purse across her shoulders.

Karina watched as Sommone walked out the club's front door. *I can't stand that girl. Ever since I saw her in Trae's office that day, I haven't been able to trust her ass.*

When Karina finally made it to Trae's office, she knocked on the door, but there was no answer. She placed her ear against the cold wood to see if she could hear anything, but there was dead silence. For some reason, she didn't trust Trae anymore either. After waiting for a few seconds, there was still no response. Karina knocked again. When someone finally opened the door, her eyes almost popped out of her head.

"Can I help you?" Carmen asked.

"Is Trae here?" Karina snapped, with her hands on her hips.

Carmen turned to Trae, who was already on his heels after hearing Karina's voice.

"Hey baby," he said nervously. "Come on in." He opened the door as wide as he could.

"Hey, I thought we could go grab something to eat. That's if you're not too busy," she said, eyèing Carmen from head to toe.

"No..." Before Trae could finish his sentence, Karina placed her hands on her hips again. "Naw, I mean, I'm not busy," he said.

"I thought so," Karina responded.

Carmen told Trae she would call him later and started to leave. "Oh, Carm, let me introduce you to my girl, Karina." Trae was relieved that he and Carmen's small love session had been interrupted. For some reason, he knew messing with her would've caused serious mayhem.

"Nice to meet you," Carmen said, with a fake smile.

Karina didn't respond. Instead, she studied Carmen all the way to the door. "Who was that bitch?" Karina asked, as soon as Carmen walked out.

"A new employee," Trae replied. "Remember I was telling you about her."

"Well, I don't like her ass already," she replied with an attitude.

"Karina, you don't even know the girl."

"I don't have to know her. I'm a good judge of character, and something tells me that she can't be trusted," Karina said, moving her head back and forth.

Trae was determined not to get into it with Karina, so he walked back to his desk and grabbed his keys. He couldn't believe she actual-

DEEP

ly wanted to spend time with him. It was a sure sign things were looking up for them.

On cloud nine, Trae whisked Karina off to The Capital Grille in
Tyson's Corner. After the hostess escorted them to their seats, she
said their waitress would be out in a few minutes to take their drink
orders. Trae thanked the pale white woman, then pulled Karina's chair
out for her. This caught her off guard. He hadn't done that since their
first date, proving that the time apart helped them.

Sitting at a cozy table for two, they ate and held a conversation
like old times. It was like they'd never been apart.

Looking across the table, Karina was direct and to the point. "Did
you sleep with her?"

"Sleep with who?" he asked, caught off guard again.

"That bitch, Sommone, that's who."

Trae looked her in the eyes," I swear to you, I've never slept with
that girl."

"And what about the new girl?"

"Who, Carm?" he asked.

"Oh, so y'all go by nicknames now?"

Trae was beginning to get frustrated. "I didn't sleep with her
either."

Karina stared at him and waited for a sign that told her he was
lying, but nothing ever came. Not even a small twitch in his eye. "Trae,
if this is gonna work, I need to know that I can trust you."

"You can. I told you that."

"You told me a lot of things. Like you're getting out of the business
and we're gonna move far away."

"I have a deal that's gonna take place, and when it does, we're on
that plane to wherever. I just need to know you're gonna be sitting
next to me."

When she asked what that meant, he wouldn't explain. Against
her better judgment, Karina made the decision to trust and stand
behind him. They held their champagne glasses in the air and toasted
to a new beginning, before giving each other a small peck on the lips.
Trae couldn't have been happier.

Just as they were finishing up their dinner, Karina's eyes zoomed
in on Trae's cell phone as it rang. He checked the number then sat it
back down on the table.

"I guess some things will never change, huh," Karina said, rolling
her eyes. "So, who is it this time?"

A NOVEL BY DANETTE MAJETTE

"It's just Kevin." He reached out for Karina's hand. "He can wait."

Karina could see the concerned look on his face when he saw that Kevin had not only left him a voicemail, but sent him a text message as well. She was impressed. This was the first time Trae had put her before business. Any other time, he would've answered and talked throughout their entire meal.

"Things have changed," he said. He planted a big juicy kiss on her lips. He glanced at the light blinking on his cell phone, wondering why Kevin was so desperate, but decided to ignore the call again.

Trae and Karina drove down Georgia Avenue past Howard University on their way back to the club. The congestion near the campus usually irritated Trae, and normally he would take back streets just to avoid sitting in traffic forever. But this time, he took full advantage of the extra time he had with Karina.

Once they arrived at Pleasures, he put the car in park, and sat back as his eyes roamed up and down Karina's body.

Damn, I missed this, he thought.

"What are you thinking about?" Karina asked.

"You."

"What about me?"

Trae blushed like a schoolboy. "Nothin'. Look, I need to drop by and get some more clothes tonight. That's if it's alright wit' you."

"Sure," Karina responded, with a slight grin. She had something special planned for him when he arrived.

After giving each other another kiss, Trae got out and walked around the car to open the door for Karina. He then walked her to her car to make sure she was safe. As she sat in the driver's seat, she rolled the window down and gave Trae a subtle smack on his ass.

"See you tonight," she said, pulling off.

Trae couldn't help but smile.

Once he walked in the club, Trae checked his message from Kevin. "Yo' man, that nigga Rico actin' up again. Don't worry 'bout it though, I'ma take care of this nigga once and for all."

Trae's heart raced. The last thing he needed was Kevin acting like a loose cannon. The heist was only a few months away, and they needed to stay low key. He tried several times to get Kevin on the phone, but he wasn't picking up.

"Shit!" he yelled, as he called Carmen. "Hey, you know where Kevin at?" he asked, as soon as she answered.

"Yeah. He said he was on his way to Rico's," Carmen responded.

Something wasn't sitting right with Trae. Kevin never missed a call

DEEP

from him. He could be knee deep in pussy, but if his phone rang he would pump the breaks and pick up if he saw Trae's number.

"Trae, what's goin' on?" Carmen asked.

"Look, I think somethin's wrong. Meet me at the club right now!" he yelled.

"I'll be there in a minute, I'm right down the street."

A few minutes later, she raced into the parking lot on two wheels. As soon as she stopped, Trae jumped in. "We gotta get to Rico's!"

"Why, what's up?" Carmen asked.

Trae looked at Carmen with a worried look on his face. "I don't know, but I have a feelin' some shit is about to go down."

DEEP

THE MASTER PLAN

With Biggie Smalls blasting throughout the house, Rico and his crew sat in the living room counting the money they had collected from the streets that week. Standing with a stack of twenties in his hand, Rico laughed at his boy Tariq, who was picking on their toothless friend, Buggs.

"You a stupid ass nigga, man. Leave that dude alone before he bite yo' ass," Rico said, laughing wildly.

"I'm sayin', you know that nigga can't eat spaghetti because it'll slide right through his teeth," Tariq said, about to bust a gut.

"Nigga, shut the fuck up! I can eat spaghetti," Buggs replied, sounding like a two year old. "You always clowning on somebody," he said, throwing a stack of money on the table.

Everyone looked at Tariq, waiting to see what his crazy ass was about to do.

"Alright, y'all chill," Rico said, still laughing.

However, Tariq didn't find it amusing. He walked right over to Buggs and stood so close to him he could smell what he had for lunch. "What'chu say bitch ass nigga?" he yelled. He looked Buggs right in his eyes.

"You heard what the fuck I said, nigga," Buggs answered, not backing down.

Rico walked over and stood between the two. "Shorty, come on. Seriously, we got too much work to do. Y'all can handle this shit later. We need to count this loot up, so I can give that nigga, Trae, his money before he sends his bitch, Kevin, looking for me." When everyone got quiet, Rico wondered what was going on.

"So, I'm Trae's bitch, huh?"

Rico turned around quickly after hearing the sound of Kevin's voice coming from behind him. He had no idea Kevin, Big Paul and Ice Man had been hiding upstairs for hours and waited patiently for

A NOVEL BY DANETTE MAJETTE

Rico and his boys to get there.

"Hey man, you know I ain't mean that shit. I was just trippin' wit' these…" Before he could finish his sentence, Kevin pulled out his 45.

"Well, trip off this, nigga," Kevin said, pointing his gun straight at Rico's right eye.

"Kev, man, calm down," Rico pleaded.

"What if I don't want to calm down?" Kevin asked.

"Please man. Look, I got all yo' paper."

"Shut the fuck up. Yo' ass got a free pass with Trae the last time, but I ain't him. I ain't got no problem blowin' yo' muthafuckin' wig off. No problem at all."

Rico was shook. He and his boys were known to ride for the cause, but they were no match for Kevin and his crew.

"Big Paul, grab up all this shit. The dope, the money, and the gats," Kevin ordered.

"Shorty, all that shit ain't y'alls," Rico replied, as his voice went in and out.

"What you tryna to do, commit suicide?" Kevin asked, looking at Rico like he'd just lost all his God given sense.

Big Paul didn't let Rico's comment bother him, as he followed Kevin's orders. After scooping up the stacks of money, he grabbed the garbage bag that was sitting on the floor, and put the money and the guns inside, while Kevin and Ice Man stood guard. Once they had everything, Kevin told Rico and his boys to get down on the floor.

"Shorty, come on. You ain't gotta do this," Rico pleaded, talking fast.

Kevin cocked his gun. "Keep talkin', your ass is gonna be the first to go."

Out of nowhere, Big Paul heard an unusual sound. "What's that?" he asked, looking around.

Kevin and Ice Man looked down on the floor at Rico's boys only to find Buggs, the craziest one out the bunch, crying like a baby.

Kevin held a huge smile. "Ice, this is classic, ain't it? This nigga cryin' like a little bi-aaa-tch." When Kevin looked down and saw a watery substance flowing, he quickly jumped out the way. "Nigga, I know you ain't pissin' on yo' self too?" Kevin was laughing his ass off. "You niggas runnin' round here like y'all some gangstas and shit, but for real y'all a bunch of pussies."

Big Paul and Ice Man headed toward the back door with two garbage bags full of money and guns as Kevin stayed behind.

"Y'all say yo' prayers," Kevin said, aiming his gun at the group. He

DEEP

was just about to pull the trigger when he saw Big Paul and Ice Man stumbling back into the living room. "What y'all doin', man?" he asked. He turned his gun toward the group of strangers in all black, who walked behind his crew.

"Get down muthafucka!" one of them demanded.

"Hell naw you get down, bitch," Kevin countered, about to set it off.

The guy grabbed Big Paul and pointed his .357 toward Paul's temple. Ice Man immediately held his head down. Big Paul was his best friend and the sight of a gun pointed to his head made him nervous, which was an emotion he rarely had.

"I'm not gonna tell you again. Get the fuck down and everybody empty yo' pockets." The masked man walked along the wall with his gun still pointed at Big Paul until he got to a safe spot. "That's it. Now take out what you packin'."

Still talking shit, Kevin followed the stranger's directions. "Y'all some dead muthafucka's. Watch."

"Shut the fuck up!" the stranger yelled.

Kevin smiled as he reached in his boot and pulled out his .22. He slipped it under his body when the goon turned his head slightly.

"Make sure you keep an eye on him," the stranger ordered, to one of the guys in his crew.

"I don't think so," Kevin replied, as he shot the stranger in the nuts. In agony, the guy dropped his A16 rifle down on the floor right next to Big Paul, which instantly set things into motion.

"Nigga, you wanna put a gun to my head," Big Paul said, as he retrieved the rifle and filled the guy's body up with holes.

Pandemonium set in as the two crews fired at one another. Pieces of wood flew all over the place as the bullets tore through the walls. Pictures cracked and fell to the floor, as blood splattered against them. All the noise sent Rico and his boys, who were without weapons in a corner out the line of fire. Ice Man charged across the table at one of the gunmen. His fist collided with the guy's jaw, instantly making the gunman drop his weapon. Ice Man bent down and picked up the .357 then chimed in on the gunfight.

Driving like they were in a high-speed chase, Carmen and Trae sped down Rico's street. Not wanting to be noticed, Trae instructed

Carmen to park the car a block away from the house. As soon as Carmen whipped the car into a spot, they hopped out and ran toward the rear of Rico's house. Once they reached the back door, Trae put his hand in the air, as a signal for Carmen to be still so he could listen. When he put his ear against the door, surprisingly it was quiet. This really made him suspicious, because Rico always kept a house full of loud mouth niggas. When he twisted the door knob, it opened with ease. Trae looked back at Carmen and gestured with his head to follow him.

Leaning against the wall of the kitchen, with their guns drawn, they entered the house quietly. However, as soon as they made it to the living room, the smell of blood told them it was too late. The mystery men in black were all dead, except the one guy Kevin had shot in the balls. But he wasn't moving either, so Kevin assumed he was dead too.

When Trae walked in the house, he saw his crew standing over the dead bodies. He lowered his gun. "I knew some shit was gonna go down!" he yelled.

Kevin quickly turned around and pointed his gun, but once he saw that it was Trae he pointed the gun back toward the floor. "How did you get in here?"

Trae ignored his question. "Big Paul, you and Ice Man get the hell out of here. We'll catch up with y'all later. Carm, go back to your car, and get it started. Me and Kevin will meet you in a minute," he ordered. As they all left, Trae inched along the wall toward the front of the house to make sure it was clear.

"Ain't nobody else in here, packin'," Kevin said, as he sat on the couch and pulled out his blunt.

Trae looked at Rico and his crew, who seemed terrified. "Man, what the fuck is goin' on?" he asked, walking over to his friend. Kevin didn't know how to answer. It was obvious from the expression on his face that he was distraught. Rico and his boys still didn't move. They felt it was in their best interest to stay low until Kevin came back to his senses.

Kevin is fuckin' up, Trae thought to himself as he looked back at Rico.

With Trae and Kevin's attention focused on something else, the one guy who was still alive saw his opportunity and rose up. Only six inches away from where Trae was standing, he reached in his pocket then sprang at Trae. However, before he could finish his superhero attempt, Trae quickly shot off a round, which landed in the middle of

DEEP

the guy's forehead. His body dropped instantly.

When Trae walked over to his victim, he immediately noticed the familiar face. After walking over to each member of the man's entourage, his thoughts were confirmed.

Trae knew that it was only a matter of time before the cops arrived, so he walked over to Kevin. "We gotta go. Can you walk?" he asked.

Kevin laughed. "Yeah, that's their blood." He stood and turned to Rico. "We just got one loose end to tie up." He cocked his gun, and with one quick swoop, he shot Rico and his boys.

At the same moment, Trae heard sirens, which were faint at first, but were getting louder by the second. "What the fuck you do that for?" he asked panicking.

"We can't afford to leave no witnesses!" Kevin shouted.

Trae was pissed, but he knew Kevin was right. "Let's get the fuck out of here!"

With a burst of speed, they ran down the block to Carmen's waiting car. "Where to?" Carmen asked.

"Go to the club," Trae said, out of breath.

Kevin looked at Trae. He couldn't read the expression in his eyes, but he knew what he was thinking.

"Look, man, I went to pick up the money from Rico, then out of nowhere these niggas just came in blazin'. That wasn't my doin' back there. Big Paul will tell you," Kevin stated.

Trae reassured his friend that he knew it wasn't his fault. Surprised by Trae's calm demeanor toward him, Kevin looked at his friend in confusion.

"What did you see back there?" Kevin asked.

Trae shook his head. "Those were the niggas from Anacostia Park, who were poppin' off at us that day."

Kevin's face lit up. "Are you sure?"

"Yes, I'm sure. I recognized the nigga who was wit' Courtney."

"Dirty muthafuckas. That's why they all goin' home in body bags," Kevin said unremorseful.

Carmen felt her blood pressure rise. *You're gonna regret saying that, you piece of shit.* "This wouldn't have happened if you weren't so out of control," she said.

"Fuck you, bitch!" Kevin barked.

Trae told them both to shut up. "Kev, she has a point. This shit is gonna bring us some major heat."

A NOVEL BY DANETTE MAJETTE

Trying hard to stay focused on the road, Carmen couldn't help but think about what had just happened. "Trae, why do you think those niggas were there?"

"I don't know what the fuck is goin' on," he replied, scratching his head. "I do know that if they the cops connect us to this shit, everything we worked on is gonna go up in smoke."

Kevin let out a heavy sigh. "Trae, they can't connect us to this. No one saw us go in and the niggas who can ID us are dead."

"Rico and them dead too!" Carmen asked, turning around quickly.

"Damn right they dead," Kevin said, in cocky tone. "I wasn't gonna let them niggas live so they could snitch."

Trae's brain went into freeze mode. All he wanted to do was carry out this last job, so he could retire and leave this life of crime behind him. Pondering his next move, he sat silent, trying to piece together the events that had taken place. Staring out the window, he spotted his grandmother's face. She looked disappointed in him. *I told you that fool was gonna cause you nothin' but problems.*

An hour later, everyone was in Trae's office at the club. They all took a seat like they were in school.

"What we gonna do now?" Big Paul asked.

"We ain't gonna do nothin'," Trae said. He walked over to his bar, grabbed a beer, and guzzled it. "We just gonna lay low and let this shit die down."

"What if it doesn't?" Ice Man asked.

"Then we all gonna be sharin' a cell together," Trae responded, throwing his beer bottle in the trash.

"A'ight man, I'ma go get some rest," Big Paul said, standing up and heading toward the door.

"Cool. I need to go over to my house anyway and pick up some more clothes before I head to my hotel room," Trae said, giving them all a pound.

"Hopefully I'll see y'all tomorrow if the cops don't come pick us up tonight," Kevin joked.

You got that right, asshole, Carmen thought.

DEEP

HOMECOMING

Karina made one last check to make sure everything was in place, then picked up the phone and called Trae. "Hey, where you at?" she asked.

"I'm right down the street," he informed.

"Good. The front door is open, just come in," she said, in a sexy-like tone.

Trae couldn't believe his ears. He didn't want to get his hopes up too high, but at the same time, he felt like he and Karina had made some progress over dinner. Stepping out of his car, he walked up to the door and slowly turned the knob. As soon as he entered, Trae stood in the doorway absolutely floored. He couldn't help but smile at the sprinkled rose petal trail that led from the front door, up the stairs, and into the bedroom. As he made his way up the stairs, he could hear the sounds of Anthony Hamilton playing softly from the Bose surround sound system. His smile became even larger when he saw a bottle of champagne on one of the nightstands along with several candles.

"Karina," he called out.

"I'm in here!" she yelled from the bathroom.

The anticipation of what he was about to see next filled his body with excitement as he opened the bathroom door. "Care to join me," she said seductively, soaking in their Jacuzzi tub.

Trae's dick began to jump. "No doubt." He quickly got undressed and joined her in the hot soothing water. Caressing her made him feel like he was in heaven.

"Taste," she said, feeding him a strawberry covered in whipped cream.

Trae licked his lips. "Umm…that's good."

"I love strawberries," she said, biting into what was left of the fruit.

A NOVEL BY DANETTE MAJETTE

"Karina, this is really nice..."

She had a concerned look. "I hear a but comin'."

"'Cuz I don't know what to make of all this. I mean I love what you did, but if it don't mean we're gettin' back together, then I don't see the point."

Karina understood exactly where Trae was coming from. He was the only one who made an effort to salvage the relationship. As far as she was concerned, she didn't think their relationship could survive. He spent way too much time in the street, and not enough time with her. She also blamed him for the death of their baby, and not to mention the suspected cheating. All the excitement, warmth, and passion they had when they first met was gone.

"The time I've spent alone has given me the chance to step back and gain some insight on what went wrong between us," Karina said.

Trae nodded his head. "Me too."

"Trae, I need to know I'm gonna be your number one priority from now on."

"You are. I promise I'm gonna try harder this time, but I need you to promise me that when problems come up, we can sit down and talk them out. No more leaving. We're gonna deal wit' it head on, alright?" he said.

When Karina agreed, they kissed to seal the deal.

Once the water got cold, Trae stood and lifted Karina up into his arms. Carrying her into the room, his smooth lips glided over hers. She wanted to melt as Trae laid her down on the bed. Karina let out a heavy sigh as he spread her legs far as an eagle's wings, kissing her inner thighs, until he found her cave. He caressed her skin and ran his fingers over her hairs. Karina was perfectly trimmed, and he loved to feel her this way.

Using both hands, Trae gently opened the lips of her pussy. With his index and middle fingers, he placed them around the outer perimeter of her clitoris and wiggled his fingers in a circular motion. He inserted one finger to feel her wetness. With one finger inside, he pushed it back and forth, and rubbed her clit at the same time causing Karina to squirm. When Trae pulled his finger out and sampled her flavor, it was so delightful he wanted to taste more. He placed his tongue inside her inner pussy, and licked every inch then stopped to suck on her clit. Karina continued to squirm, but Trae was hungry and wasn't stopping until he was full. Seeing Karina's reaction was a complete turn on for him.

After pleasing her for several more minutes, he decided it was time

DEEP

to feel her inside. He rose up and entered her cave with full force. Karina raised her ass, and was in sync with Trae's movements like it had been rehearsed. Trae went deep to feel her vaginal wall, causing her to let out a delightful moan. He grabbed her legs and lifted her ass up off the bed. She placed her legs on his shoulders as he continued to explore inside her body. She rubbed his chest and played in her own joy to keep it moist for him. Trae liked seeing her play with herself. He bent Karina's legs back like she was about to give birth, then teased her by patting her clit with his dick.

"Trae, stop playing and make me cum," she whined.

He continued to tap her clit with a few more times before re-entering her place of sexual satisfaction. He let her legs relax, but she kept them planted firmly on the bed. Trae pumped deep in a circular motion. Karina, feeling her climax arriving, worked her hips, rising off the bed to meet Trae as he went deeper.

"Oh shit, you feel so good," Karina moaned.

At that moment, Trae grabbed her breast and rubbed her nipple as he continued to hit her walls.

"Suck it baby," she begged.

Trae obliged, by sucking like a baby while diving inside her wet pussy. Karina didn't stop moving. She pumped back at Trae harder and harder, ready to reach her climax.

"Right there, Trae, Rrr-iii-ght there!" Karina shouted. A few seconds later, she exploded!

Trae pursued his own climax, and after a few more strokes he fell limp on her breast.

The night was so magical that Trae had forgotten all about his problems. Reaching over to the nightstand, he grabbed his cell phone and saw there was text message from Sam at the club saying that Courtney had called several times. .

What the fuck does that bitch want? he thought.

"What are you doing?" Karina asked.

"I'm turning my phone off. Tonight belongs to you," he replied, kissing her on the lips.

"It better belong to me," Karina said, climbing on Trae. "Now, let's get round two started."

DEEP

MAKE IT HAPPEN

Watching the news in her small apartment in the southeast section of D.C., Carmen chowed down on Captain Crunch cereal. Gulping the last of her milk, her cell phone rang. She picked it up and saw it was a blocked number. She knew it was Willie.

"Hello," she answered.

"Check in," Willie responded.

"I'll be there in a hour."

She quickly took a shower, and headed to the store on M Street. Sitting on the subway, Carmen began to think about the night at Rico's house. *We gotta hurry up and put an end to Trae and his crew. Shit, who knows I could be next.*

"Next stop, Foggy Bottom," the metro driver announced over the intercom.

A few minutes later, the train doors opened and Carmen got off. She pulled her baseball cap down over her forehead and quickly strutted toward the store.

Pushing open the doors, Carmen made eye contact with the new store clerk, who was an old friend from the academy. After ten minutes of making casual conversation about the clothes to distract a customer, the clerk gave her the okay to go in the back. With three pairs of jeans and two shirts in her hands, Carmen walked in the dressing room as the clerk locked the door behind her.

Once at the end of the hallway, she turned and knocked three times to let Willie know she was at the secret door. When she walked in, she plopped down in the chair at the table and gave Willie a nod.

"This shit is getting out of hand," Carmen said as she let out a huge sigh. She looked exhausted.

"I know," Willie said. He took a seat next to her. "We did some research, and found out the guys who were killed at Rico's were responsible for that little girls death at Anacostia Park. My guess is that they were there to rob Rico, but obviously they underestimated him."

Carmen laughed. "Rico...Rico didn't kill those dudes. Kevin and his lynch men did it."

"Wait...Wait. What do you mean Kevin did it?"

Carmen stood up and poured herself a cup of coffee. "Kevin and his boys were there to pick up the money Rico owed, when the other dudes came busting in."

She stared at the ceiling, and wondered how the city she loved could be filled with so much corruption and hate. She wondered how all this happened. Children were being killed, there were homeless people camped out on every corner, and unemployment was at an all time high.

Willie took his fist and drove it right through the wall. "Those bastards are taking over the city. We need to bring them down now!" he yelled, breathing hard.

"Without some hard evidence, I don't see that happening. I mean the shootout would be my word against theirs," Carmen said.

Willie shifted his glance to Carmen. "What about the heist?"

"As far as I know it's still on."

Willie sat nursing his hand. "I'm starting to lose my patience, besides we can't wait any longer. If we don't get something soon, the State's Attorney's office is going to shut the whole operation down, and that piece of shit is going to keep playing God," he said, making the muscles in his face hardened.

The two sat and tried to come up with a plan to move the heist along. They felt that was their best shot at getting Trae off the streets once and for all.

"He's trying to get out the game. He wanted to pull this one last thing off so he and his girlfriend can leave town," Carmen added.

Willie rocked back and forth in his chair. "If we turn up the heat on his ass, that might force him to make things happen sooner."

"Does that brain of yours ever stop working?" Carmen asked, shaking her head.

"No. You go see what you can find out, while me and my brain work on some counter attacks," Willie replied.

"I'm almost scared to ask what that means," Carmen said, as she walked to the door.

She walked out of the dressing room and up to the counter. "I'll take these. The other ones are too tight."

DEEP

"Cool," the clerk said, folding the jeans.

Carmen paid for her item, then walked back to the subway in route to Pleasures.

It was three o'clock in the afternoon and the club was packed, as men dressed in business suits, filled almost every table.

"What's going on?" Carmen asked the bartender on duty.

"Private party for some big wig corporate type," he said. He handed her a Corona. "If you looking for Trae, he ain't here yet."

"That's cool. I'll wait." Carmen took a seat and watched as a raunchy old man got a lap dance. "I bet he's married with children."

"No doubt. His wife's probably at home, thinking he's working hard on some business deal." He laughed. "When in reality, the only thing he's working hard on is that big ass." He threw his hand towel over his shoulder. "By the way, I'm Sam. I've seen you with Trae a couple times."

"Nice to meet you, Sam. I'm Carmen."

Carmen was on her second beer when Sommone walked in.

"Hey Mone," Sam yelled over the music. "What you tastin'?"

"Just water. I'm not staying. I just came to pick up my check. The show's tonight."

Carmen looked in Sommone's direction. It was hard acting like she didn't know her when in fact they'd been partners for a few years. "Excuse me. I couldn't help but overhear that there's some type of show tonight."

"Oh, Sommone, this is Carmen. She's a friend of Trae's, so be nice to her," Sam said.

Sommone smiled. "Nice to meet you Carmen. Yes, the Ne-Yo show."

Not wanting to appear out of the loop, Sam said, "Oh yeah, that's right."

The three of them continued to have a conversation until Trae arrived. He walked in, smiling like he'd just won the lottery.

"Well, you sure look better than you did yesterday," Sommone said. "Trae I came to get my check. Is it in the office?"

"Actually no, I have it right here," Trae replied reaching in his pocket. He pulled out the white envelope and placed it in Sommone's hand. "I wanted to give it to you personally."

Carmen couldn't help but notice the obvious attraction between Trae and her partner. *She better not be falling for this dude.*

A NOVEL BY DANETTE MAJETTE

When Sommone saw Carmen looking at her with a strange expression, she thanked Trae and quickly walked away.

Trae sat down at the bar next to Carmen. "What's up?"

"Nothin', I just came to make sure you were straight," she said.

"I'm cool. I just went and checked out of my hotel room."

Carmen was confused. "I thought you and your girl were beefing."

"We were but we got back together last night." Trae slid closer to Carmen so no one could hear him. "I guess things are finally lookin' up for me. Now all I need is for this job to go through without a hitch, so we can leave town."

"I hear you. I'm thinkin' 'bout goin' back to Jamaica. I was livin' large over there," Carmen said.

"I don't care where we go as long as it's far away from here." Trae responded.

"You should go to Senegal. I hear it's beautiful there."

"Where's that?" Trae asked.

"In Africa, you know the motherland."

Trae laughed. Senegal, huh? That would be different. Oh, well, I gotta go home. We're goin' to the Ne-Yo concert tonight." Trae paused for a second. "Hey, you should come roll with us," he said, standing up.

Carmen thought about it. "Um...I can do that. But I have a few things to take care of, so I'll meet y'all there."

"A'ight. I'll put you on the VIP list, so you don't have to wait in no long ass line," Trae said.

He was about to leave when he felt a tap on his shoulder. He turned around and almost lost it when he saw Courtney standing there with a sneaky grin on her face.

He told Carmen to excuse him as he grabbed Courtney by the arm and pulled her toward the front door.

"What are you doing? I haven't had my drink yet!" she yelled, trying to pull away from him.

When they got to the front of the club, Trae threw her up against the wall.

"I'm not sure what you really want, but don't come around here anymore," he whispered. "And stop calling here too. The next time I might not be so nice." He wanted to question whether Courtney had anything to do with her dude from the park being at Rico's house that night or if she knew he was dead, but decided not to entertain the thought. He wanted to get away from her as soon as possible.

"Is that the way you treat the..." She stopped. "Never mind, I'll tell

DEEP

you about it at a later date."

"Tell me what?" Trae asked.

Courtney snickered. "If I tell you now then I'll spoil the surprise."

Trae was tired of playing games with her, so he pushed her out the front door. Courtney, caught off guard, lost her balance and ended up on the ground as a couple of guys were coming inside.

"Damn bitch, you got tossed out like Jazz from the Fresh Prince," one of the guys joked. The guys laughed as they stepped over her to get in.

Courtney was so embarrassed, she started crying. "That's alright muthafucka. We'll see who has the last laugh," she said, as she got up and brushed herself off.

DEEP

NOT YOU AGAIN

Brand new clothes were thrown across the bed, draped over the chaise, and spilling out of shopping bags when Trae walked in the bedroom. "What happened in here?" he asked.

"Good, you're home." Karina swallowed the last of her wine. "Which ones should I wear?" she said, holding up her new True Religion and Joe's jeans.

"Wear those," he replied, pointing to the True Religions. "They make yo' ass sit up in the air."

"You're crazy, you know that?"

"Crazy 'bout you." He threw Karina on the bed. "Can I get some lovin' before we leave?"

Karina glanced at the clock on the nightstand. "Trae, it's eight o clock, we gotta get ready."

"We got time."

"No, we don't. You know it takes me forever to get dressed."

"A'ight...but you owe me when we get home."

Karina kissed him on the lips. "Deal."

An hour later, Karina studied herself in the mirror and liked what she saw. The jeans looked great on her and the shirt she was wearing complemented her complexion. Her Jimmy Choo pumps also gave her a tall and lean model look. Trae however, settled for a more casual look, jeans and a black t-shirt.

"That's what you're wearing," Karina said frowning.

"Hell yeah, I ain't gettin' all dressed up for that dude."

"I know it's just a show, but can't you wear a dressier shirt."

"What's wrong wit' my shirt? It's from LL's new Todd Smith line."

Karina laughed. "I know. I do work in the fashion industry."

"Well then you know it's stylish and can be worn anywhere."

Karina laughed. "What, are you, LL's new spokesperson now?"

A NOVEL BY DANETTE MAJETTE

"Naw, but I should be. Come on, we gotta go," he said, walking out the room.

Men, Karina thought, *they are absolutely clueless.*

While she locked up, Trae pulled his Cadillac into the garage and pulled out his Range. He hadn't driven his new car in a while, so he thought this would be the perfect opportunity.

All the way to the nightclub called Love, Trae cracked jokes that kept Karina laughing. It was just like old times. By the time they arrived, Okie Street looked like a block party. The streets were lined with cars, fine dressed guys, and girls from every section of D.C.

Once they got through the traffic jam, Trae pulled up to the valet parking sign, and handed his keys over to the attendant.

"Shorty, you betta not get one fuckin' scratch on my ride or that's yo' ass." After helping Karina out of the truck, they made their way to the front of the line.

"Everybody step back!" the bouncer yelled when he saw Trae.

"Good lookin' out," Trae said, slipping the bouncer a hundred dollar bill.

"Come on, I'll escort you to the VIP section," the bouncer responded.

As soon as they entered the club, all eyes were on them, but Trae wasn't one for attention. That was more like Kevin's deal, he loved being in the spotlight. Something Trae warned would bring them down.

There must've been a hundred people in the VIP room, so it took Trae and Karina some time to make it to their reserved tables. When they finally arrived, they greeted Kevin, Big Paul and Ice Man, who were already on their third bottle of Cristal.

"Trae, I ain't seen this many phat ass bitches in one spot in a long time," Kevin whispered, eyeing every big booty that walked by. "Too bad you ain't still single."

"Shorty, these chicks can't do nothin' for me," Trae said, pouring Karina a glass of champagne. He handed her the glass, then suggested they go mingle before the show.

Just as they got up out of their seats, Carmen walked in looking like a black Barbie. Trae was in a trance. It was the first time he'd seen her dressed so seductively. From the angle where he stood, he could see right through the sheer black dress that clung to every curve he didn't know she had.

"Damn," Trae mumbled. He quickly walked over and greeted her with a huge smile. Obviously completing forgetting about Karina. "I'm glad you made it," he said, as his dick stiffened.

DEEP

She ran her tongue across her lips gently. "Me too."

Trae's concentration was blown. "Okay...I betta go before my girl starts actin' up in here."

"Alright, I'll talk to you later," Carmen said, grabbing his glass of champagne from him.

Trae could see the suspicious look in Karina's eyes when he walked back in her direction. "I'm glad you almost broke your fuckin' neck to speak to her," she said, with an attitude.

"Baby, don't start. Nothin' is goin' on between us. You gotta lighten up," Trae responded, kissing Karina on the cheek.

After trying to convince her for a few more minutes, Trae finally took Karina around and introduced her to some of his friends, who she hadn't met before. She soon found herself engaged in a conversation with the sister of an old college roommate. When she finally looked up, Trae was gone.

With so many people calling out his name, and pulling him in all directions, Karina was left on her own. She retreated to the bar, and watched as girls made complete fools of themselves. Out the corner of her eye, she spotted Trae talking to a girl whom she had never seen before. She was stylish and her hair hung well past her shoulders. It was obvious it wasn't a weave from the way she kept running her fingers through it. It was also clear to Karina that she and Trae knew each other well, because she kept falling all over him every time he would say something.

Here we go again. Who the fuck is this bitch? Karina thought to herself. When her curiosity reached it's peak, she walked over, slipping her arm around his waist.

"I was wondering where you were," Trae said, kissing her on the cheek.

"I'm right here," Karina said, gritting her teeth.

The two women stared at each other for a moment before Trae realized they didn't know each other, "That's right, you never met my girlfriend."

"No, I haven't," the woman answered.

"Karina, this is Ice Man's sister, Bridget. She's a school teacher."

"Trae, she didn't ask you what I do for a living," Bridget said, pushing him.

Karina extended her hand. "Hi, Bridget, nice to meet you."

"Same here. Well, Trae, I have to go find that brother of mine. I'll talk to you later."

A NOVEL BY DANETTE MAJETTE

Karina felt stupid. Here she was claiming her territory when there wasn't a need. "You know I was about to go off. I thought she was another one of your hoochies," she said.

Suddenly the lights dimmed, and the band began to play as Ne-Yo stepped from behind from the right side of the stage.

With a black fedora hat, black sports coat, and jeans, Ne-Yo greeted the crowd. "What's up, D.C.!" he yelled, as groupies fell all over one another screaming.

He cued the band and started to sing. After performing three of his songs, he signaled for the band to stop.

"Hey, check this out. While I was sitting in the dressing room, I got a message from my assistant that someone named Trae wanted me to dedicate this next song to his girlfriend, Karina." The crowd went wild. "So Karina, this one's for you."

Karina was stunned as she listened to Ne-Yo perform *When You're Mad*.

She wiped away tears as thoughts about how she and Trae struggled to keep their relationship together entered her mind. Even though they had been through a lot and there were always things threatening to tear them apart, they managed to keep it together. That's when she finally realized that those obstacles were only making their love stronger.

At three a.m., the club was finally starting the wind down, so Trae and Karina decided to leave. When Karina had to use the restroom, she told Trae she would meet him outside. While he waited for his truck, he noticed a familiar face walking in his direction.

He turned to see if Karina was coming. Then looked down the street to see what was taking the valet attendant so long.

"Hi Trae. Bet you thought you'd never see me again."

Trae didn't respond immediately. His heart started to beat double-time as he cleared his throat. "What the fuck is it wit' you? You're like a nagging cold that won't go away."

"Why are you actin' like that? Especially since the night we spent together was so special," Courtney replied.

"Special...bitch, what the fuck is wrong wit' you? I just hit that shit and bounced."

Courtney laughed. "Well, when you hit it, that was special to me." She stepped closer to Trae and brushed her hand across his chest.

DEEP

He turned and looked for Karina. "Look, my girl is about to come out here, so beat it," he ordered.

"Where was your girl when you were fuckin' me?" Courtney asked. She was finally starting to get an attitude.

"Look, I told you that I had a girl, so you need to forget about that night cause I have," he replied.

"Well, I can't," she said, holding her stomach.

Trae almost lost it. "I don't know what kinda game you runnin', but I ain't the one. As a matter of fact, why don't you call your man that stepped to me at the park?" Trae watched closely to see how Courtney would react.

"Oh, that nigga wasn't my man, just my flavor of the month. But you, it looks like me and you will be connected for a long time," Courtney replied with a devilish grin.

Trae clenched his jaw. "Fuckin' wit' me is the wrong thing to do, shorty."

"I'm not fuckin' with you, this is real."

When Karina walked up, she noticed Trae's uneasiness. But after the way she acted in the club about Ice Man's sister, she thought it was best not to fly off the handle. Instead, she stood silent as Courtney walked off laughing. She couldn't explain it, but there was something about the way Courtney smiled over her shoulder that made her feel uneasy. Minutes later, the valet returned with Trae's truck. They both climbed in and headed home.

"Was that the girl I got into it with the first day we met?" Karina asked after riding in silence for a while.

Trae shook his head. "Yeah, she comes to the club wit' her girl-friends sometimes, and asked me if I could start lettin' her in for free," he lied.

"So, is she still trying to get you to call her?"

"Naw, she fuck wit' some nigga with dough uptown now," Trae lied again.

"That's good to know. Now I don't have to worry about her trying anything with you." Karina knew what she'd just said was a lie.

In actuality, she was extremely worried. Even though she and Trae had worked out their problems, the fact that she didn't trust him was eating away at her, big time.

DEEP

HERE WE GO AGAIN

The next day, Karina was behind the register at work handing a bag to a customer, when she noticed Courtney standing in her department. She walked over and asked, "What are you doing here? Get out of my department!"

"Oh, I'm sorry, is this your department or does the whole store belong to Nordstrom's." Courtney asked sarcastically

Karina wanted to slap Courtney right there on the spot. Instead, she turned and walked away.

Courtney gave a slight smirk and followed Karina. "So, how's Trae?"

Karina turned around slowly and bit her lip. It took all her strength to keep her composure. "He's doing just fine," she said. "Look, stop worrying about my man and worry about your own. You know your baller from uptown."

"What?" Courtney asked with a confused expression. "Someone gave you fucked up information. I don't have a man. Not yet anyway, but I got my eye on one."

Karina was confused. She was sure Trae told her that Courtney had a boyfriend. "Whether or not you have a man is really none of my concern. I'm just warning you to stay away from mine."

Courtney laughed. "Too late."

"Bitch, what do you mean too late?"

"Just what I said. And the next time you call me a bitch you better be ready to get your ass kicked. Better yet, get ready to lose your job, after I drag your ass all over this floor."

Karina almost went off on Courtney, but she had to remember where she was. She simply reminded her again to leave Trae alone or she would be the one getting the ass whipping. She then told Courtney to leave before she called security. When Courtney didn't move, Karina walked over to the register and picked up the phone.

At that point, Courtney started to leave, but couldn't resist the urge to get under Karina's skin one last time. "You really need to stop walking around like you're Trae's one and only, because I know for a fact that you aren't."

"Just get the fuck out!" Karina shouted.

"Don't forget to tell Trae I said hello," Courtney responded, with a sneaky grin.

"Whatever!" Karina said, looking at her with disgust. Although she given Trae her word that she would discuss anything that was bothering her, she felt she couldn't talk to him about this. Their relationship was finally starting to heal and if she said something about Courtney, he might think she didn't trust him again. Even though it was obvious he'd lied about her having a boyfriend.

As Courtney walked away a man dressed in a nice suit and tie greeted Karina. She could tell from the conversation he was having on his cell-phone, that he was a businessman.

The man who was tall, and well built finished his conversation, and then started looking at the jeans. "Hi, can I help you with something?" Karina asked.

"Yeah, my one day business trip has turned into a three day trip, so I'm in need of a few things," the man replied.

"Well, those jeans fit really nice. They're a boot cut fit, with a thirty eight inseam to accommodate your height." She handed him a pair. "Is there any particular style of shirt you prefer?"

"Yes, definitely something with a collar and long sleeves."

Karina walked over to the sports shirts and pulled a few styles. "Do you like any of these?" she asked.

The man looked at the shirts, studying each one's sleeve length. "These are fine...I'll take two of them."

Karina proceeded to the register to ring him up. "So, what type of business are you in, if I'm not being too nosey?"

"No...no, I'm a producer," he said, handing Karina his credit card.

"Wow, that sounds interesting."

"It has its good days and its bad."

"A bad day being when you make an awful song, huh?" Karina responded, cracking a smile.

"Exactly. By the way, my name is Dazmon, but please call me Daz," he said.

DEEP

"I'm Karina. Nice to meet you, Daz," she responded, shaking his hand.

Their conversation was interesting. He made Karina laugh when he talked about some of the artists who were absolute nut cases. It wasn't until a new customer came up and asked her for help that she realized how long they'd been talking.

"I better get back to work," Karina said. She walked around the counter and handed him his bag. "Let me know if you ever need any assistance." She handed him her business card.

He looked at the card. "Thank you. I will. Have a nice day."

"You too." Karina couldn't help but glance at the nice looking gentl-men as he walked away.

When the new customer decided not to buy anything, Karina start-ed straightening up. She was almost finished folding the unorganized jean table when she spotted Trae standing outside watching her through the window. He walked in and stood beside her.

"Hey baby," she said, grabbing his hand. He immediately pulled away. "What's wrong?"

"Who was that nigga smilin' all in yo' face earlier?" he asked.

Karina looked confused. "What are you talking about?"

"The dude you thought was so funny," he said loudly.

Karina noticed people watching. Scared he would lose control and blow up in front of everyone, she stepped over to the counter, called Ashley and asked her to come over and watch her department. When Ashley finally arrived, Karina headed straight for the front entrance as Trae followed closely behind.

She found an isolated spot then tore into Trae's shit. "First of all, don't ever come to my job and embarrass me like that again. Second, talking to customers is part of my job. I have to build a repore with them if I want them to spend their money with me. Third, I work in the men's department, so it's kinda hard not to talk to any men."

"Whatever. You was feeling that nigga!" he said, yelling at her. "You even looked back at the dude when he walked away."

Damn he saw all that? Where in the hell was he? I hope Trae's ass isn't some sort of stalker. "I don't even know him, Trae," she replied, yelling back.

"I told you this job was gonna be a problem. Niggas just waitin' for you to fuck up so they can throw that shit in my face."

She took a deep breath, trying to compose herself. "You know what, you need to just be honest with yourself. You just hate that I'm working around men period!"

"Yeah, cause I know how these dudes are out here!"

This dude has some fuckin' nerve. "I could say the same about your place of employment," she said, with her hands on her hips. "I don't say anything when women are always throwing their pussy in your face!"

Trae was so bent, he grabbed Karina around the throat. "Let me tell you something. That place of employment pays for that big ass house you live in, the expensive clothes you like to wear, and the fancy restaurants you like to eat in. If you have a problem wit' what I do you can always pack your bags and leave."

One of Karina's co-workers who was out having a cigarette noticed Trae and Karina arguing. He walked over. "Hey, do you need me to call security?" he asked Karina.

"No, I'm okay. We're just having a disagreement."

Trae turned and looked at the guy. "Nigga, take yo' ass back in the store and sell somethin' before you get fucked up out here."

The guy was scared to death, and as much as he liked Karina he felt she wasn't worth getting hurt for, so he quickly went back to work and never turned around.

Later that evening, the rain was coming down so hard it had caused two major accidents and a dozen fender benders. Barely able to see out of her windows, Karina slowly pulled her Jaguar into the driveway. Dripping wet, she got out of her work clothes, emptied a can of soup into a pot and flipped on the television. Several minutes later, the phone rang.

"Hello," Karina answered.

"We still beefin'?" Trae asked..

"I don't know. Are we?" she questioned, with an attitude.

"I hope not, cause if we are, I'ma have to take this back."

"Take what back?"

"Come to the door and find out."

When Karina opened the door, Trae was standing there looking like a lost puppy.

"This," he said, handing Karina a silver and gold gift wrapped box.

DEEP

"I'm sorry," he said, pressing up against her.

She cut her eyes and smirked. "You should be." When she opened the box, she screamed, "Oh my God!" She placed her hand over her mouth as she pulled out a white vintage fur coat. "I can't believe you bought me this."

"Does that mean you forgive me?" Trae asked.

She smiled. "I guess I can forgive you."

After walking back into the house, he led Karina to the living room. He kissed her so deep and hard, she instantly dropped the fur on the floor.

"Let's go upstairs," Karina suggested.

"Un...un, I want it right here," he said, throwing her back onto the couch. After taking off her jeans along with her panties, Trae entered her from behind and filled her treasure with every inch of him. "I love you...I love you...," he repeated, with every thrust.

"I love you too," she whispered, pushing her ass back against him.

Karina's breathing grew heavier as Trae slid in and out of her nest. His powerful thrusts were driving her crazy.

"Does it feel good?" he asked, sucking on her neck.

Barely able to speak, she muttered the word, "Yeeeah..." Her heart rate increased.

Trae pulled Karina's hips back toward him in a rhythm. He then grabbed her hair, as he forcefully pounded his dick into her pussy Trae was near his end, but Karina pounded back even harder. Within a few more strokes, Trae had collapsed on her back

After showering, Karina and Trae laid in bed tangled in each other's arms.

"I hate to bring this up, but we need to talk about what happened today," Karina said, looking at Trae.

He turned the television off. "I told you I was sorry," he said.

"I know, but I still feel like you don't trust me."

"It's not you, it's me. I'm just stressed and I took it out on you."

"What are you stressed about?"

"Shit ain't goin' right in the streets. But it's gonna be a'ight."

"Are you sure?"

"I'm positive, baby."

Karina wanted to tell Trae about her run in with Courtney, but she didn't want to mess up a goodnight. Instead, she leaned over and kissed him goodnight.

Trae tried to go to sleep, but with everything that was going on he couldn't. If this deal didn't go through, he would never get out of the game.

DEEP

CLOSE CALL

It was a busy Friday night and Valentine's day was a week away. The girls at Pleasures were working overtime, because most of them had men they wanted to impress. In between her sets, Sommone kept tabs on Trae. Taking mental notes of his comings, goings, and anything she thought was out of the ordinary.

Just as Sommone was putting on her skimpy police officer outfit, Trae walked into the dressing room with a wife beater on. She found herself staring at his powerful biceps, so she lowered her eyes to the floor.

"Even though I don't care for that particular costume, it looks good on you. But it's gonna look even better when you take it off," Trae said.

Sommone's eyes grew big. "Excuse me?"

"I'm just kiddin'," Trae said giggling.

"What do you say we have a drink after the show?"

"Maybe, I'll see," he said.

Sommone made a face and started to walk away, taking long, fast struts that made her ass wiggle. *What about now?* she thought.

She stood in the wings off stage, waiting to go on. As she peeked out, she could see the club was packed with some shady characters. Her eyes were immediately drawn to a fair skinned, foreign looking gentleman carrying a briefcase, and being escorted by a bouncer to Trae's table. After Trae greeted him, the man puffed on a huge cigar as they discussed business.

"So, are your people ready?" Trae asked.

"Not quite. That's a lot of money to get together, so we need a little bit more time, the Dominican responded."

"Come on Rafael, you're killin' me. I need to make this happen."

"Don't worry it won't be long, my friend."

"I'ma tell you right now. I don't want no shit from your folks," Trae warned.

Trae had to keep his eye on Rafael. He was a smart, Dominican mobster, who was part of the Dominican Federation, an organization known for extortion, murder and drugs. Rafael was always running from place to place, making illegal deals. That's how he and Trae met in the first place.

"They'll be no problems, my friend. Now let's enjoy the show."

After their meeting, the two men toasted.

Who is he? Sommone thought, almost missing her introductory cue.

She slid out onto the stage allowing her alluring moves to captivate the men, who were hissing and making loud noises. Covered in the blue police jacket, she removed it seductively, and threw it out into the crowd, exposing her sequin bra. An intoxicated man waved a five dollar bill up at her, giving Sommone the opportunity to get a better view of who Trae was sitting with. As soon as she looked at the dangerous looking guy, who had a scar on his face, they locked eyes. He stared at her for a few seconds, then leaned over to Trae and said something.

Trae walked to the end of the stage and motioned for Sommone to kneel down. "He likes you, so give him a little something more than the usual," he whispered into her ear.

She gave him a faint smile, then swirled back to the center of the stage and worked her magic on the long silver pole.

After her set, Sommone met up with Trae at the bar as soon as she left the stage. Sam poured them a drink, as Trae imagined her bent over his desk naked.

"Trae, you alright?" Sommone asked, tossing back the first drink, and asking for another. She couldn't believe how good he looked at that moment.

"Mmm…yeah, I'm sorry. I just got a lot on my mind."

"I bet I can fix all that if you let me."

Trae almost choked on his drink. "Are you serious," he asked in shock.

"I meant, I could give you one of my famous massages."

When Trae asked Sommone to come back to his office with him, she smiled. This was the break she'd been waiting for. Sommone was sure she could get some information out of him if she played her cards

DEEP

right.

When they walked into the office, Sommone immediately took a seat on Trae's couch, as he sat behind his desk.

"You gonna make me sit over here by myself," she said smiling.

He shook his head as a grin formed in the corners of his mouth. He got up, fixed two shots of Patron, and sat down next to her. "You gonna get me into trouble," he said, his eyes roaming up and down her body.

"And just how am I gonna do that?" she asked, with a hint of mischief in her eyes.

He knew being in his office with Sommone was a bad idea. Every time he was close to her, he couldn't help but want her. Although he denied it to Karina, he was very much attracted to Sommone. He felt guilty about it. In his mind, their conversations were innocent. She was fun and easy to talk to.

Trae talked about his life growing up, and his relationship with Karina. When he thought she was comfortable enough, he started asking her questions about her life.

"So, what brought you to D.C.?" Trae asked.

"I just wanted a change of scenery."

"You got family here?" he asked, handing Sommone her second shot.

"Naw, my family's from Miami."

Trae sat quiet for a moment. His mind flashed back to the first day Sommone came into his office. The story she told him then wasn't the same story she was telling him now. Then he remembered Kevin saying he'd seen her somewhere before. At the time, he thought Kevin was just running his mouth, but now he was afraid that his friend might be right.

"Um…so what did you do in Miami?"

"I was a dancer. Can't you tell?" she said slurring a little.

"So, you were doin' yo' thang on stage, huh?"

"Yeah, I put in work."

"So Miami …I thought you were from ATL?" Trae asked.

Sommone's hands started to shake. "I moved to Atlanta when I was about thirteen, but I'm originally from Miami."

Trae looked at her with suspicion. "I see…I see."

Sommone knew she'd fucked up big time, and the only way to rectify the situation was to get Trae's mind off her and on to something else.

A NOVEL BY DANETTE MAJETTE

"Look we've done enough talking. Let's do what we really came in here to do," she said, unbuttoning his jeans.

Although Trae was still suspicious, he couldn't resist her. He began to remove his shirt then fell back on the couch, as Sommone kissed him and rubbed his chest.

"We really shouldn't be doin' this," he said.

"I won't tell if you won't."

Trae still couldn't resist, especially after she took his tongue into her mouth and sucked on it. The smell of her skin aroused him and made his dick stiff as a board. He reached in the cabinet next to the couch and pulled out a condom. He ripped it open with his teeth and threw the package to the side. After securely placing it on, he told Sommone to get on top.

He grabbed her ass and entered her halfway, alternating shallow and deep thrusts that left Sommone begging for more.

"Damn, you feel good," she whispered, as she dug her nails into his back. For Sommone, this wasn't a cover up. This was real.

"You feel good too, baby," Trae replied.

Gasping in delight, Trae placed one of Sommone's breast in his mouth and sucked on her nipple. It took everything for him not to lose control.

With her arms wrapped around his neck, she swung her hips as if she was on stage giving a show.

"Come on, Trae, fuck me harder!" she shouted.

"You sure you want that," he grunted.

"Yeah, baby, I like it hard."

Trae held her tight as he picked up his tempo. Digging deeper, Sommone cried out and threw her head back.

"Damn!" she yelled.

Trae covered her mouth. "Not so loud. Someone might hear you."

Sommone ignored him. "Yes…yes…yes," she repeated, as her juices flowed down on Trae's dick.

"Don't stop yet. I'm cummin,'" Trae demanded.

Sommone clamped down on his shaft, grinding her hips.

"Ohh…shit," he cried, bringing him to a point of no return.

As soon as Trae squirted, he hopped up still dripping.

"What's wrong," Sommone asked.

"I think you better go. The last thing I need is my girl walkin' in."

"Okay," she said, quickly grabbing her clothes. "I can't believe you got a conscious all of a sudden."

Trae realized how his attitude must've come across as crazy, so

DEEP

he explained to Sommone that he wasn't trying to play her. "I just don't want my girl goin' off on you again or me for that matter."

Sommone told Trae she understood, then got dressed and went back to work like nothing ever happened.

I gotta stop lettin' pussy take over all the time," he said.

DEEP

SHE SAID IT'S YOUR CHILD

In much need of some pampering, Karina decided to spend the day at her favorite spa in Georgetown. While she was there, she ran into her co-worker, Dominique. As soon as Karina saw her, she knew she wasn't ready for the conversation.

"What's going on, girl? How you doing?" Dominque asked.

"I'm doing great! Trae bought me this beauty for Valentine's Day," Karina replied, exposing her new three-carat diamond bracelet. It was no sense in beating around the bush. Karina knew Dominique was well aware about her and Trae.

"Um...that's nice. But how are you really doing?"

"What do you mean?" Karina asked, giving Dominque a serious look. She hoped Ashley wasn't running her mouth at work.

"Well, I thought you would be upset about Trae's new girl."

Karina looked at her like she was crazy. "What girl?"

Dominique saw that Karina had no idea what she was talking about, so she tried to change the subject. "Oh, don't worry about it. So...have you ever been to this spa before?"

"No, I want to know what you're talking about. What girl?" Karina asked. This time there was more of a demand in her voice.

"I'm sorry I thought you knew. There's a girl in my neighborhood named Courtney who's been running around telling everybody that she messes with Trae, so I assumed it was true. But from the look on your face I guess it isn't."

Karina let out a slight laugh. "Girl, puh-leez! That's a joke. Trae would never cheat on me."

"Look Karina, stop being so naive. Trae hurts every woman he deals with. Shit, I should know." Karina didn't respond. "Listen, I'm not here to throw salt in your game. From what I hear you and Trae love each other, but I still think you should be careful. Let's not forget he's

A NOVEL BY DANETTE MAJETTE

still a man."

"Thanks for the advice," Karina said in a low tone.

"Well, I gotta go. It's almost time for my facial. I'll talk to you later," Dominique responded as she walked away.

Karina was so upset she left the spa without even being seen. She quickly walked to her car and rode off. Almost in tears, she pulled over on the side of the road to get herself together before she drove home. She knew the rumor was probably a lie, but Dominique's words still haunted her. *Trae wouldn't cheat on me after all we've been through.* It was just out of the question.

When she pulled in the driveway, a few minutes later, Trae was already home.

"Hi baby. How was your day?" he asked as Karina walked through the door.

"It was okay. I went to the spa."

"Sounds relaxing."

"Well, it would've been if I hadn't run into this girl from work. You're not gonna believe what she told me." Karina didn't want to mention that the girl she was talking about was one of his many hoochies.

Trae shook his head. "What did she say?"

"Never mind. I'm not even gonna entertain you with today's gossip." Trying not to let on that something was bothering her, Karina retired to the bedroom, with Trae following closely behind.

"Okay what's wrong?" he asked.

"What makes you think something's wrong?"

"Because first, I ain't get any sugar when you walked in. Second, you ain't even notice the shopping bags from your favorite store right beside the door."

"I'm sorry. It's just been one of those days."

"If you give me my sugar, I might forgive you," he said, with a snicker.

Karina planted a small peck on his lips. When he tried to take it a step further, she pulled away.

"Not today, Trae. I'm not feeling too well," she said.

"You need me to go get you something from the store?"

"No, I just need to get some rest."

"Well, I'll be out in the garage messin' wit' my bike if you need anythin'."

Karina didn't respond as Trae walked out the room. When he closed the door, she laid on the bed and stared up at the ceiling.

DEEP

I don't know how much more of this I can take. Karina began to wonder if all the stress of being with Trae was worth all the material things. It was beginning to be one thing after another with him.

The next morning, Karina didn't feel like going to work, so she decided to stay at home. She was in the middle of a phone call with her mother when the doorbell rang. Karina hadn't spoken with her mother in weeks, so she kept talking, hoping the person would go away, but they seemed relentless. Frustrated, Karina told her mother she would call her back then went to answer the door.

When she looked out the peephole and noticed a delivery man holding a bouquet of flowers, she smiled. Trae was always sending her roses.

"Hello," Karina said, opening the door.

"I have a delivery for Mr. Trae Keal," the delivery man replied. "Can you sign for him?"

Karina displayed a weird expression. "Sure," she said, signing the piece of paper. When she was finished, the delivery man handed her the beautiful long stemmed flowers.

"Have a nice day," he said walking away.

Karina didn't respond as she closed the door and wondered what was going on. *Why in the hell is someone sending him flowers*? As she sat the vase on the table, she couldn't wait to read the small white card that was attached.

When she opened the envelope and read the contents, she nearly collapsed on the floor. It was a note from Courtney congratulating him on being a father, along with a copy of the positive test results from her doctor, and her phone number.

Karina couldn't believe her eyes. After reading the paper at least three more times, she sat still on the floor and sobbed. "There has to be some mistake," she said aloud. "Trae would never do this."

However, reality soon set in, and Karina quickly realized that Trae could do something like that to her. *He's lied to me about so many things, what difference does this make.*

By the time Sommone showed up for her shift at the club, word

A NOVEL BY DANETTE MAJETTE

had already spread about her night with Trae. She was terrified and embarrassed. If word got outside the club, she would be finished.

I didn't have a choice, she thought, trying to rationalize. She'd been given strict instructions to do whatever she had to do in order to get Trae to trust her, so sleeping with him was the only way to do that, especially since he suspected she had lied about where she was from.

Sommone went straight to Trae's office and knocked on the door.

"Come in," he yelled.

"Hi. Sorry for bothering you," she said.

"It's okay."

She closed the door and sat down. "I don't know if you've heard, but it seems a few people are talking about what happened between us the other night."

"I swear I didn't tell anyone," Trae said defensively.

"Well, we were the only people in the room, Trae."

"Look, everybody around here runs their mouth. Plus, they just hatin' on you because you're the new girl," he said, coming over and sitting next to her. "Don't worry, I'll make sure they stop talkin' shit."

Sommone smiled. "What if your girlfriend finds out?"

"She won't. They wouldn't dare say anthin' to her. You just leave them to me."

"Okay. Well, I better get to work." She kissed him on the cheek. "Talk to you later."

She got up to leave, but Trae grabbed her by the arm. "Since you're here, how about a replay of the other night?" he said, trying to undress her.

"I don't think that's a good idea," Sommone replied, rubbing his hand.

As much as he wanted her, he knew she was right. Having sex with her in his office was playing it close, so he kissed her good bye instead.

When Trae came home later that night, he yelled several times for Karina, but she didn't answer.

"Baby, where are you," he yelled as he wondered through the house.

He looked in the family room. "Oh, there you are. What you doin' on the floor?"

When she looked up, her eyes were blood shot red from crying.

DEEP

"What's wrong?" he asked, kneeling down.

Not able to pull herself together, she handed him the note along with the test results. When he read it, he became enraged, but knew he had to convince Karina that the note wasn't true.

"Baby, listen to me," Trae pleaded.

"I'm not listening to shit you have to say!" Karina screamed.

"Please, you have to hear me out."

Tears ran down Karina's cheeks. "Why, so you can tell me more fuckin' lies? Is Courtney the girl from the Ne-Yo show?" She wanted to see if he was going to tell the truth.

"Yeah she is, but you can't believe anythin' that crazy ass girl says," Trae replied.

"Fuck all the games at this point, Trae. Did you sleep with this girl?" she asked.

Trae knew he couldn't possibly tell Karina the truth. If he did, their relationship was sure to be over. "No, I never slept wit' that bitch. I told you, she mess wit' a dude I know from uptown."

Karina was furious. "Stop fuckin' telling lies right to my face. Courtney came by my job recently, and told me that she didn't have a boyfriend, who lives uptown!"

I'm gonna kill that bitch, Trae thought as he got himself together. I can't believe you're gonna believe her dumb ass over me Karina. Courtney is just out to get me, that's all. Trust me, I'll do whatever it takes to prove to you that baby is not mine," Trae said. "Hell, I'll even take a test to prove it."

Karina was shocked. She hadn't expected Trae to say that. "Well, how am I supposed to handle this?"

At that point, Trae knew he might have a chance of convincing her. "We'll handle it together. I promise."

After reassuring Karina, Trae pulled her close to him and started kissing her. When Karina didn't resist, Trae felt he had her right where he wanted. He immediately pulled her shirt up, exposing her breasts. He fondled them for a second, stroking her nipples with his fingers. He then tugged at the buttons of her jeans until they were open. With her jeans and panties pulled down, Trae cupped her ass hard. He then slid his fingers between her thighs to explore her lips. She was purring as he stroked her, sending her into ecstasy. Karina was eager for him to enter, so she motioned for him to lie on the floor, and guided his dick into her pussy. Karina bounced on Trae's dick, as he grunted and smacked her cheeks. However after a few more strokes, she buried her face in his chest to hide her tears.

"Baby, what's wrong?" Trae asked.

". I just love you so much, and don't want to get hurt."

He caressed her face. "I love you too."

"If you love me, then tell me the truth. Is that your baby?"

"I swear to you on my mother's grave that I didn't fuck her."

As soon as the words escaped his mouth, he made a silent prayer. *Please forgive me for lying, ma.*

Two weeks later, Trae drove around all day going nowhere, so he could mellow out. He even contemplated having Courtney taken out for the stunt she pulled. *That would be stupid. I'll be the first mutha-fucker the police come looking for,* he thought. To ease his mind, he went to Pleasures to have a drink. He needed something to take his mind off of all the drama he was going through.

"Your usual, Trae?" Sam asked when he sat down at the bar.

"Yeah, main man. Make it a double," Trae replied referring to the Hennessy and Coke.

"You look like you kinda stressed."

"Man, you don't know the half of it."

Worried how the outcome of the test would affect his relationship with Karina was taking its toll on Trae. True, he was a womanizer, but his heart and sole belonged to her. He loved her more than anything.

After having three more drinks, Trae went home. Drunk and mad as hell, he wondered how his life got so messed up. For some reason Trae knew he was about to pay the ultimate price for sleeping with Courtney, and if he had it all to do over again, he would've went straight home that night. *Damn, I really fucked up this time.*

DEEP

IF ONLY FOR ONE NIGHT

The undercover work was finally starting to take its toll on Carmen. She'd been on the case for over six months, and missed her husband. However, she knew seeing him would be too dangerous, so she decided to settle for a phone call instead.

When she heard her husband's voice, she was caught between her body's needs and her minds awareness. "Hey, babe. I miss you," she said.

"I miss you too," Damien responded.

"Let me come see you. I'll be careful," Carmen said, against her better judgment.

"It's too dangerous. If they see us together, it's no telling what they'll do."

Even though Carmen knew Damien was right, she was still disappointed. It had been so long since she felt her husband's arms around her, that she began to wonder if she ever would again. Carmen's jobs, which were supposed to be short assignments, always turned into months, sometimes years. Her husband supported her, but often wished they could live a normal life.

Although it was scary and frustrating sometimes, Damien understood how much Carmen loved her job and liked to live on the edge.

"I don't know how much more I can take of this. This assignment is taking longer then Willie told us it would," Carmen said. "Shit, I wish I could just catch him doing one major drug transaction or something, so we can get this show on the road."

"That'll never happened. You said he never touches any of his own product," Damien replied. "I thought for sure we would have him in custody by now. Willie was right, these guys are smarter than we thought."

"I'm tired of this shit. I need to see you, and I need to see you

A NOVEL BY DANETTE MAJETTE

now. So stay by your phone, I'm gonna make a few calls, then I'll call you back," Carmen said.

Damien yelled out her name, but she had already hung up.

Twenty minutes later, she called him back and gave him instructions to meet her at the Courtyard Marriott hotel on the Eastern Shore of Maryland later on that evening. She wanted to make sure their meeting location was as far away from D.C as possible, to reduce the risk of running into anyone. Damien was hesitant at first, but he knew Carmen wasn't going to take no for an answer.

Damien circled the parking lot of the hotel several times before he finally parked. Once he make sure that he wasn't followed, he threw on his Maryland Terrapin basketball hat, and checked the perimeter one last time before making his way through the hotel lobby doors and into the elevator.

He watched as the elevator lights lit up when he passed each floor. Once he reached the fourth floor, he quickly walked down the hall and knocked on the door of room 421.

Damien looked his wife up and down as she opened the door. "Damn," he said, closing the gap between them. "I really missed you."

"I missed you too."

He kissed her lips while caressing her. Sucking on her neck, he moved her negligee slightly, exposing her shoulder.

"I'm so glad we did this," she said, watching as he moved down past her navel. He pulled her bikini down, and positioned his nose right in her center.

He placed a tender kiss on her hairy mound, before using his fingers to stroke her. His tongue and fingers were hard at work. Whenever his fingers stroked, his tongue went deeper. Carmen moaned.

Laying on her back, Carmen legs were tangled around her husband's body like a pretzel. She slid her hands down his ass, as he glided in and out. Her breathing got heavy.

"Baby, get on top," he demanded.

"Whatever you want," she replied.

Damien pulled her down, as she started to grind back and forth. His forcefulness was a turn on. She bounced faster.

"How does it feel?" Carmen asked.

She waited for a response. Instead, he let out a loud moaning

DEEP

sound that echoed throughout the room.

Moments later, Carmen collapsed on her husband's chest as waves of pleasure flowed through her body.

The next morning, Carmen woke up to her husband staring at her. "What's wrong?" she asked.

"Nothing. I just miss watching you sleep," Damien said, playing with her hair.

"After this case is over you can watch me sleep every night." Carmen smiled. "I really can't wait for all of this to be over. I want to go back to being the real me...Selena Nichols. You know, sometimes when people call me Carmen, I forget they're talking to me."

"That's understandable, but you have to be careful. Someone might pick up on that." Damien threw the covers back, then slid onto his wife. "I'm such a lucky man."

"Why?" Carmen asked.

Damien held a huge smile. "Because I get to sleep with two women at the same time."

Carmen and Damien tried to enjoy the little time they managed to steal from all the craziness. They ordered room service and laid in bed cuddling each other, but their good time was interrupted by a knock at the door.

"Who could that be?" Carmen asked silently.

"I don't know." Damien grabbed his gun, walked over and looked through the peephole. "There's no one there. Maybe it was house-keeping," he said, whispering.

"Yeah, maybe you're right."

There was another knock, and this time it was louder and even harder. "Ask who it is," she whispered.

Damien walked over to the door. "Who is it?"

"Open the damn door."

The two immediately recognized the voice. "Shit!" Luckily, they both had on robes.

Caught, Damien slowly opened the door and waited for the wrath of God to come down on them.

"What the fuck are you two thinking? What if Trae or one of his boys had followed you here?" Willie yelled, scolding them like kids.

Carmen and her husband looked at each other. They knew what

A NOVEL BY DANETTE MAJETTE

they'd done was a stupid move on their part, but they were desperate to see one another. They figured what's life without a few risks.

"We're sorry," they said in unison. Willie's look told Carmen that he expected more. "We're really sorry," she repeated.

"How did you know we were here?" Carmen asked, as she took a seat on the bed.

"It doesn't matter how I found out. What matters is both of you could have jeopardized this whole case if someone had saw you."

Carmen told Willie she was sure that she was the last thing Trae was thinking about these days.

"Why do you think that?" he asked.

"He's going through some serious personal issues."

Willie laughed. "So, she took my advice."

Carmen and Damien were thrown for a loop. "Who took your advice?"

Willie slipped his hands in his Khaki pants, "Courtney, his mistress."

"How did you know she was pregnant?" Carmen asked.

Willie wouldn't reveal his source. All he would say is that he was the one who planted the seed in her ear to send the flowers to his house along with the test results.

"I also got a tip that he was the one who killed that pimp named Pretty Tony on H Street. A witness who was there that day, gave us a license plate number."

"Trae doesn't strike me as the kind of guy that would register his cars in his own name," Damien said.

"You're right. It's registered to the sister of one of Trae's junkies. We brought her in. She didn't waste anytime giving Trae up after we threatened to give her twenty to life."

"You want him bad, don't you?" Carmen asked.

"You know it. Now back to you two. I don't care how occupied you think he is with his personal affairs, you can't take chances like this."

As mad as Willie was, he understood the emotional strain Carmen and her husband had been under, so he let them off with a smack on the hand. "Okay, since I'm here, are there any updates?"

"Naw, he's being pretty secretive about when the heist is going down," Carmen said.

"What about you?" Willie asked, turning to Damien.

"Nothing much. I've been following him, but there's been nothing out of the ordinary."

Willie was quiet for a minute. "I think we need to push it a little fur-

DEEP

ther," he said.

"What do you suggest?" Carmen asked.

Willie pulled out his cell phone and dialed. "Hey Courtney, let's turn up the heat a little bit." After talking a few more minutes, he closed his cell phone.

"What is that going to do?" Damien asked.

"It might just scare him enough to want to get out of town earlier."

"Are they still threatening to pull the plug on the investigation?" Carmen asked.

"Yeah, if we don't give them something concrete soon. They're way over budget as it is, and we haven't given them anything to show for it," Willie said, with a shimmer of anger. "We have got to get Trae and his whole crew off the streets." Willie was about to leave, when he turned around and looked at his two agents. "I told you the money I took off Trae that day would come in handy."

All Carmen and Damien could do was shake their heads, say goodbye, and head back to D.C.

DEEP

D-DAY

March 5th was the day Trae turned twenty-eight, and Karina planned to have a very romantic dinner for him. She went to the store and got everything she needed to make his favorite meal. Then she went to Bath and Body Works to get some scented candles. On the way home, she stopped at a flower shop and picked up some red roses to decorate the house, which were her favorite. She wanted to make it a night he wouldn't forget. Little did she know, it would be a night she wouldn't forget.

When Karina pulled into her driveway a old black Jeep Cherokee was in the driveway. *Who the hell is that*? she thought. When he got out the car, she immediately recognized Courtney in the driver's seat.

"What the fuck are you doing here!" Karina yelled as Courtney rolled down the window. At this point, Courtney was becoming a thorn in her side. "How did you know where we lived anyway?"

"I have my sources. Besides, where is my man anyway? I'm waitin' for him to get home,' Courtney replied with a sneaky grin.

Karina was furious. "Why do you insist on saying that shit? He's not your man, bitch!"

"Actually, he's more than just my man now. He's actually the father of my baby." Courtney rubbed her stomach in circular motions. "Oh, by the way, did he get my flowers?"

"Look, you need to play these games with somebody your own age. I know you're not pregnant, and I know you've never slept with Trae."

"Oh, so is that what you think?" Courtney asked. "Well honey I hate to give you the bad news, but we've definitely fucked. As a matter of fact, we did it in his office."

Karina frowned. "I don't believe you."

"Well would you believe it if I told you that he has a birth mark on his dick?"

Karina's heart almost fell in her shoes. At that point she knew Courtney had to be telling the truth. *How else would she know that*? "Get the fuck off my property!" she yelled at Courtney.

"Oh, I see you finally believe me, huh?"

"What did I just say, slut? Can't you follow fuckin' directions?" As Karina made her way toward the truck, she heard it when Courtney locked her door.

"Yeah, I gotta get going anyway. I need to go and pick out some stuff for the baby. Tell Trae I said call me when he gets home," Courtney responded after starting her truck. When she pulled off, she let out a piercing laugh.

Now I know I can't do this. After getting the bags in the house, Karina sat down at the kitchen table and placed her hands over her face. With tears flowing, she suddenly became enraged, and ran to her bedroom, then pulled out the .22 Trae had given her for protection. This was the first time she'd even touched it. After retrieving the gun she sat on the bed and patiently waited for him to come home.

It was nine o'clock when Trae finally came home. All the lights were off and the house was silent. After looking in the family room, and not finding her there, he pushed the door open to their bedroom and found her sitting on the edge of the bed.

"Hey, baby. What you doin' in the dark?" Trae asked turning on the light. He handed Karina the Neiman Marcus bag he bought in. "Look what yo' man got you today."

Karina's reaction was immediate. "Why didn't you just kill me? It would've been easier than doing this to me," she said. She'd come to her senses and put the gun away.

"What the hell are you talkin' about?"

"You had me fooled, didn't you? I thought we had the ultimate relationship. Trust, honesty and love. But that was just all a lie. Well, you can drop the act now. I see exactly what you are. You're a piece of shit!"

"Baby, what is wrong with you? You scarin' me!"

"I find it funny how every time we saw that bitch, Courtney you tried to play it off like you didn't know her. But I find it funny how someone who was supposed to have a man uptown, knows that you have a birthmark on your dick!"

Trae looked like he'd seen a ghost. He was speechless as he sat on the bed. *I'm gonna kill that bitch Courtney.* "How did you find that out?"

"That bitch was in the driveway when I got home today and told me *everything.*"

Trae's mouth fell open. "The driveway? How does she know where we live?"

"Some sources she has," Karina replied. "But you know what, that's not even important right now. What's important is the fact that you fucked her."

Fuck it, I can't get out of this one. "I'm sorry" he mumbled. "I never meant for this shit to happen."

"What the fuck were you thinking? I mean did you really think you could hide a damn baby from me!"

"Karina, I know. I fucked up, baby, but please give me a chance to make it up to you."

"It's too late! You've destroyed any chance of me forgiving you."

"Please don't say that. Just listen to me," he pleaded, as she started to pack her bags.

"Say what the hell you got to say, and then get the fuck out of my life."

"It only happened one time."

"Well, Trae, it only takes one time. Not that I believe you."

"Karina, I swear it only happened one time."

"Okay. If that was the case, why didn't you just come clean and tell me what was going on?" she asked before hitting herself in the head. "What am I thinking? Then you would've had to explain sleeping with her in the first damn place."

"Karina I love you."

"You should've thought about that before you fucked that stank bitch. Now get out my way," she said, as she put her suitcase on the bed.

After Karina finished packing she grabbed her car keys and headed for the door. Distraught, Trae stood there rubbing his baldhead and swearing at the top of his lungs. He knew he had fucked up big time. Most of all, he was pissed at Courtney for fucking up his life.

After Karina left, Trae tried calling her cell phone several times, but there was no answer. That didn't surprise him. He knew he was be the last person in the world she wanted to talk to. Anxious, he called back about ten minutes later. But there was still no answer. He started to worry, so he decided to drive to Ashley's house. When he got there, Ashley was on her way out.

"Hey, Trae! Where's Karina?" Ashley asked.

"I don't know, I thought she was here," he replied, looking around her condo.

"Naw, I haven't seen her. Is everything alright?"

"Not really!" He held his head down and sighed.

"Okay you're scaring me. What's going on?" Ashley asked.

"I'll let her tell you. Please, if you hear from Karina, can you please tell her to call me?"

"Yeah, but I want to know what the hell is going on! If my friend is in trouble or something, I want to know."

"Ashley, it's nothin' like that. It's me, I fucked up! I really fucked up this time," he said, with tears in his eyes.

Trae's comment and a display of emotion was something Ashley had never seen before. She tried to act like she was sympathizing with him, but what she really wanted to do is jump his ass like an alley cat. She just couldn't understand how a love that strong could make him do something so stupid.

"You know I was against your relationship in the beginning, but I knew how much she loved you, so I supported her decision. I knew it was only a matter of time before you did something to fuck it up!"

"What?" He grabbed Ashley and threw her up against the wall. Kissing her hard on the lips, he grabbed her breasts.

"Let me go, Trae!" she yelled, struggling to break free.

"Why? The reason you always throwin' salt in my game is because you want me. Well, here I am," he said, unzipping his pants. "You've been wantin' some of this dick every since you met me."

He ripped open her blouse, pulled up her bra, and then bit her neck. After she cried out for help a few times,he finally let go of her. Laughing, he strolled toward the front door.

"I'm gonna call Karina and tell her what you did you, dirty mutha-fucka," she threatened, after throwing her shoe at him.

Trae turned around and walked back over to her. He grabbed her arm and held it tightly behind her back. Ashley screamed in agony. "You gonna do what!" he yelled, applying pressure.

"Nothing!" she screamed.

"I thought so," he said, letting her go.

DEEP

Karina drove her car up to the front of the Ritz Carlton in Arlington, Virginia and put her car in park. The valet ran over, took her keys and gave her a ticket. Exhausted, Karina checked into her room. As soon as she unpacked, she jumped in the shower and stood under the steamy hot water. *Why do I keep making the same mistakes?* she thought.

After showering, she sat on the bed and cried until the pain subsided. She tried to deal with the situation on her own, but that wasn't working so she called Ashley.

"Hey, has Trae been by there looking for me?" she asked, as soon as Ashley answered the phone.

"Yeah," Ashley answered. She took a deep breath. What happened?"She wanted to tell Karina what happened between her and Trae before he tried to turn the story around, but feared for her life.

"Oh, honey you have no idea."

"He cheated on you, right?"

"Yeah, but that's not all. He got another bitch pregnant."

"What?"

"Yeah, he's gonna be a daddy," Karina cried.

Ashley was speechless for a moment. "Oh Karina, I'm so sorry!"

"I'm okay."

"What are you gonna do?"

"I don't know. I want to tell him to go to hell so bad, but I love him too much."

Ashley wanted badly to tell Karina to leave Trae alone and move on with her life, but she knew all too well what he was capable of, so she kept quiet.

After days of crying and feeling sorry for herself, Karina decided it was time for her to go home. She knew she couldn't avoid Trae forever, so she hopped in her car and headed up Highway 395. When she reached the driveway it was empty. Trae was obviously not home. But as soon as she started to unpack her car, he pulled up. Elated to see her, he jumped out without closing his door or even shutting off the engine.

"Baby, I'm so glad you came back. I was going crazy without you," he said.

"Good. Don't get too excited though, I don't know how long I'm staying, or if I'm even gonna stay for that matter," Karina responded.

She took her bags in the house and plopped on the couch. Trae followed.

"I know there's nothing I can do or say to change what happened. Trust me, if I could go back to that night, I wouldn't have did what I did. But I can't. If I'm the father, I'ma just have to deal wit' it. Like old folks would say, I made my bed now I gotta lie in it."

"You're right about that," Karina replied, with a spark of sarcasm.

"So, where do we go from here?"

"I don't know, Trae. I don't know if I can deal with this anymore."

"Baby we can get through this. It's gonna take some time, but we can do it."

"Do you love her?" she asked.

"Hell no! I don't even like the bitch!"

"You don't like her, but you fucked her. Explain that to me. This time I want the truth or I'm out the door."

Scared, he began to confess. "I met her the night we lost the baby. You were blaming me, and that made me feel like shit. I was drinking and she came on to me. I should've just left, but I started talkin' to her, then one thing led to another."

"So, you went out and fucked some bitch the night we lost our baby and you didn't use a condom!" she yelled.

"I did, but it broke," he lied.

Karina looked at him like he was crazy. "It broke. How convenient."

"I'm serious."

"None of this shit would be happening if you had just kept your dick in your pants. How do you expect me to ever want to make love to you again?" Karina asked.

"I'm sorry I hurt you."

"No, Trae, I think you're sorry you got caught!" Karina shouted.

In exasperation, he threw up his hands. It was useless for him to argue with her about it. He just had to accept the fact that she was right and he was dead wrong.

After hours of talking, Karina was still not convinced that Trae was telling the truth. She wanted to believe him and try to move on, but something just wasn't sitting right, with her. That night Trae slept in the guest room. Before Karina went to sleep, she knelt down and prayed for God to give her the answers to her unanswered questions.

DEEP

The next morning, the sun beamed through the blinds into the bedroom. Still tired from the day before, Karina rolled over to look at the clock. It was eleven o'clock and as usual, Trae was gone. After making breakfast, Karina sat down at the table. As she ate, she played back Trae's version of what happened with Courtney.

"Something's not right," she said to herself.

Realizing she would never be able to continue her relationship with Trae until she was satisfied that he was telling the truth, she trashed the house, and stormed through every room until she finally found the card that came with the flowers that day. She remembered that Courtney's number was at the bottom.

Karina sat and stared at the card for a few minutes, then finally got up the courage to call her.

When the phone rang, Karina's heart began to race rapidly.

"Hello," a soft voice answered.

"Umm yes. May I speak to Courtney?"

"Speaking."

"Courtney, this is Karina. Trae's girlfriend."

Courtney laughed. 'I gave my number to Trae, not you. What do you want?"

"How long have you and Trae been seeing each other?"

"Does that really matter? I mean, the only thing that should matter to you is the fact that yo' man got me pregnant while you were laying up in a hospital bed," Courtney said, trying to get a rise out of Karina.

"Did he tell you about me that night?"

Courtney laughed again. "Hell no! Why would he tell me about a penny when he had a dime right in front of him?"

Karina was furious, but she wanted to know more, so she kept he cool. "Look. I'm not trying to start anything with you, I just need to ask you one more question."

"What do you want to know?"

"Did the condom break?" Karina asked.

"What fuckin' condom? We didn't use one."

Karina's mind started to spin as the pieces were starting to fit now. She slammed the receiver down. Trae had lied to her for the last time. Infuriated, Karina could feel the temperature rising in her body. She was so vexed she felt that she could kill him with her bare hands.

A NOVEL BY DANETTE MAJETTE

Crying, she went into the bedroom and laid down. Before long she was asleep.

When she woke up an hour later, she went downstairs and found Trae in the living room on the phone. Without wasting any time, she grabbed a bottle of Bacardi from the bar.

"You liar," she said, as she raised the bottle over her shoulders and tried to smash it over his head.

Trae immediately grabbed the bottle from her hand and pinned her down on the couch. Screaming, she began to claw his face with her nails until he let her go.

"What the fuck you talkin' 'bout now?" he asked.

"I will never forgive you for this," she said, as she ran to the room to pack her belongings.

As quick as Karina packed her things, Trae unpacked them.

"I'm not lettin' you leave me again, so you might as well sit your ass down and listen to me," he said, as he threw her on the bed and held her down with his body.

"I don't want to hear anything that comes out of your mouth!" she shouted.

"Too bad!"

"Get off of me!"

"Not until you listen to me. I cheated and then I lied because I didn't want to lose you. I was scared! For the first time in my life I was scared of something. And that was losing you. I love you, I love you," he said, as he kissed her.

After Karina mellowed out, Trae told her that if she wanted to leave he wouldn't stop her.

"Just know that you mean more to me than anythin'. I'm telling you the truth. I never slept with Courtney after that night. I bet she ain't tell you that though. And as far as her not knowing about you, she lied. She knew all about you. I told her. She's just mad at me because I told her us sleeping together was a mistake. And you know what's so fucked up, she won. She got exactly what she wanted...you out of my life."

By night fall, Karina and Trae had both cooled down. Trae was in the living room nursing his wounds ,while Karina sat in their bedroom trying to figure out what she should do. After hours of intense silence, Trae went into the bedroom.

"I'ma make this shit up to you if it's the last thing I do. Just please give me the chance. Can you do that for me? For us?" Trae asked.

"I don't know. How am I supposed to just forget about all this? It

DEEP

would be one thing if you had just cheated, but you might be the father of another child. We don't even have a baby together."

"I know I'm asking a lot, but we can get through this. I'm telling you we can. I just need you to tell me we can at least try."

"I don't know. I just need some time to myself to think about this."

"Baby, I don't think us being apart from each other is the answer," he pleaded. "We need to work this out together. Here under one roof. I'll even sleep in the guest room."

It took a lot of convincing, but Karina finally agreed.

DEEP

MISSING IN ACTION

Sommone woke up to the smell of fresh brewed coffee, and instantly became nervous because her coffee pot shouldn't have been on. She jumped up and ran in the kitchen with her gun, only to find Willie adding sugar to his cup. Her heart almost jumped out of her chest.

"Shit, you scared me. What are you doing here?" she asked putting the 9mm away.

"I wouldn't have to be here if you would check in like you're supposed to," Willie said, taking a seat at the kitchen table. He placed his coffee on the table and crossed his legs. "What's going on with you?"

Sommone poured herself a cup then sat down next to him. "I'm sorry. It's been crazy at the club," she stated, sipping on her coffee.

"Really? Well, don't forget you're not really a stripper, Melanie," Willie replied calling her by her real name."

She shook her head. "Yeah, I know, but this is harder than I thought it was going to be."

"So, have you found out anything?"

"No, just what we already know. Trae definitely never touches any drugs personally. His boys just bring back money majority of the time. But he was talking to some Spanish looking guy in the club not too long ago."

"What did he look like?"Willie asked.

Sommone tried to describe the man as best she could. "I've never seen him before, but he looked like the fuckin' Godfather or somebody the way he smoked his cigar. Who do you think he was?"

Willie sat back. "I don't know," he said, with an attitude. "Maybe his connect or something."

Sommone could tell her boss wasn't happy that she didn't have more information on Trae. Especially since he was hell bent on destroying him.

She tried to put his mind at ease. "I made a lot of progress with him the other night. He's starting to trust me a little more now."

Willie gave her a disapproving glance. "Okay, so we're on the same page. You're only there to get information on Trae, that's it. Do I make myself clear?"

Sommone caught a serious attitude. She'd never heard him use that tone of voice before, and didn't like it. "I know what I'm supposed to be doing. I can't help it if the guy has a thing for me."

"I don't care about him. I'm worried about you. You haven't checked in for days, you don't answer your phone when I call, and you've been spending a lot of time at that club. Keep your eyes on the prize. I don't want anything to fuck this up. If we play this right, Trae Keal won't know what hit him."

Sommone looked directly into Willie's eyes. "I'm very good at what I do. So you don't have to worry about me," she responded.

"That's good to know. Now get to work. Time is running out."

He finished off his coffee, pulled his skull cap down over his head then left.

As soon as Sommone locked the door, she exhaled. *That was close. If he knew I slept with Trae he would have my ass.*

Sommone stripped out her pajamas then went into the bathroom. As soon as she stepped into the shower, she leaned up against the shower tiles and closed her eyes as the hot water poured over her body.

Minutes later, she was so deep in thought that she didn't notice the water was ice cold. *Damn, am I ever gonna get a decent shower in this rat hole?*

She turned the water off, and slid down the cold tiles. It was time for her to be honest with herself. She was playing a dangerous game sleeping with Trae, but for some reason she was willing to take that chance. She had to play this one just right.

DEEP

EVERYTHING SHE MISSED AT HOME

It was eleven o'clock and the store had been open for an hour before Karina got her first customer. She walked over to the gentleman who fumbling through the Seven Jeans table, and smiled.

"Can I help you find a size?" she asked.

"Yeah, do y'all have a thirty eight in these?" the man asked, holding up a pair of jeans.

"Hey, I didn't know that was you," Karina replied. "I see you're doing more shopping." She looked at Daz and remembered how good he looked the last time he was in the store.

"Well, you told me to come back if I ever needed more help picking out some things, so here I am."

"Great. I'm glad you came back, I'll get a dressing room started for you while you finishing looking around. Oh, those jeans run a little small, so you might want to go up a size."

"Thanks, but I'll take a chance with the thirty-eight," Daz said, holding the pants in the air.

After setting up the dressing room, Karina returned to the floor. She wanted to offer her help again, but didn't want to seem to overbearing. Customers hated that, especially black customers.

When Daz was ready to go into the dressing room, Karina led the way, and told him that if he needed anything to let her know. After trying on the jeans, he came out and handed Karina the jeans.

"You were right. They do run small," he admitted.

"So, I take it you want the forty's?" Karina asked with a smile.

"Yes, please."

After getting the correct size, they went to the wrap stand to ring up his purchase.

"Your total is $203.45."

Daz handed Karina his credit card and then thanked her for help-

A NOVEL BY DANETTE MAJETTE

ing him.

"No need to thank me. It's my job," she replied.

"Can I ask you something?" he asked.

"Sure, as long as it's not too personal."

Daz smiled. "How long have you been working here?"

"About four years, why?"

He went on to tell Karina he had a small clothing company in Maryland. "You think maybe you can give me some tips on how to increase my business?" he asked.

"I'd love to," she said. "Wow, a producer and a store owner. You must stay pretty busy."

"Yeah, I do."

After talking for a few more minutes, they exchanged numbers. Karina knew she would be headed down a dangerous road if she called Daz. Trae would never approve of her working with him under any circumstance, but she wasn't going to let that stop her. After all, Trae came and went as he wanted to. He dealt with people Karina definitely didn't approve of, and he cheated on her, so all bets were off.

A few days passed before Karina heard from Daz on her way home from work.

"Sorry, I haven't called," he said.

"That's alright. I know you've been busy."

"What about you, are you busy today?"

"Oh, no not at all."

"Well, do you think you can you meet me at my store in about a half an hour?"

"Sure. Give me directions."

Karina wrote down the directions, and then called Trae to let him know she would be home late. By her surprise, he didn't even ask her any questions. *He probably could care less, since he*'s never home anyway.

When Karina arrived at the store in Forestville, Maryland Daz was sitting behind the counter. He stood up and greeted her with a handshake.

"So what do you think of my store?" he asked.

Karina glanced around. She was impressed at the colorful lighting that gave the store its unique urban yet elegant atmosphere.

DEEP

"It's really nice. I think the only improvement I would make is your merchandising," Karina said.

"See, I knew you would know exactly what I needed."

His compliments were followed by a smile, that told Karina he enjoyed her company.

Karina walked over to one of the racks."So, did you design these t-shirts yourself?"

"Yep! Me and my partner."

"Wow, that's really impressive," she replied.

Karina continued walking around the store admiring Daz's work. They chatted for a while, then she gave him a few pointers on merchandising. After helping him for over an hour, they said their goodbyes.

Talking to Daz sparked something in Karina she hadn't felt in a long time. He made her feel sexy, an area Trae seemed to be slacking in.

After driving home, Karina walked into the house and immediately went into the kitchen. About to start dinner, she turned to find Trae standing right behind her.

"Hey baby. Where you been?" Trae asked.

"I went to this clothing store to help the owner with a few things," she said.

"Oh, where?"

"In Maryland." Karina knew her answer was vague, but she didn't care.

"Oh," Trae said, grabbing his coat. He didn't seem too interested.

"It looks like you're headed back out."

"Yeah, me and the fellas are gonna check out this party at Republic Gardens."

"Didn't y'all just go out last night?" she asked.

"Yeah, but it's Big Paul's birthday, so I told him I'd slide through."

"It seems you're there for everyone but me these days."

Trae frowned. "What's that suppose to mean?"

"Nothing, Trae. Nothing."

Furious about Karina's comment, Trae stormed out the house. It had only been a few weeks since Karina agreed to try and work things out. She was sure that the situation would bring them closer, but it didn't. Instead of Trae going out one night a week, he went out almost every night. He never took her anywhere. And when people would invite them to parties, he would neglect to mention them to her and go by himself.

Still dealing with the fact that Trae cheated on her. Karina was very insecure, and she didn't understand why he wasn't spending his nights at home trying to reassure her. It was truly a depressing time for her. With no one to turn to, she tried to keep herself occupied by working.

Three days after seeing Daz at his shop. Karina decided to give him a call on her day off, but there was no answer. Moments later, her phone rang. She was pleasantly surprised to see it was Daz's number.

"What are you doing tonight?" he asked, in a sexy tone.

"My usual. Nothing," she replied.

"Why don't you come and see me at my studio?"

Karina thought for a moment before answering. "Okay. Let me change, and then I'll meet you there. Where is it?"

"On U Street."

"Great, I'll see you then."

As soon as she hung up, she slipped out of her sweat suit and jumped in the shower. After showering, she threw on some jeans along with her favorite sweater. After a final check in the mirror, she sprayed Jean Paul Gautier on her neck and applied her MAC lip-gloss.

When Karina saw Daz almost forty minutes later, she thought she was going to melt. She stood in the door of his studio admiring him for so long, he had to wave his hands in front of her face to get her attention.

"Oh my God, I'm sorry. I was thinking about something," Karina said embarrassed.

"That's okay. Come in," Daz said.

"Wow, so this is what a studio looks like."

"Yeah, you've never been in a studio before."

"No. I don't get out a lot," she replied, as she sat down on his soft leather couch.

"Your man don't take you out?" Daz asked.

Karina sighed. "No, he's too tied up with the boys most of the time."

DEEP

"That's a shame. Some niggas don't know how good they got it."

"Amen, brotha," she said, with laughter. "So, what about your girl-friend?"

"How do you know I have one?"

"Please! A fine man like you single. I think not."

"Umm…she's at home most of the time with my daughters. They're my life," he said.

Karina thought about how up front Daz was with her and how she wished Trae could be that way.

Daz made Karina forget about all her problems. They sat on his couch, and talked about everything from love to politics. He was such a well-rounded guy. She was enjoying herself so much she completely lost track of time.

"Oh shit! It's almost twelve thirty," Karina said, in a panic.

"I guess you got to go home before your man comes lookin' for you."

"Yeah."

"That's cool. Let me walk you to your car. But before I do let me give you this."

Standing in the doorway of the studio, Daz wrapped his arms around Karina and kissed her. Shocked, she didn't respond,and just stood there staring at him. He felt her body respond to her, so he pressed himself closer. There was no denying her feelings, she want-ed him. Karina knew it was wrong, but she was going to take it all the way with Daz.

Kissing passionately, he tugged at her top and bra until her breast fell out. Her jeans and thongs followed, falling past her thighs. Karina excited with anticipation, tugged at his pants and unzipped them. She fumbled for his zipper and freed his erect dick. After she had his penis in her hand, she gently massaged it. She couldn't believe what she was feeling. Needing to see it for herself, she nudged him to back up. Her eyes widened.

"Damn." *That has to be at least ten inches.*

Amused, he started laughing. "Don't worry, I promise I'll take it easy," he said.

"I…don't know."

"Trust me."

Sucking on her breasts, he covered his dick and slid it in. Moving in and out, he grunted as he forced his dick deeper and deeper. The feeling sent shivers down Karina's spine. Her legs shook, she gritted her teeth to stop herself from screaming. Moving rhythmically together, they both erupted into ecstatic orgasms.

"I hope I didn't hurt you," Daz said.

"It was a little intense at first, but I'm alright."

Karina got dressed, then glanced at the diamond bezel on her watch and panicked when she saw it was almost two in the morning.

"Oh shit, I have to go!" she yelled.

"Okay at least let me get dressed so I can walk you out."

Sure that Trae was home by now, Karina quickly got dressed. She sat on the couch, trying to think of an excuse for being out so late. When she looked up, she saw Daz sitting in his studio chair with a far-away gaze in his eyes. Not wanting to break his concentration, she got up to leave.

"Wait!" he yelled.

"Daz, I already know what you're gonna say. I understand this was just a fuck," Karina said.

"No, it's not that. I just think we shouldn't do this. As much as I enjoyed it, we can't let that happen again. I have a family that I love, and if my girl found out about this she would leave me. No one is worth that."

"I agree. I feel the same way." Feeling like a fool, Karina left.

Driving well past the speed limit all Karina could think about was getting home and taking a shower. Before she got to her street, she called Ashley to ask her to cover for her.

When Karina walked in the door, Trae was sitting on the couch talking business. As soon as he saw her, he hung up without even telling the person goodbye.

"Where you been?" Trae asked.

"Ashley and I went out," she answered.

"Went out where?"

"Do I ask you where you've been," she snapped.

"Whoa! What the fuck is wrong wit' you?"

"Nothing!"

"I ask you a simple question and you get all fired up and nothin' is wrong?"

"You right. I'm mad. You go and hang out, and it's alright. I go out, and I get the third degree."

Trae was furious. "Ain't nobody givin' yo' ass the third degree. I just asked you a damn question," he said, slamming his phone down on the coffee table. "It's always somethin' wit' you."

Feeling guilty, Karina immediately took a shower. She wanted to

DEEP

wash away the dirt she felt. After all the grief she gave Trae about cheating, she couldn't believe she went out and did the same thing. She tried to excuse her behavior by telling herself that they were even. Trae had cheated on her, but that was no excuse. She had a choice to leave him and she didn't. In her eyes, she was no better than he was.

After getting into bed, Karina clung to the edge, hinting that she didn't want to be bothered with Trae. Her odd behavior made him feel that there was something wrong, but he couldn't figure it out. He assumed she was still feeling the wrath of his deception. So, he wrapped his arms around her body and kissed her neck. Little did he know she had her own dirty little secret.

"I love you," Trae whispered.

Feeling like shit, Karina mumbled, "I love you too."

DEEP

KEEP YOUR EYES ON THE PRIZE

The next morning, Kevin told Trae to meet him at the chop shop. Karina was still asleep, so he gulped down some breakfast, took a shower, and got dressed. Before he left, he went over to Karina's side of the bed and kissed her forehead.

"I love you," he whispered. Karina never moved.

Driving slowly, Trae glanced at the people walking down the street, and began to think about his problems. He had so many thoughts about the Courtney situation bouncing around in his head, that he was starting to get a migraine.

When he reached the gate at the chop shop, he noticed a white van with a Smith's Electric logo on it.

"Shorty, what the fuck is this truck doin' here?" Trae asked as he stepped out of the car.

Kevin laughed. "Man, see this is exactly what I thought. You've been so caught up in your own bullshit, you forgot about the job we're suppose to be doin'."

Kevin was right. Trae was so preoccupied with Courtney and Karina, he'd totally forgotten about the heist for a minute.

"Good lookin' out," Trae said, walking in the back of the shop. He took a seat behind the dusty desk that was located in a small cramped room as Kevin sat in the chair.

"Man, what's goin' on? Is that baby yours?" Kevin asked.

"I think so," Trae replied, kicking the trash can across the floor. "Man, I've always been on top of my game. How did I let this grimey ass bitch play me?"

"I told you these chicks ain't shit. That's why I fuck 'em then roll out."

Talking about Courtney made Trae's temperature rise, and the migraine he had earlier was now even more painful. Even though he was just as responsible for what happened, he still blamed her. "I can't believe I let that bitch set me up," Trae said, rubbing his temples.

Kevin felt what Trae was saying. "Shorty, that bitch needs to be shut down. Know what I mean?"

Trae knew exactly what Kevin was talking about.

"You want me to take care of it?" Kevin asked.

As Trae thought about what Kevin was suggesting, his grandmother's face appeared. *Baby, how can you even think about killing the mother of your child?*

"Trae...Trae!" Kevin yelled. "Did you hear me? What are you thinkin' 'bout?"

Trae shook his head. "Nothin'. Look, any other time I would take you up on your offer, but she might be the mother of my kid, so just leave it alone."

Kevin shook his head. "A'ight, but let me know if you want me to handle that."

As the two continued to talk, Big Paul, Ice Man and Carmen walked in.

"What's good wit' you?" Big Paul asked, giving Kevin a pound.

"Same ole same ole," Kevin responded.

Big Paul pulled Trae to the side. It had been a while since they talked, and Big Paul wanted to give Trae an update on how Carmen was working out. "Can I holla at you outside?"

When Carmen heard Big Paul say that, she became extremely nervous. She couldn't wait until this case was over, so she could stop stressing about her cover being blown.

"Sure, Big P," Trae said as he stood up. They both walked out the room and stood a few feet away from the door.

"So what's been up?" Trae asked.

"Nothin' much. Just thought you'd like to know Carmen has been handlin' her business."

"Word."

"Yeah, man. She got us a hook up with the camouflage uniforms and even got us a map of alternate routes just in case somethin' goes wrong when we leave the base," Big Paul said.

Trae was disappointed in himself. He was so wrapped up in his personal life, that he'd forgotten about getting the things they needed for the heist.

Kevin and Carmen exchanged dirty looks as they waited for Trae and Big Paul to come back. Although they tried hard to work together without any problems, Kevin still didn't give her the respect she wanted.

"What the fuck you lookin' at?" Kevin spat.

Carmen looked Kevin up and down. "Absolutely nothin'," she replied with an attitude.

"Oh, that's supposed to be funny?" Kevin asked, looking at Ice Man.

"Man, chill," Ice Man said, still laughing.

They all got quiet, when Big Paul and Trae walked back in the room.

"So is everyone straight?" Trae asked, looking at each of them.

"Yeah, some of us are," Kevin sneered, staring at Carmen.

"You know what, I'm tired of you. So what is your bitch ass tryin' to say?" Carmen asked. "You've made little comments since I been down with y'all, but remember, I wouldn't have to be here if you were doing your job."

Kevin was enraged. He pulled out his .45 and aimed it at Carmen's head. Any other person would have been terrified, but not Carmen. She returned the favor, so to speak.

She pulled out her nine and aimed it at his chest. "Now what muthafucka?" she asked.

Kevin was impressed. "You got some big balls to be a chick."

"You got that shit right." Carmen said, looking straight in Kevin's eyes.

Trae looked at them like they had lost their minds. "We got a job to do, and y'all stupid muthafuckas wanna kill each other. Man, put those guns down and let's get back to business."

Carmen slowly lowered her weapon first, then Kevin followed suit. Although they still hated one another, they had to remember what they were there for.

DEEP

SEXY LADY

It was a Saturday afternoon, and Karina couldn't seem to concentrate, so she decided to leave work early. Although she hadn't heard from Daz since they'd slept together, she couldn't stop thinking about him.

Maybe I should 've kept it platonic. I would still have someone to confide in. She continued to think about Daz for the next few minutes until her thoughts were suddenly interrupted by a silky, familiar voice.

"What's up, beautiful?" Daz asked.

Karina's eyes lit up. "Hi. What are you doing here?"

"I thought I'd drop by and see how you doin'."

"I'm doing great! How about you?"

"I'm a'ight."

"Look, I'm really sorry about the other night. I don't usually act like that. I think my lack of affection at home is causing me to act foolishly," Karina said.

"You don't have to apologize. It takes two to tango."

Karina was excited to see Daz again, although he seemed remorseful for cheating on his girlfriend. This led her to believe he wanted nothing more to do with her. But she was wrong.

"Hey, I'm about to get off. Why don't you walk me out?" Karina asked.

"Cool," Daz replied with a smile.

Karina went up to the second floor and clocked out. When she returned, Daz walked her to her car.

"I've missed talkin' to you," he said.

Karina told him she felt the same way. Leaning against her car, their conversation lasted for almost an hour. He made her smile and thanks to him, she had a whole new outlook on some things. She could talk to him about anything, something she felt was hard to do

A NOVEL BY DANETTE MAJETTE

with Trae. Daz was perfect, but he was already taken.

After realizing how long they'd talked, she told Daz she needed to get home.

"Can I see you later?" she asked.

"Are you sure you can get away?"

"I don't have those problems. He's never home, so he won't even miss me."

"Great, I'll be at the studio."

Not wanting to miss another minute without seeing Daz, Karina went straight home, showered, changed and headed off to his studio with a smile that wouldn't go away. A few minutes after she walked in, Daz's father and brother greeted her.

"Who are you?" Daz's father asked.

"I'm Karina." She held out her hand, but he looked at her like she was on crack.

"What are you, a dancer?" he asked.

Karina cleared her throat. "No."

"Singer?"

"Oh, God no!" she said laughing.

"Then what are you doing here?"

Looking at Daz for help, she answered him, "I'm just a friend."

His father gave a disapproving look then walked out followed by his brother. As soon as Karina was sure they were gone, she asked Daz if she'd done something wrong. He assured Karina that was just the way his father reacted to new people.

"Don't worry about that. Just make yourself comfortable," Daz suggested.

Karina took his advice, and curled up on couch as she watched him work on his new track.

"Have you always been interested in music?" she screamed, over the loud beats coming from the speakers.

"Every since I was a kid. Have you always been interested in fashion?" he asked, turning the music down.

"No. I actually wanted to be a lawyer when I was a kid, but the thought of being in school that long made me change my mind. So, I tried to find something else I love. I couldn't think of anything I loved more than shopping, so I got into retail."

"Yeah, that figures. Women love to break a niggas pocket."

DEEP

"The only pocket I break is my own," Karina countered.

"Oh really. So you one of those independent women?"

"Most definitely!"

As time passed, Karina found herself wanting to kiss Daz. But she wasn't sure if that's what he wanted, so she waited for a sign. After he finished recording his track, he sat on the couch next to her. Talking and rubbing his leg at the same time, she leaned over to kiss him. Much to her surprise, he didn't resist. Instead, he undressed her and let nature take its course.

Over the next few days, being with Daz made Karina feel alive again. He was fun, and always seemed to make time for her when she called. Sometimes they would sit for hours and just talk. This made Karina feel special since she could never hold a decent conversation with Trae without the phone ringing.

Soon, Karina started spending every moment she could with Daz. She would even leave work early sometimes to meet him at his studio. Karina knew she was playing a dangerous game, but she was convinced she would never get caught. Every precaution was taken when she would go and see him. She always had Ashley as her alibi, and would call her job to see if Trae had called before she went home. As the weeks followed, she was drifting further and further from Trae, and closer toward Daz. Besides,Trae was so self-absorbed in other things, he didn't even notice. Eventually, Karina just started coming and going as she pleased. She completely threw caution to the wind. That's when the shit hit the fan.

DEEP

THE PLAYA GETS PLAYED

After living a double life for weeks, Karina seemed to be caught between her feelings for Daz and her security with Trae. However, Daz made it very clear to her that he would never leave his family under any circumstances, which made Karina wonder why she was jeopardizing what she had at home. So after debating with herself, she finally made the decision to work on her relationship with Trae.

One night, instead of going to see Daz, she called Trae and asked what time he would be home.

"Umm. I'm not sure. Why?" he asked.

"Well, I thought we could go have dinner together and talk. I feel like we're drifting apart and I don't want us to lose sight of our love for one another," Karina said.

"A'ight, I'll be home at nine."

"Okay. Don't be late!"

Her words alarmed Trae, but he dismissed them as her just being sentimental. If there was anything Trae could count on, it was Karina being faithful. As far as he was concerned, he had nothing to worry about. He had Karina locked down. Everything she had was because of his wallet. The house, the cars, and the jewelry were all compliments of him. That arrogance is what led him to believe that he could do whatever he wanted.

Wanting to look her best for Trae, Karina took a shower and then got dressed in her Seven jeans that made her butt look bootylious, and a Michael Stars shirt that always accentuated her breasts. She wanted tonight to be special. She had to find a way to reconnect with Trae, even though she knew it would be a challenge.

After getting dressed, Karina looked down at her watch to see what time it was. When she saw it was nine forty-five, she was livid.

A NOVEL BY DANETTE MAJETTE

It was around 12:00 a.m. when Trae finally got home. By that time, Karina was in the bed. Creeping in the room so he wouldn't wake her, Trae got undressed and tried to slip into bed.

"You mean to tell me you think that little of me that you couldn't even call and let me know you weren't coming," Karina said, sitting up.

"Baby, I'm sorry! I started gamblin' with those niggas and lost track of time. Shit, I lost about $5,000," Trae replied.

"If you don't start paying your girlfriend some attention, you're gonna lose more than that."

Trae stared at her for a minute. "What the fuck is that shit supposed to mean?"

"It means that what you won't do someone else will!" Karina yelled.

"Yeah right!" Trae said, dismissing her comment.

Pissed at Trae for his lack of concern about their strained relationship, Karina planned a trip out of town with Ashley for the next weekend. She decided to stop trying to win a losing battle. Her relationship was over. She just needed the strength to walk away.

The day before her trip, Karina went to the nail salon to get a manicure and pedicure. On her way back home, her phone rang. It was Daz. She hadn't heard from him in a while, and was surprised he'd called.

"Hey you," Karina answered with a sexy voice.

"Hey, what's up? I was wondering if I could see you," Daz said in a suggestive tone.

"I don't know. I was on my way home. I'm going out of town tomorrow," Karina answered.

"Please. I miss you."

After thinking for a few minutes, she finally gave in. "Alright. Where are you?"

"I'm at the studio."

"Fine, I'll be there shortly."

"Cool."

When Karina walked into the studio minutes later, there were candles lit, R.Kelly playing in the background, and champagne chilling. To top it off, Daz was looking fine as ever.

"What's all this?" she asked looking around.

"I told you that I missed you. But I know telling you don't mean shit

DEEP

if I don't show it," Daz said.

"You're something else you know that?"

"You ain't seen nothin' yet!"

After Karina got comfortable on the couch, Daz poured her a glass of Moet. "So how's the home front?"

"Fucked up as usual," she replied. "How about you?"

Daz tok a sip of champagne. "It's alright."

"If it's alright why are you here with me?" Karina asked, rolling her eyes.

"I know. This shit is crazy! I love her to death, yet I can't get you off my mind."

"I can't seem to get you off my mind either, but we both know we can't be together. I mean, I can't keep coming over here and having sex with you. Some people can do the no strings attached shit, but I can't. I want to be in a meaningful relationship with someone who loves me the way I love them."

"I feel you. So I guess this is it, huh?"

Karina nodded. "I guess it is."

"Friends," Daz said.

"Friends," she replied in a somber tone.

The mood was broken for both of them, so they decided to call it a night. As Karina stood up to leave, Daz pulled her close to him and kissed her. His kisses grew more passionate as he eased her onto his black leather couch. It was so intense, her legs began to tremble and her pussy felt ticklish and ready to be touched. In a rush to get him inside her, she undid his jeans and slipped her hand down onto his manhood. With her eyes closed, she began to kiss his neck while stroking him.

Forced into position, Karina's pants and thongs were stripped down.Then Daz strapped on a condom and began to work his magic. All attempts to make it sensitive and romantic were brushed aside. Her body obviously was affecting him, because he began to push up inside her harder and harder as he pulled her hair and grabbed her breasts. Soon, he was groaning and gasping for air. After minutes of him punishing her, she felt his cock gush with a flurry of jerks.

In the aftermath of their sinfully fulfilling sex, Daz and Karina snuggled. Karina had never felt so satisfied, so safe, and so in love. Daz was everything she ever wanted in a man.

Moments later, Daz went into the bathroom to clean up. Not knowing if she would have the courage to say goodbye and mean it, Karina got dressed quickly and left before he returned. It was too much for her to have to say goodbye to the one man who made her feel alive again. She needed her trip with Ashley now more than ever.

Back at home, Karina started to pack. Halfway into her packing, Trae came home. He immediately went to the refrigerator and grabbed a beer. He was about to go upstairs when he was met by Karina struggling down the stairs with her luggage.

"Let me help you with that," he said, sitting his beer down. "You ready for your trip?"

"Yep!"

"Look, baby, I know things haven't been good between us lately. But believe me when I tell you that I love you with all my heart. I promise you, as soon as this deal goes though, we're gonna leave D.C. like we planned so we can get our relationship back on track," Trae said.

Choked up, Karina began to cry.

"Why are you cryin'? I just said..."

"I know what you said. Why couldn't you have said this a week ago? Hell, months ago!"

"You're right. But all that matters now is today. Now come on upstairs so I can make love to my woman before she leaves tomorrow."

Karina didn't put up a fight, but when they reached the room, she became edgy and nervous. She knew once Trae was inside her, he would know she'd been fucking someone else. She needed time to think, but there wasn't any. For Trae, it had been definitely too long since he had made love to his woman and he was planning on making up for lost time.

Like the control freak he was, he threw her down on the bed, pulled her pants down then removed her panties, eager to get her butt naked. Then he nudged her hips to make her move down. Playing with her nipples, he smothered his face into her pussy licking, smearing her wetness all over his mouth.

Trae wasn't the affectionate type, but he sure could lick pussy and was good at it. Whenever he would make Karina mad, he would just go down on her, and all was forgiven.

After Karina's second orgasm, Trae rolled on his back and pulled her on top of him. Running his hands up and down her back he eased in and out of her, sending her into a whirlwind of ecstasy. Kissing him

DEEP

made Karina aware how she missed the intimacy of their relationship, and wanted things to be the way they used to be.

Interrupting her thoughts, Trae asked her to get up for a minute.

"Why, baby? What's wrong?" she asked.

"I don't know, I feel somethin'."

"You feel something where?"she asked.

"Hold on. Let me turn on the light."

Confused, Karina complied.

When the light came on, Karina glanced over to Trae, who was peeling something off of his dick. She couldn't make out what it was, but he could. With the look of shock and disgust on his face, he held the small particle up to the light to explain it. Then he turned to Karina.

"You been fuckin' somebody!" he screamed.

Karina's heart felt like it was running a marathon. "No! What are you talking about?"

"I'm talkin' about this piece of rubber that just came off my dick!"

"What? Let me see," Karina said, trying to play it off.

"Karina, that is a piece of condom, and it came from you!" Trae shouted.

Karina knew she had to try and turn the tables. "You sure it ain't come from you! You think I don't know you out there fucking around on me! It must be yours, cause it sure as hell ain't mine!"

"You mean to tell me you let some clown ass nigga leave a piece of condom in your dumb ass. Then to make matters worse, you let me eat you! Oh my God! I ought to...!"

Scared, and without any excuse for her behavior, Karina got dressed and went downstairs. Cussing and throwing shit all over the place, Trae followed.

"Who the fuck is he? Who is he!" he yelled as he grabbed her by her hair.

"Trae, stop it!"

"Naw, bitch, you stop it! Stop actin' like yo' ass is innocent! I should've known your ass was fuckin' around. You was gettin' a little too cocky, and you been sayin' a lot of slick shit lately. But I ain't pay it no attention. I should've though because women only act like that when they got new dick in they life. You nasty bitch," he said, turning his back on her and grabbing the back of his head. "I should fuck yo' ass up!"

All Karina could get out of her mouth was, "I'm sorry" in a faint voice before Trae shot her a look of contempt. Her words meant nothing to him and she knew it. For minutes they were silent and said nothing, as Trae paced the floor back and forth in anger.

"You better start talkin'. Who is the nigga?" he said, grabbing her by the arms.

"It doesn't matter!"

"It does matter. The condom broke, so that means that nigga came in you. Then I ate you! That means this nigga is in my life now!"

Convinced Trae would find out the truth anyway, Karina told him Daz's real name. "His name is Dazmon."

"Dazmon! Where the fuck does he live?" Trae asked, throwing Karina down on the couch.

"I don't know."

He ran over to the closet and snatched his gun from a shoe box. He checked to see if it was loaded, then grabbed Karina by the hair and told her to take him to Daz. "You gonna take me to this nigga or I'ma kill yo' ass," he threatened.

Karina was stunned by Trae's behavior. Her fear soon turned into anger. She started swinging like a maniac.

"Not too long ago the shoe was on the other foot. You went out and cheated and I was supposed to forgive and forget, I cheat and now I'm the scum of the earth. Fuck you! Yeah, I cheated and guess what. It was good!"

Trae stopped and looked at her. "What did you say? Bitch did you just say it was good?"

"Yes. It was..."

Before she could get the last word out, Trae hit her with the back of his hand. He was just about to hit her again, when the sight of his mother lying on the floor being hit by Pretty Tony flashed before his eyes. He grabbed his head and yelled, "No!"

When Karina got up off the floor, she ran back up the stairs and locked their bedroom door.

Trae followed, demanding that she open the door. When she kept refusing, he kicked it in, and started waving his gun in her direction.

"Where did you meet him?"

Karina was terrified. "At the store."

"I should've known. Does Ashley know him? What the hell am I thinkin'? Of course she knows him. Y'all bitches tell each other everything. Where did he fuck you at?"

"We were at his studio."

"Oh, so he some fake ass music nigga!"

"No! Look, we were just friends at first. He would come to the

DEEP

store and we would just talk."

"I'm a fuckin' fool, man!"

"No one at my job knows who he is. They just think he's a customer of mine."

After hours of interrogation, and a few broken household items, Trae finally calmed down.

"You know what gets me? You treated me like shit when I cheated on you. Every chance you got, you threw that shit in my face. Talkin' about how you don't understand how someone could do somethin' like that to someone they love. And how I wasn't shit for sleepin' wit' Courtney. The truth is, you ain't no better than I am. As a matter of fact, yo' shit was worse!"

Karina had never seen him this way. It was at that moment she realized how much he loved her and how deeply she'd hurt him. But there was no taking it back. What was done was done and all she could do was apologize.

The next day, Karina picked Ashley up and left for Virginia Beach. After what went down the night before, all she could think about was getting out of town.

"Girl, what's going on?" Ashley asked.

"I don't even know where to start," Karina replied..

"What'chu talking 'bout?"

"I got caught last night."

Ashley's eyes got big. "What!"

"Yeah, Trae found out about me and Daz."

"How?"

"It's too embarrassing to talk about."

"Wait a minute, bitch! We been friends for how long? Not to mention all the shit I tell you!"

After getting all the sorted details, Ashley fell all over Karina laughing. She was laughing so hard she almost caused Karina to wreck her car.

"Girl, how you let that happen?" Ashley asked.

"I don't know. What the hell was I thinking?" she said frustrated.

"Look, you have nothing to be ashamed of. I mean, he cheated on you and probably gonna be a daddy soon."

"I know what you're saying, but I did the exact same thing I chastised him for."

"Karina you were lonely. Daz gave you the attention you needed. The attention Trae wouldn't give you. Sweetie, there is nothing wrong with that."

Ashley's words could never convince Karina that her actions were justified. She was wrong, and now she had to face the consequences of her actions.

DEEP

IN NEED OF A FRIEND

It was three o'clock in the afternoon the next day, when Trae showed up at Pleasures. Word spread quickly throughout the club that he was in a bad mood, so everyone steered clear, except Sommone. She marched right into his office and asked him what was up.

"You might not want to be in here right now," he snapped.

"That's alright. I think I'll take my chances," she responded.

Trae couldn't concentrate on the paperwork he was filling out, so he threw it across the floor. "I need a drink," he said. He walked over to his bar and threw back two shots of vodka.

"Is there anything I can do to make you feel better?" she said, locking the door. Sommone started dancing for Trae. "Why don't you let Mone' make you feel better?"

Trae shook his head and smiled. "What is it about you?" he asked. "Maybe some of Mone' is exactly what I need." He grabbed at her velour shorts, but Sommone moved his hands.

"Wait a minute, daddy. This is my show. Now give me a kiss."

Trae quickly obliged. Slowly, they locked lips, and Sommone slid her tongue inside his mouth. Using her skills, she began sucking his tongue with such force, at times it hurt the back of his throat. She then released, and used her tongue to lick the outline of his lips and nose.

Sommone gave Trae tiny kisses on his left eye lid, around his forehead and to his right eye lid. Slowly, her tongue twirled down his nose and back into his mouth. He moaned softly, as his hands explored her body. Feeling the heat, Sommone assisted Trae in taking off her shorts.

"Lay down on the floor," Trae demanded, as he threw her shorts across the room. Lifting her legs to get a better view, he studied her pussy.

"C'mon, stop teasing me," she begged.

A NOVEL BY DANETTE MAJETTE

Trae crawled up Sommone's body, and rubbed his dick between her breasts until it was fully erect. He moved further up until it was close to her mouth, then he dipped his hips to press his dick against her thick soft lips.

Sommone smiled as she released her tongue to lick his head in a circular motion. Trae let out a low moan of satisfaction when she started to take long strokes. She pushed him back.

"I want to feel you in me," she whispered.

Trae obliged, pulling Sommone's legs over his shoulders. He playfully rubbed his dick on her lips before inserting it. Her juices began to overflow onto the floor as he moved in and out with force.

"Yeah, c'mon fuck me," she moaned, thrusting her hips.

He arched his back, to give him the position to speed up the pace. After he felt her legs start to vibrate, he knew she was about to have an orgasm.

"Oh yeah, yeah," she muttered.

With a few more quick thrusts, he started wailing as his eyes rolled in the back of his eyes. He drilled in deeper. "Mmm…yeah that's it! Cum for mama."

DEEP

OFFICIALLY MISSING YOU

Once Karina and Ashley got to Virginia Beach, they checked into their room and got settled. Ashley, ready to hit the streets asked what they should do first. Karina didn't feel like going out, so she told Ashley she would have to go out by herself.

"Oh hell no! I didn't come all the way down here to do nothing. So I suggest you get yourself together, Miss Thang," she said to Karina.

"I can't even think straight right now. I don't know what I'm gonna do when I get back home. What if he moved my shit out?"

"Then you'll just have to move back in with me. Shit, I could use help with the rent," Ashley joked. "Oh, by the way, did you go to the bank and get your money out. I would suggest you do that first. You know how shiesty niggas get."

Karina assured her Trae would never do anything like that and even if he did, they had separate accounts. She had her own account that Trae had no knowledge of. Karina was no dummy. She knew she needed to save some money for a rainy day, just in case Trae got locked up or something.

"You's a sneaky bitch! But a smart one never the less," Ashley said with laughter. "So, have you talked to Daz?"

"No. I tried to call him to let him know what happened, but he's not answering."

"Umm, what about Trae?"

Just as Karina was about to answer Ashley her cell phone rang. "Speak of the devil," Karina said, looking at her caller ID.

"Don't answer it!"

"I have to. If I don't he'll keep calling." She took a deep breath. "Hello," she answered.

"What's up?" Trae asked.

"Nothing. We just checked into our room."

"So, did you call your man today?"

"Trae, he's not my man."

"What would you call him then? Especially since you were fuckin' the nigga!"

"Look, if this is what you called for then we have nothing else to talk about."

"What the hell do you mean we don't have nothin' to talk about? When I cheated, you ain't miss a chance to throw that shit in my face. That's all we talked about. Now that yo' ass went out and cheated, we ain't got shit to talk about. You a funny bitch, you know that!"

"You got one more time to call me a bitch, a'ight. I know you're mad, but that shit ain't necessary."

"Are you in love wit' that nigga?"

Karina yelled. "No!" She told Trae once again how they were only friends and how things just got out of hand.

Trae let out a hugh sigh. "So, where do we go from here, Karina?"

"I don't know, but it's obvious we just need to go our separate ways. We've hurt each other enough."

"Why is it when things don't go your way, you always ready to throw in the towel?" he asked.

"I'm just trying to do what I think is best. You're never going to fully trust me again, just like I don't trust you. Without trust what do we have?"

"We got each other! Yeah, this shit got me fucked up right now, but I ain't ready to give up on us! Are you?"

Deep down inside, Karina wasn't ready to give up on their relationship either, but she felt they needed some time apart once again, if they had any chance of working their problems out.

"How many times do I have to tell you this? You can't work your problems when you're in two different places. So, I'll see you when you get home."

Click!

"What did he say?" Ashley asked, ready for a play by play of the conversation.

"He wants us to work it out."

"What!"

"Yeah, he said he'll see me when I get home. I guess I still have one."

"Damn, girl what the fuck you be doing to him? I need to take a few notes."

"Shut up crazy!" Karina said, throwing a pillow at Ashley.

DEEP

After talking to Trae, Karina was ready to go out and get some-thing to eat. Ashley, on the other hand, was ready to get her freak on, so they went to a restaurant in the hotel lobby for some appetizers and a few Apple Martinis. After getting pissy drunk, the two went back to their room and went to sleep.

The next morning, Karina awoke to the sound of her cell phone ringing. It was Daz.

"What's up, cutie?" he asked.

"Hi."

"You still sleep?"

"Yeah. Look, my boyfriend found out about us."

There was silence for a few moments. "How?"

Karina explained the whole embarrassing scene to Daz, who was shocked.

"Shit!" What did he say?"

"What didn't he say? He's angry and I don't blame him, so until this blows over, I don't think we should talk."

"No doubt! I'll give you your space. I just wanted to tell you I got signed to a major record company out in L.A."

"Wow, that's great! I'm really happy for you. I know how hard you've been working to get a deal. I wish you luck!"

"Thanks. Well, I guess this is good-bye."

"I guess so."

When Karina hung up, she felt depressed. As much as she tried to convince herself that she wasn't, she couldn't...She had fallen in love with Daz. Now it was over.

DEEP

A CHANGE OF HEART

The weeks of fighting had run its course with Trae and Karina. Although they weren't back at a hundred percent, they were slowly starting to find their way back to one another. Karina could think of several reasons why she should leave Trae, but she couldn't do it. Even their lovemaking was starting to be more of a physical connection, rather than a chore Karina felt was barely worth attempting.

One evening Trae came home early, and asked Karina if she wanted to take a drive down to the Georgetown waterfront.

"Sure, but I was just about to start dinner," she said.

"We'll grab somethin' while we're out."

Trae and Karina spent hours milling through the exclusive shops on Wisconsin Avenue before stopping for a bite to eat. The pub style café, with a forties theme covering the walls, offered a variety of foods, from steaks to hamburgers. They both order New York Strip steaks, salads, and wine.

For the next hour or two, they sat laughing and talking like old times. When they left, they drove to a nearby park and sat in the grass to talk some more.

"So, you still wanna leave D.C.?" Trae asked.

"Why? You don't want to leave now?" Karina asked.

"Naw. I still want to go, but I don't want to roll if you're not goin' wit' me."

Karina tossed her hair back with her fingers. "Crazy as it seemed, I knew exactly what I was getting into when I met you. Although I hoped like hell you would change."

He cut her off before she could go any further. His eyebrows arched. "I thought we were gonna leave the past in the past," he said.

"We are. I'm just saying, I thought once we got together, you would change. But you didn't."

A NOVEL BY DANETTE MAJETTE

"I know, but I won't let you down this time."

"Trae, how many times have you said that?"

Trae knew Karina was right, and even though he had let her down in the past, he was sure he wouldn't do it again. The problem was convincing her of that.

Karina watched as Trae drifted off into his own little world. She nudged him. "Why all this sudden talk about leaving town?"

Trae wasn't sure if he should tell Karina what was going on, but he felt that was the only way she would leave with him.

"My sources tell me the Feds have been watchin' us. I think they're about to bring me in," Trae replied.

Karina was shocked."Why didn't you tell me what was going on?"

"To be honest, I thought you would think I was just lyin' to get you to leave with me. Man, I'm in some shit that I just can't get out of. So, I guess you could say I'm in too deep," he sighed.

Karina's mind raced. "Come to think of it, I've noticed this same black car parked down the street all week. Do you think it's them?"

"It could be. I haven't seen it."

"Oh my God. What are we going to do?"Karina asked.

Trae reached out his hand and smoothed Karina's hair. "We've got to get out of here. You wit me?"

Even though her head was spinning and everything seemed to be happening so fast, she agreed to go with Trae.

"Okay, this is what we have to do," he said, grabbing her hand.

Trae ran down his plan to Karina. She was glad to be leaving all their problems behind them and starting a new life with Trae. Even if it meant assuming a whole new identity. Of course, she had a plan of her own.

DEEP

HOLDIN HIM DOWN

Karina finished packing her belongings then went downstairs to secure the house. She took one last look around at the home she and Trae shared, before piling her bags by the door. A few minutes later, she saw a pair of headlights in the driveway. In the midst of the rain, she eagerly opened the door and turned on the porch light thinking it was Trae. However, Karina gasped when she saw a white man in a dark trench coat exit the car. She jumped back into the house and slammed the door shut, then peeked out the window.

Once the man was at the door, he knocked forcefully a few times before Karina finally looked out the peephole. He must've known she was there because he took a step back, to show her he meant no harm. Her heart pounded when he raised his hand and showed her his badge. Karina hesitated a few seconds, then finally opened the door.

"What do you want?" she asked.

"Sorry if I startled you," the man said, in a raspy voice. "I'm Agent Ford of the FBI. Is Trae Keal home?"

Through the rain, Karina could see a black Plymouth parked on the side of the street as Agent Ford continued to hold up his badge.

"No, he's not," Karina said hesitantly, staring in his ice blue eyes. They stared back at her as if they were looking right through her.

"Can I ask you a couple of questions?" he asked Karina.

She nodded her head, then opened the door a little wider. He lowered his badge, and then shoved it back into his coat pocket. "It will only take a second," he said. He stepped onto the mat, wiping his feet.

Raising his hand, he brushed the rain from his hair, before following Karina into the living room.

"What's your name?" he asked.

"Why?" she asked, taking a seat on the couch. "What's this

A NOVEL BY DANETTE MAJETTE

about?"

"Well, I've been assigned to a few unsolved murders, and we think Trae might have some vital information that might help us solve the cases."

"Why Trae?" Karina asked, crossing her arms.

"I don't know how familiar you are with what happened, with the officer who was shot in a parking garage downtown. We have information that he was friends with Trae and frequented his club. Have you ever seen him before?" Agent Ford said, handing Karina a photo of Monty.

"No, I don't recognize him," she said, handing to the photo back to him.

"Do you know anything about the trip to Vegas Trae took right after the officer was shot?"

"I...I really don't recall that. It's been a rough year for me," she said unable to keep her voice from trembling.

Agent Ford studied her reaction. "You know withholding evidence is a federal offense," he replied.

Agent Ford shifted his weight, then shoved his hands into his coat pockets. He constantly stared at Karina, like he expected her to say something. She uncrossed her arms, but she didn't know what to do with them, so she crossed them again. She leaned back on the couch feeling very nervous about the whole situation. Agent Ford picked up on Karina's uneasiness. It was obvious to him that she knew something.

Pulling out a small note pad and a ballpoint pen from his shirt pocket, Agent Ford began to question Karina about Trae and Kevin. He then scribbled her words on the pad.

"Is there any reason why Trae is avoiding us? We've been by his club several times, but no one ever seems to know where he is or when he'll be back," he said, keeping his eyes on the notepad. "I think it's really strange, especially since we just want to ask him a few questions."

"What are you implying?" Karina asked loudly.

"I'm not trying to imply anything, I was just wondering where he is."

"Trae is a very busy man. He doesn't go to the club every night." Karina was fired up like a grill. "Look, I've told you everything I know. Now, if you don't mind, I'd like for you to leave. "

"Okay. Well, thanks, you've been very helpful," he said.

Agent Ford shoved his pen and notebook back into his shirt, and

DEEP

handed Karina a business card. "If you think of anything that might be helpful, please call me. My number is on the card."

"Okay," Karina replied, holding the card in her hand.

Agent Ford glanced outside and saw that the rain had stopped before he opened the door. "Thank you for your time."

Karina watched as Agent Ford took strides, his trench coat flapping behind him. Relieved, she locked the door, and leaned her back against it. She closed her eyes, still gripping the agent's card in her hand. She had no idea what she should do. All she could remember was Trae's words to make sure she was on the plane no matter what and he would meet her at the secret spot in a couple of days.

Then she had a frightening thought: *What if he doesn't make it? What if the Fed's pick himup before he can leave? What would I do then?*

After making his way down a crowded hallway at FBI Headquarters, Agent Ford stuck his head into Willie's office. "Got a minute?" Ford asked.

"Sure thing," Willie said, looking up. Ford walked over to Willie and dropped the photo on his desk. "How did it go?" Willie asked.

Agent Ford sat down. "She fell for it. You should've seen her. I thought she was going to have a nervous breakdown right in front of me."

Willie chuckled. "I kinda thought she would."

"She probably called him as soon as I left. He's definitely going to pull off this heist sooner so he can get out of town."

"Yeah, well when he does, we'll be right there," Willie said. "Shit, at this point I hope they hurry up myself. We've only been waiting for a fuckin' year," he joked.

Willie was really feeling himself. Unlike the other investigations, this time they had audio, video, and live testimony from a federal agent. He knew that this time Trae would not be able to walk, no matter who he had representing him.

A novel by DANETTE MAJETTE

DEEP

IT'S GOIN DOWN

It was the one o'clock in the morning when Trae summoned Carmen, Kevin, Ice Man and Big Paul to his office at Pleasures. One by one they showed up curious about Trae's urgent phone call.

"What's up wit' you?" Kevin asked, sipping on a beer he picked up from the bar on the way in.

"It's goin' down tonight," Trae said.

"Tonight?" Carmen looked puzzled.

"Yeah tonight. I already have the truck outside, we just have to wait for Greg to call."

"Shorty, I thought we were gonna wait until next week," Big Paul said.

"Well, there's been a change in plans, and luckily when I called the Dominicans, they were finally ready, so we have to hit now."

Fuck! Carmen thought. *How am I gonna let Willie know what's going on?"* She was thinking so hard, she didn't even hear Trae telling her to hand over her cell phone.

"My cell?" she asked.

"Yeah, We're not takin' anythin' that might be evidence against us later, so we're all leavin' our cell phones here. Don't worry, I'ma lock 'em in the safe. I'll have Sam bring them to us later," Trae said.

"Carm, you and Kevin sit tight while we load up the truck."

It was fine with Kevin, because he wanted to finish his beer. Carmen, on the other hand, was trying to figure out how she was going to call Willie. She needed to use the office phone, but how could she with Kevin watching her like a hawk?

When the truck was finally loaded, Trae's crew went through the plan one last time, to make sure they were all on the same page. They sat shooting the shit until Greg called and Trae gave the word. Carmen could tell from the look on Trae's face that he was worried. At

A NOVEL BY **DANETTE MAJETTE**

that point, she began to feel for Trae, and hoped he would change his mind. Without the heist, the Fed's really didn't have anything on him, at least nothing air tight.

At exactly four a.m., the crew loaded up in the van and finally headed toward the base. The drive was intense. They were taking a big risk. If they didn't do everything exactly as planned, they all could be looking at some serious jail time.

Armed with fake ID's, weapons and uniforms, they all let out a sigh of relief as a young looking military policeman waved them in after checking their fake credentials. Once they entered the base, Kevin shook his head.

"See, this is why muthafuckas from other countries be comin' over here tearin' our asses up. You see how easy that was?" Everyone laughed lightening the mood.

"Well, just be glad today the dummies ain't do they job or we would all be in handcuffs right about now," Trae replied. "Shit, I'm glad they had a kid at the gate."

Carmen pulled into an empty parking lot next to the armory, so they could change into their uniforms. Once they were ready, Trae waited for the signal from Greg. Thirty minutes later, Greg pulled up in a Five Ton truck with Corporal Riviera. He got out slowly, giving Trae and the boys enough time to get out and position themselves.

With Corporal Riviera waiting outside the locked cage doors, Greg finally said the words Trae and his crew had been waiting to hear for months. "All clear!" Greg yelled.

"Let's go!" Trae ordered to the crew.

The men ran in with a vengeance overpowering Greg and Corporal Riviera, throwing them both to the ground.

"Gimme the code to the weapons room," Kevin ordered. The two didn't bulge. "Gimme the fuckin' code," Kevin repeated, pointing the gun to Riviera's head.

"Alright...alright...," Greg said, going along with the plan. "424*611."

Kevin smacked him just to make it look convincing. He then went to the room to turn off the alarm.

"Why is the weapons room unlocked this soon," Riviera whispered to Greg.

"I don't know. The soldier on duty last night must've forgot to lock it," Greg lied. He could tell from the look on Riviera's face that he thought something was up.

When Kevin returned he told Ice Man to give Carmen the signal to

DEEP

back the truck up to the door. "Remember, we don't have much time!" he yelled.

With their adrenaline flowing, Trae and his crew loaded up the truck, while Kevin watched Greg and Riviera. Everything was going as planned, except Greg's theory that Riviera wouldn't be a problem.

He saw how distracted Kevin was with all the chaos going on in the cage, that he tried to charge him. Caught off guard, Kevin fell back on the floor. Carmen and Trae stopped in their tracks to see what the commotion was all about.

Kevin managed to kick Riviera back up against the wall, giving Greg the perfect opportunity to let one off right in Riviera's head with his M9. Luckily, it had a silencer.

Kevin was pissed. "I thought you said that nigga wasn't gonna be a problem," he said, getting up.

"My bad. I guess he took that die for your country shit to heart," Greg replied with no remorse. "We need to get the fuck outta here, we only got five minutes left," he said, looking at his watch.

Trae ran to the door and made sure no one heard anything. Once the coast was clear, the men made sure there was no evidence to link them to the robbery.

"Let's go!" Trae ordered, carrying the last of the weapons.

Greg drove the Five Ton, just in case they got stopped, since he was the only one with a military identification card as Trae at the rest of his crew followed in the fake contractor van.

When they reached the front of the base, Trae prayed that they would get back through without a problem. As soon as the same young guard waived them through, he let out a huge sigh then smiled. *Retirement, here I come.*

News of the heist quickly spread. It was on every major news channel in the United States by 11 o' clock that afternoon. Sitting safely in a suite at the Renaissance downtown, Trae and his crew watched the news coverage.

"A Staff Non-Commissioned officer, on his way to clean his weapon opened the door to the armory on the 8th Marines base and found the body of a twenty-year old corporal. He was shot in the head and there were signs of a struggle. Military police say the armory was completely emptied of its weapons."

A NOVEL BY DANETTE MAJETTE

Trae and his crew listened attentively as the Commanding Officer of the base spoke. "Whoever opened it, stole the weapons, relocked it and fled. We believe this murder and theft was carried out by career criminals."

"There a lot of strange faces on this base everyday," a woman said, who declined to give her name. "With so many different contractors and civilians working here, it's actually kind of easy to get in and off the base, I'm sad to say."

They returned to the Commanding Officer of the base. "The government has a hard job ahead of them, but since it involves the theft of hundreds of weapons, I'm sure there will be an intense manhunt."

With his nerves shot to hell, Trae sat on the couch in their suite. This was the first time he'd ever had second thoughts about anything he'd done.

"It's too late to turn back now, Shorty," Kevin said to Trae.

"What'chu talkin' 'bout?" Trae asked.

"I see the look on your face. I'm tellin' you, after we unload them off on the Dominicans, we home free."

"I hope so," Trae said.

Back at the FBI headquarters, Willie was on the phone with everyone he knew, trying to get information on Carmen's whereabouts when an agent walked into the room.

"What do you have?" Willie asked.

"Nothing yet, sir. I've been on the phone with our contact at the club, and there's been no activity there. No one has seen or talked to them. But we have a few men staking the place out."

"Shit!" Willie yelled, pushing over his desk. "That bastard may have slipped right through our hands!"

Willie began picking up the huge stack of papers when his phone rang. "Hi, it's me. Has there been any word yet?" Damien asked. He was worried sick about Carmen.

"No, not yet. I don't understand what happened. They weren't supposed to hit the armory for a couple days, why the change of plans?" Willie said, scratching his head.

"I don't know, but I'm worried."

"Don't be, we're going to find her. I have every available man out there looking for her," Willie assured.

"Thanks, but that's not helping me right now. It's your fault she's

DEEP

missing in the first place."

"I agree. We dropped the ball on this one, but I can assure you we're doing everything in our power to find her."

The fact that everyone was out looking for Carmen didn't help ease Damien's fears. Although he was used to her being in dangerous situations, the thought of her being out there with no communication scared him. The only obvious explanation was she was in trouble. He needed answers, and he needed them now. So he went to the only place he felt could give them to him.

Still uneasy, Trae walked down to the hotel's lobby with a baseball cap pulled down over his forehead. He looked around, found the pay phones, and dialed the Dominican.

"Trae, my friend, I see you and your comrades are headliners on every major news channel across the U.S.," Rafael said, when he answered the phone.

"Yeah, that's why we need to do this, so I can get the hell out of here," Trae said, fidgeting with the phone.

"Trust me, I understand. What do you say we meet tomorrow?"

"Where?"

Rafael thought for a moment. "How about in the wholesale district off of Florida Ave…say around three."

"That's good. See you then. Oh…make sure everything is straight on your end," Trae said. "You got my girl's information right?"

Rafael laughed. "Stop worrying. Ah…you Americans have such a sense of humor." He hung up.

Pulling off the heist was one thing Trae had to worry about, but Rafael was another. Although Trae was sure he was on the up and up, he still had to keep in mind Rafael could try to double cross him at any moment.

Before he went back up to the room, Trae called Sam at the club and told him to meet him the next day with their cell phones a block away from the hotel. He also told him that it was very important that he make sure he wasn't being followed.

"Don't tell anyone that you talked to me." Sam assured him that he wouldn't.

When Trae walked back in the room, Carmen was sitting on the couch. She'd been sleep most of the day and desperately needed to

A NOVEL BY DANETTE MAJETTE

talk to Willie.

"So, what time are we meeting the Domincans tomorrow? I want to get this over with so I can fly those friendly skies by tomorrow evening," Carmen asked.

Just as Trae was about to divulge the information, Kevin interrupted. "Trae, I think we should call in some reinforcement, just in case those fools start wildin' out."

"You think those niggas might try somethin'?" Ice Man asked.

"Ice, one of the seven deadly sins is greed. So, yeah, they might try somethin', but they better come ready to die if they do," Trae replied.

For the rest of the day, Carmen tried to figure out how she was going to call Willie. She knew he was probably going crazy not knowing what was going on. She made several attempts to go down to the lobby, but Trae wouldn't let anyone leave the room. After all, there was no need to. He had already ordered room service and had it delivered before they arrived, so no one would see what they looked like. Talk about paranoid, Trae was past it. He didn't even sleep that night, and hadn't planned on resting until he was home free.

DEEP

SOMEBODY'S WATCHING ME

The next day, it was almost time for Trae and his crew to go meet Rafael. Knowing this would be the last time they talked to each other in a while, Trae and Kevin sat huddled in a corner of the suite.

"You a'ight?" Kevin asked.

Trae shook his head, yes, but Kevin could tell it meant no.

"Shorty, what's up? And don't tell me nothin', cause I don't wanna hear that shit," Kevin added.

Trae smiled. He looked at his friend of more than twenty years, and wondered what he would do without him. Kevin drove Trae insane at times, but Trae never had to wonder about Kevin's loyalty. "I just got a bad feeling about this. I keep havin' these visions that my plane is leavin', but I ain't on it."

"You think Rafael is gonna try some bullshit?"

Trae got up and stood over by the window. "I can't explain it, but I feel like some shit is gonna go down."

Kevin stood up and walked over to his friend. "You remember what I told you when we first met?"

"Yeah, you told me I was a bitch."

Kevin laughed. "Besides that."

"Yeah, you told me I didn't have the heart for this, but you did and you would always take care of me."

"That's right. I'll always take care of you." He embraced Trae. "But, I did somethin' and I've been keepin' it from you for a while now."

Trae looked at Kevin with a confused expression "What is it?"

"I hope you don't get mad, but the night after the Ne-Yo show, I ran into Courtney and..."

"And what?" Trae asked with anticipation.

"I fucked her that night."

Trae smiled. "Oh, is that all? Who cares, she's a slut anyway."

A NOVEL BY DANETTE MAJETTE

"Umm...no that's not all. I'm really the father of her baby."

Trae's smile turned into laughter. "Are you serious? Shit, that's the best news that I've heard in a while. But I still can't believe Courtney did that shit to me if she knew I wasn't the father."

"I think she chose you over me because you have more money," Kevin said, with a slight laugh.

"Well it doesn't even matter now. All I care about is that's your crazy ass baby mother now, and not mine."

Trae and Kevin continued to talk about Courtney for a few more minutes before the got back to business. "I love you like a brother, Trae. That's why I think we need to go to plan B," Kevin said.

Trae walked away. "Man, there is no way in hell I'm leaving you here to deal with this."

"Shorty, you don't have a choice. If we both get locked up, we fucked. At least one of us should be on the outside, to look out for the other one."

Kevin lived for drama, and if anyone was going to be at that party, it was going to be him.

Sam opened up the club, then went into Trae's office to get the bag he had to deliver. He walked out to the parking lot took a look around, then got in his truck, headed for the hotel to meet Trae. Just as he was pulling off, he ran into Sommone.

"Hey Mone, You can go in. I already opened up," he said.

"Okay. Where's Trae?" she asked.

"Um...I'm not sure. I gotta go. I'll be back in a minute," he said, driving away.

Sam acted so strangely about Trae's whereabouts that Sommone, like a true stalker, followed him to find out why.

Following Sam closely, she picked up her cell phone and called Willie, "Sam just left the club."

"Where are you?"

"I'm following him now. He's acting really strange. I think he knows where Trae is."

"What's his location?"

"He just pulled into the parking garage at the Renaissance Hotel on 9th and L," Sommone said, trying to find somewhere to park.

"Good work. I'm on my way. Make sure you stay in your car until we get there."

DEEP

"Okay."

Sommone sat in her car for about ten minutes when she saw a man wearing dreads and a hat walk out the garage elevator door. Sam immediately got out and greeted him. He then handed the man a bag and got back into his car.

Talking to Sam through the window, the man told Sam to be in the wholesale district at two o'clock. "Make sure no one sees you."

"Okay," Sam replied.

Sommone quickly picked up her phone and hit the redial button.

"Hey, he's about to leave. What should I do?"

"Did you see who he met?"

"Yeah, some guy with dreads," she said, trying to get a closer look. Sommone prayed there was some way she could keep Trae from getting caught.

"You stay put, we'll keep an eye on things from here."

"How are you gonna keep an eye on things when you're not here?" Sommone asked.

"Oh, but we are, sweetie. Look to your left."

Sommone looked to her left. "Where? All I see is a laundry truck."

"That's us."

With her cell phone back in her possession, Carmen walked into the bathroom and sent Willie a text message. *At the Renaissance Hotel 9 St. Deal bout to go down. Don't know where.* She hit the send button and waited for a response.

Carmen was waiting for a reply, when she heard a knock at the bathroom door.

"You a'ight in there?" Trae yelled, from the other side.

"Yeah, I'm cool," Carmen said, checking her phone for messages.

She knew she had to get back out there before Trae got suspicious, so she turned her cell phone off and went back to join the rest of the crew. After sitting for nearly ten minutes in silence, there was a knock at the door. When Kevin answered it, a large and unfamilair man walked in and gave Trae a hug.

"What's up wit'chu?" the man asked.

"Nothin' much You sure you wanna do this shit' Shorty?" Trae asked. When Trae looked around the room, he realized everybody knew the guy expect Carmen. "Yo', Carm this my man Dre. Dre this

Carm."

"What's up?"Carmen asked. She noticed how much Dre looked like Trae.

Dre shook his head. "Nigga, you wild as shit. You got a bitch on the team now."

"Shorty, watch yo' language man, she's family."

"My bad. My bad," Dre said, laughing.

Trae led Dre off to a secluded area of the suite. They were deep in conversation, when Trae's phone rang nearly sending Carmen into a state of panic. She watched as Trae wrote down the instructions he was given onto a piece of paper.

Trae rounded up the crew and gave them their last minute instructions. "I'll see y'all at the spot," Trae said, as he grabbed his bag.

"Where you goin'?" Carmen asked.

"I gotta make a stop, but I'll catch up with y'all later." He gave them all a heartfelt hug and walked out the door. Carmen was beginning to think she was on her own when it was time for them to leave and there was still no sign of Willie.

An hour later, Trae called Kevin and told him that he was safe, so they could leave. As soon as Carmen walked out of the elevator into the parking structure, she silently thanked God when she saw Damien walking toward her with a suitcase in his hand. He looked like a real guest coming to check into the hotel as he nodded at the entire group and stepped onto the elevator. Carmen wanted to turn around so badly, but knew that would put up a red flag, so she continued.

"Where's Trae?" Carmen asked, looking around.

"He's gonna meet us there," Kevin said. "I'ma drive the contractor truck, you ride wit' Big Paul."

Over in the laundry truck, Willie was beginning to get nervous. "Where's Keal?" Willie asked.

"I'm not sure," one of the agents replied.

A few seconds later, another man walked out of the elevator.

"Oh, I think that's him right there," Willie said, looking through his binoculars. The crew piled into Big Paul's truck and drove out the parking structure with Kevin leading the way. As soon as they turned the corner, Willie and his agents followed.

As they drove toward Florida Avenue, Carmen wondered why Trae wasn't with them, and how much of a coincidence that Dre looked just

DEEP

like him. Then it hit her. Dre was a decoy. Carmen was beginning to think that her cover was blown. *First he calls the heist early, then he took our cell phones, and now a decoy. Does he know who I really am?* she thought.

When they pulled into the wholesale district, Carmen noticed a limousine waiting outside one of the shops. They stopped, circled the block one more time, then pulled up next to the limo.

Kevin rolled down his window.

"Follow us," Rafael commanded.

Kevin rolled his window back up then did as he was instructed. Seconds later, the driver of the limo pulled into an abandoned warehouse and got out. He walked to the opposite side of the car and opened the door for Rafael. Dressed to kill, Rafael straightened his suit, then pulled out a briefcase.

After making sure they were strapped properly, Kevin, Big Paul, Ice Man, Carmen, and Dre got out of their trucks as well.

Kevin walked over and introduced himself. "It's about time I got to put a face with the voice." He asked Rafael to walk with him over to the truck, where the stolen weapons were. "Everything is here," he said. "Now, are you sure you got the right account information?"

Rafael smiled. "Yes, my friend. I'm sure. He took his laptop out of the case and began the transaction. Everyone appeared visibly nervous. Little did they know, it was alot to be nervous about.

With the building surrounded, Willie and his agents swarmed the place. But It was too late, Rafael had already hit the send button, transferring over five million dollars into an off shore account set up by Karina.

"Freeze!" Sommone yelled, running over to Kevin and Rafael.

Everyone stood still. That's when Carmen walked over to Willie's side, and pointed her gun directly at Kevin.

"You two bitches set us up!" Kevin yelled. "I knew it. I knew there was something up wit' y'all." He pulled out his burner and started to blast at anyone who was in the way.

Sommone ran for cover, but was hit once in the chest. Willie and his agents returned shots as Big Paul and Ice Man joined Kevin in the gun battle. Dre, still in the truck, started the engine and rammed the pedal, breaking through the warehouse doors. Carmen quickly applied pressure to Sommone's gunshot wound.

"I'm alright. Go get him," Sommone whispered, barely able to speak.

A NOVEL BY DANETTE MAJETTE

Carmen quickly ran to one of the agent's car and followed Dre.

Still blasting shots at one another, the Feds seemed to be on the brink of defeat as Kevin, Ice Man, Big Paul, Rafael and his cohorts gave them a run for their money with their high performance weaponry. But just as they were about to call this a defeat, SWAT swarmed in and shut everyone down. First, they took out Big Paul who was causing the most damage with a grenade launcher. Then a sniper took out Ice Man, Kevin and Rafael. Kevin continued to fire back shots, even though he knew he didn't have a chance in hell. With his ride or die mentally, Kevin got up from behind the truck and blazed as he ran towards Willie and his men. With fifteen shots to the body, Kevin dropped about ten yards from the man who was responsible for his death.

Carmen had been following Dre for miles before he started shooting at her. This made Carmen very concerned for the innocent bystanders who were going about their everyday business. Chasing Dre through residential areas, Carmen got on the radio and requested back up.

"Air control, this is Agent Carmen Nichols. I need a visual on a Black Chevrolet SUV. Suspect is headed westbound on New York Avenue," she yelled. "Suspect is a black male, and considered armed and dangerous. I repeat armed and dangerous."

She tailed Dre for miles, as a helicopter followed in the air, giving a dispatcher a point by point account of where he was headed.

Dre couldn't get the helicopter or Carmen off his tail, so he started firing shots in the air instantly making Carmen and the helicopter pull back a little. After dropping his cell phone a few times, Dre was finally able to call Trae's number.

"Pick up, pick up!" he yelled, trying to keep his eye on the road. When Trae's phone went to voicemail, he left him a disturbing message.

"Yo' girl Carmen, is a fuckin' FED. She's a FBI Agent!" Dre yelled, before slamming the SUV into the rear of another car at top speed.

Carmen quickly jumped out of her vehicle and ran with her weapon drawn toward the truck. She yelled for Dre to throw his weapon out the window, but he didn't move. When she got closer, she saw blood covering his face. She walked over slowly and opened the door. She pulled Dre out and laid his body on the ground. While calling for an ambulance, she stuck two fingers on the side of his throat.

"Shit, he's dead," Carmen said. She immediately checked on the occupants of the other car. "Are you guys alright?" she asked, opening the driver's side door.

The driver was unresponsive, but the passenger was alert and answered, "My husband's hurt, please help us."

"This is Agent Nichols, I need an ambulance on the corner of Bladensburg and New York Avenue," Carmen said to her radio.

Willie showed up on the scene within minutes. He headed straight to the SUV. When he looked in and saw Dre's body, he looked over at Carmen and yelled, "Where's Keal?"

"I don't know they used a decoy, he could be anywhere by now," she said.

"Shit! Shit! Shit!" Willie yelled, as he kicked the side of the SUV's door.

"What about Sommone, is she okay?" Carmen asked.

Willie held his head down. "I'm afraid not, she's gone."

Disguised in an African Dashiki, Trae got off a plane in Chicago and waited for his first connecting flight inside a restaurant. While he waited, Trae decided to check his voice messages one last time before he left the country.

"You have three messages," the recording said.

The first message was from Karina, saying she had made it safely. The second one was from Sam saying everything was in place. The third message was from Dre. He could barely make out what he was saying, so he stepped out of the restaurant so he could hear it clearer.

"Yo' girl Carmen, is a fuckin' FED. She's a FBI Agent," he heard Dre say. Trae couldn't believe what he was hearing, so he replayed it again. This time he heard the message and the crash clearly. Shocked, Trae took a seat. After a few minutes of disbelief, Trae wanted to call someone to get the 411. Scared that the phones at the club might be tapped, he called Sam's cell phone. The phone rang about four times before Sam picked up.

"I'm so glad you called. Shit is all fucked up, man." Sam said.

"What the fuck is goin' on. Dre left me a message sayin' Carmen works for the Feds," Trae said.

"It's true. So did Sommone. When I saw her pull out her badge, I was in shock."

Trae was in awe. He couldn't believe how he'd managed to let not one but two women infiltrate his crew. "What! I can't believe that I was fuckin' that bitch," Trae responded then paused. "Hold up, you just said Sommone did work for the Feds. What the fuck did she do quit?"

"Yeah, let's just say she won't be workin' for anybody else because her ass got popped."

Trae was in shock. Before he could ask about his crew, Sam blurted out, "Trae, I got the fuck out of there, man."

"Did anyone see you?"

"Naw, I did just what you told me to do. As soon as I saw Rafael hit the button, I left you a message. Shorty, as soon as I saw them get killed, I hauled ass out of there and jumped on the next plane. I just bought a ticket. I don't even know where the fuck I'm goin'. I'm really fucked up right now."

"Who got killed?"Trae yelled.

"Big Paul, Ice and...," Sam could barely get his words out.

"Where's Kev?" Trae asked.

Sam took a deep breath. "He's...he's gone too."

"Shorty, don't tell me that," Trae said, rocking back and forth in his chair. "Don't tell me that."

"It's true. He's gone."

Trae dropped his cell phone. He felt numb and filled with guilt about leaving Kevin behind to deal with Rafael. Trae and Kevin always lived life as though they would never die, so he was unprepared for this.*That bitch, Carmen better hope I never see her ass again*.

When he got himself together, Trae picked his cell phone back up. "Are you still there, Sam?" he asked.

"Yeah, man. I'm here."

"Get back on the plane. I know where you can go."

DEEP

WHEN THERE'S NO TRUST

Once the crime scene was sealed, Carmen and Willie headed back to FBI's Headquarters, to see if they could get any leads on Trae. The office was in an uproar, and the media was all over the place. Sitting in Willie's office, they brainstormed.

"Can you think of any place he could be?" Willie asked.

As Carmen racked her brain, thoughts of Sommone kept entering her mind. She couldn't help but to think that could've been her "I have no idea. What about his girlfriend, Karina?"

"It looks like she has disappeared off the face of the earth too. We've questioned her best friend, Ashley, and she doesn't have a clue either. All she could tell us is that Karina called her a few days before the heist and said she was taking a trip. She said she was a little concerned because she seemed sad about leaving."

"That's probably because she knew she wasn't coming back," Carmen added.

Willie could feel his face growing hot about Trae getting away, but he was mad at himself, mostly for not bringing him in when he had the chance. The State's Attorney's office was on his ass for not bringing him in after the heist. They felt with the magnitude of the crime on the base, they would have had more than enough evidence to send him away for a long time. Willie knew, without a doubt, his job was on the line, so he sat down at his desk and started to type his resignation.

Carmen kept digging through evidence that could possibly lead them to Trae. She stared up at the clock, and saw they had been combing through paperwork and listening to tapes for hours. Little did Trae know Carmen was wired most of the time. *His ass was too stupid to even pat me down*, she thought. Tired, she decided they should call it a night. Willie agreed, but insisted they all stay in a hotel near headquarters, just in case they got a break in the case.

A NOVEL BY DANETTE MAJETTE

With Trae still on the loose, Willie had some agents from his office guard Carmen's door. As soon as Carmen got in the room, she was surprised to see Damien waiting for her on the bed. She walked over and gave her husband a huge hug. In deep thought, she thought about all the time and energy she'd put into the case, only to have Trae get away. Her first concern was for Damien. She knew that Trae was well connected in the city and even if he couldn't get back at them for playing him, someone else could.

"Baby, what's wrong?" Damien asked. He waited for her to say something, but she seemed to be deep in thought. "Baby!"

"Huh…what did you say?"

"What's wrong?" he said, grabbing her hand in his.

Carmen sighed deeply. "I'm just tired of fuckin' up my cases."

"What happened wasn't your fault."

Carmen didn't agree. She felt if she hadn't let Willie use the scare tactics he did on Trae, the heist would have went off as planned. She would have had proper back up, and Trae would be in custody.

After having a quick dinner, Damien was exhausted, and within minutes of laying down on the bed he was asleep. Carmen sat on the couch beating herself up. Frustrated and sleepless, she got dressed. Opening the door quietly, so she wouldn't wake him, she slipped into the hallway of the hotel.

"Nichols, where you going this time of night?" one of the agents assigned to protect her asked.

"Look, I'm just going to headquarters. I'll be back in a flash," Carmen replied.

"I don't think that's such a good idea," the agent said, whispering so he wouldn't wake Willie up. "You know how crazy he gets."

"Don't worry I'll take care of him."

The agents looked at one another and shrugged their shoulders. "Alright, but at least let me call a car for you."

Carmen was hesitant, but agreed.

Waiting in the front of the hotel with one of the agents, Carmen tried to recall all her conversations with Trae about leaving town. It wasn't until she was walking into the FBI headquarters did she remember one place she had told Trae would be the perfect place for him to go.

"That's it. That's got to be where he went," she said out loud.

Carmen walked into Willie's office and took a seat behind his desk. She was just about to call Willie when she ran across a file with Trae's name on it. She thumbed through the information. Most of it

DEEP

was information and pictures she was already familiar with, but she noticed that Willie had ordered an additional check on Trae. The check was in some kind of code, and Carmen couldn't make it out.

Willie opened the door to his room and asked the agents if everything was alright. The two agents looked like a deer caught in headlights. "Is Agent Nichols still asleep?" They didn't know what to say. "Well, is she?" he yelled.

"No sir, she left about an hour ago," one of the agents said.

"Where the hell did she go?" Willie asked, pissed that she left the hotel without telling him.

"She went back to headquarters."

Willie's heart was pounding out of his chest. Not because he feared for Carmen's life, but because he was worried Carmen might find out he had been keeping some vital information about Trae from her.

Carmen sifted through the paperwork, but didn't see anything out of the ordinary. Convinced that Willie was hiding something about the case from her, she started to search his office more thoroughly. Minutes into her search, she was interrupted by a rookie agent, who came busting through the door. The scrawny kid with blond spiky hair looked more like a surfer than an FBI agent.

"Oh sorry, I thought you were the Assistant Director," he said.

"Naw, he's getting some rest," Carmen said, straightening up Willie's desk. "I'm Agent Nichols."

"I'm Agent Conner. Nice to meet you, I've heard all sorts of things about you. You're like a legend around here."

"I wouldn't call myself a legend," Carmen said, sounding modest.

"Well I better get back to work," Conner said, turning to leave.

"Um…wait. Willie sent me to get the copy of that file he ordered on Trae Keal. Could you get it for me?"

Conner looked puzzled, leaving Carmen to believe he didn't know what she was talking about. But then like the rookie he was, he asked Carmen how she knew about the file since it was suppose to be kept quiet. She explained to him that she was the undercover agent working the case. Agent Conner was so excited to be in Carmen's presence, that he started babbling like a three-year old.

"So, tell me what's it like assuming a whole new identity. You know pretending to be on their side," Conner said.

Carmen was about to say that she would tell him later, but just like the job she was paid to do, she gained his trust in order to get the information she needed. She then told Conner she needed to go, but she would talk to him later about some of her operations.

"You think you can go get that file for me now?" she asked.

"Sure, anything for you," Conner replied, bolting out of the room.

Within minutes, Conner was back smiling like he'd just made the winning touchdown in a football game.

"Here you go. I didn't find out much about his family here, but I did find out some pretty interesting things when I was in Florida." He handed the file to Carmen.

"If I can ever do anything for you, just let me know," Carmen said taking the file.

Agent Conner started to leave, but suddenly turned around. "You know the other agents treat us rookies, like we don't belong here. They don't understand that we're here for the same reason they are. So thanks again for the talk. That really meant a lot to me," he said, shaking Carmen's hand sternly.

She wanted to laugh, but when she saw how serious Conner was, she just smiled and nodded.

DEEP

A SECRET REVEALED

By the time Willie got to his office, he could tell Carmen knew everything by the stunned expression on her face.

"I know it was wrong of me to keep that from you, but I...I...was stunned myself," he said, closing the door.

Carmen's head spun so fast she didn't even hear a word Willie had said. "How long have you known?" she asked.

"I just found out yesterday. I wanted to tell you, but I didn't know where you were."

Carmen looked up at Willie. "And what about after you knew where I was. I mean you had all day to tell me."

"I'm sorry. You were already feeling bad about Trae getting away. I just didn't want to bother you with this right now. I was going to tell you first thing in the morning."

Carmen had trusted Willie with her life more times than she cared to remember, and had spent most of her career looking up to him. She even looked past some of the unethical things he did in order to make a case against someone. All because she believed in the work he was doing to take back the streets from violent criminals. All that changed when she was finally faced with the fact that Willie had withheld the information from her. Not because he thought she couldn't handle it, but because he feared Carmen would jeopardize his case against Trae.

"You can save the act, you've known for months according to your notes. I guess you thought that if you told me before we wrapped up the case, I would've let it cloud my judgment. You know...forget the oath I took and just let him walk."

"Carmen, I'm sorry. I admit I thought this might get a little sticky, but I never thought you wouldn't complete this assignment with the best integrity," Willie said.

A NOVEL BY DANETTE MAJETTE

Carmen punched Willie in the face. "Don't you ever use that word around me. You don't know the meaning of integrity," she said, before she left.

Willie yelled down the hall for Carmen to come back and talk, but she kept walking. "Fuck!" he yelled, wiping the blood from his mouth.

Willie sat in his office, contemplating his next move. He had already botched the case, and on top of it, he lost one of his best friends and agents. With everything he had done about to bite him in the ass, he decided he would leave on his own terms by going into early retirement. He would announce his resignation the next day.

Carmen's banging on the door startled her husband, so he grabbed his gun, and aimed at the door. "Who is it?"

"It's me, Carmen. Open up," she said.

He quickly walked to the door, and opened it. "You scared me. Where have you been?" he said, letting her in. Carmen's face was filled with gloom. When she didn't answer he became concerned. "Where have you been? You weren't supposed to leave the room." Carmen's husband was on the verge of hysteria. "What's wrong?" he asked, grabbing a bottle of water from the compact refrigerator.

"Did you know?" she asked, looking him in the eyes.

"Did I know what?"

"About Trae?"

"What about Trae?"

The mystified look on Damien's face let her know that he had no idea either. She gently laid her head on his lap and sobbed like a baby. When she wouldn't tell him why she was crying, he threatened to go to Willie.

"Baby, you're scaring me. Now tell me what happened," he said.

Carmen cleared her throat and stood pacing the floor as she told him the whole twisted story.

Her husband was floored. The news shot through him like a bolt of lighting. "I don't believe this shit!" he said, rubbing his head.

"Believe it!" Carmen screamed. She looked at her husband. "Now what am I supposed to do?"

DEEP

NOT SO PERFECT ENDING

The next morning, Carmen watched the TV as the man she respected more than anyone in the world announced at a press conference how he'd let a suspected murderer and notorious gangsta slip through his hands, and it was because of this that he'd decided to retire. Even though, Carmen was still angry about the information that fell into her lap the night before, she still felt bad for her friend.

Just as she was about to turn the TV off, her cell phone rang. "Agent Nichols speaking."

"Umm…you're looking for Trae Keal, right?" the anonymous caller asked.

"Who is this?"

"The caller refused to identify herself, only saying that she knew where Trae was.

"Well, where is he?" Carmen asked anxiously.

"He's in Senegal, Africa," the voice uttered. Carmen tried to keep the caller on the phone, but she hung up.

"I knew it!" Carmen yelled.

She was sure the call was legitimate, but it didn't matter. Even if Trae was there, he couldn't be touched since there were no extradition laws there. Plus, the bureau would never authorize the trip.

She would have to make this trip on her own, so without back up or her husband, she headed to the airport determined to close the case.

Trae arrived in Senegal grief stricken. He knew the death of one of his closest friends was all his fault. Kevin warned him several times about Sommone and Carmen, but he was too stubborn to listen.

When he walked into his hotel room, he was expecting to see

A NOVEL BY DANETTE MAJETTE

Karina there waiting for him. Instead, he found an empty room. He immediately called down to the front desk and asked if he had any messages. When the desk clerk told him no, he was confused.

After grabbing some vodka out of the mini bar, he sat in the chair and turned on the television. Frustrated because he didn't understand a word they were saying, he turned it off and sat in silence. An half an hour later, the phone rang.

Convinced it was Karina, he picked up the phone, but there was no one on the other end. Ten minutes later, there was a knock at the door.

"Who is it?" he asked.

"Room service!" someone said.

Trae looked through the door, and saw a man in a uniform with a cart standing on the other side. He cracked the door open and yelled through the slight opening that he didn't order room service.

"I know, but your wife did," the man replied, before slipping an envelope with Trae's name on it. When he saw Karina's handwriting, he opened the door and let the man in.

When the room service attendant rolled the cart inside, waited for his tip and quickly left. I guess he could tell Trae wasn't in the mood to hold a conversation.

Trae walked over to the bed, opened the envelope, and started to read the letter.

First let me start by saying that being with you has been one of the worst experiences in my life and now one of the best. Trae smiled. *On the cart in front of you, you'll find a bottle of champagne to toast to my new found wealth. That's right MY new found wealth. Correction- our newfound wealth, Daz and I that is. Did you really think I was that stupid? You cheated on me with Courtney, the biggest slut in D.C. and Sommone, the woman who set your dumb ass up. I mean really, did you think I was going to let you get away with that. Come on!*

Trae was furious. He grabbed the bottle of bubbly and threw it against the wall. He continued to read.

Now in the drawer next to the bed, you'll find a gun to shoot your-self with. Oh, by the way thanks for the money and suggesting that I put the account in my name. Chow!

Trae tore through the room like a hurricane. "That bitch!" he yelled over and over until he couldn't yell anymore. He opened the drawer, looked at the gun and for brief moment he thought about taking Karina's advice by ending it all.

DEEP

After thirteen hours and two planes later, Carmen finally arrived in Dakar, the capitol of Senegal. She checked into the Hotel La Residence, and immediately started combing the streets for anyone who may have come in contact with Trae or knew of his whereabouts. The first spot she went was the beach along the coastline. She showed a few people who were there for the art and music festival Trae's picture. No one had seen him. So Carmen headed to a cocktail-fueled resort she was told that was very popular around the corner. She walked around for an hour with the picture of Trae, showing it to anyone who would look at it. But again...nothing.

Warned about the roads after dark, she decided she would continue her search the next day. Disappointed, she hailed a cab and went back to her hotel.

Carmen didn't get much sleep that night. She was in a strange country, without a plan. She wasn't even sure what she was going to say if she even found Trae. What could she say? She had played him for a fool for months, pretending to be someone she wasn't. There were so many uncertainties, but one thing was sure. If Carmen did find Trae, she wasn't going to be welcomed with open arms.

The next morning, Carmen walked around for hours questioning people, until she spotted a guy running across the street to this nightclub. Sure she had seen him before, so she followed him.

When she marched up to the doors, she felt her heart stop. The club was vaguely familiar to Pleasures. Carmen took a deep breath before she went into the nightclub and walked down the velvet lined hallway. Once she was in the main room, she noticed how the deep red and brown interior enhanced the intimate styled booths with marble tables. It was a very stylish lounge, with the second level over looking the dance floor.

Since it was still early in the day, the club was empty, so Carmen took a seat at the bar. She had been sitting for about ten minutes when Sam came from the back. The two immediately locked eyes.

"Trae!" Sam yelled to the back of the kitchen. "Hurry up...she's here."

A NOVEL BY DANETTE MAJETTE

Trae ran out, the back with his gun in hand. When he saw
Carmen, he instantly cocked it.

"I'm unarmed," Carmen said, raising her hands.

"How the fuck did you know I was here?" Trae asked, moving
toward her.

Carmen was almost afraid to speak. Several seconds later, she
managed to get the words out. "I told you about this place, remember."

"You told me a lot of shit. But you somehow forgot to mention you
were the fuckin' Feds."

"Look, I didn't come here to cause you any problems," she pleaded.

"You already have. But you see, what you and the rest of them
dumb ass Feds didn't know was that I set this place up from back
home months ago so me and boys could lay back and chill. No more
drugs…no more lookin' over our shoulders, but all that is out the window now. My boys are gone and they ain't comin' back!" Trae yelled.

"I know and I'm sorry for your loss. But I have something really
important to tell you."

Trae looked at Sam. "Do you believe this shit, man? She wanna
tell me somethin'."

Sam laughed. "Naw, I don't."

"Bitch, tell me in hell," Trae said, before he pulled the trigger.

As soon as Carmen's body hit the floor, a manila folder fell from
her jacket. Still alive, Carmen managed to mutter the words, "Read."

Trae looked at Sam. "What the fuck is she sayin'?"

Trae knelt down beside her and picked up the folder. He opened it
and began to read. Every now and then he would look down at
Carmen, who was still alive, but fading away fast because her body
was going into shock.

Needing answers, Trae began to shake Carmen.

"What the fuck does this mean?" Trae continued to shake her.
"What does it mean?" He jumped to his feet and yelled to Sam, "Call
an ambulance. Call an ambulance!"

He got back down on the floor and assured Carmen help was on
the way.

While they waited on the ambulance, Trae watched as Carmen
tried unsuccessfully to reach into her shirt pocket.

"Why does she keep reachin' for her pocket?" Trae asked.

He stuck his hand in Carmen's pocket and pulled out a picture.
Trae's eyes started to water when he read the inscription on the back.
He looked at the photo again and then pleaded with her to hold

DEEP

on. "Don't you die on me!" he yelled holding her head. He started yelling at Sam. "Where the fuck is the ambulance?"

Carmen tried to say something, but Trae told her to save her strength. That didn't stop Carmen, she kept trying. She finally gathered up enough strength to pull Trae close to her mouth.

"I'm sorry," Carmen said, before closing her eyes.

Trae sat slumped on the floor, crying and holding Carmen's head in his lap.

Sam was at a complete loss for words. "Trae, what the fuck is going on?" he asked.

Trae looked at Sam with the strangest look in his eyes. He handed him the photo of Carmen and his mother. "She's my sister. I shot my own sister!"

"Oh shit!" Sam muttered in a low tone.

Trae, out of his mind, just kept holding Carmen's head. Sam could hear the sirens getting closer, so he told Trae they had to go.

"I can't just leave her like this," Trae said.

Sam looked around. He ran over to one of the table and pulled the tablecloth off of it. "Here use this."

Trae balled up the tablecloth, and gently placed it under his sisters head. With tears flowing, he kissed her on the forehead and told her he loved her. Sam helped his friend to his feet.

"Let's go this way," Sam said, pointing to the back door.

Trae quickly followed.

DEEP

DO THE RIGHT THING

The guilt of shooting Carmen was eating Trae alive, so after being on the run for months, he decided to turn himself in. Sitting in his hotel room in Kingston, Jamaica, he dialed the operator and got the number to the FBI headquarters in D.C.

"FBI headquarters, how may I direct your call?" the operator aoked.

Trae cleared his voice. "Yes, my name is Trae Keal. I think y'all are lookin' for me."

The operator asked Trae to hold on. She immediately dialed Damien's extension. "Agent Nichols, I have a man on the line who claims to be Trae Keal."

"What? Put him through." The operator transferred the call. "This is Agent Nichols."

"Yes, this is Trae Keal."

"Hello, Trae. This is Selena's...I mean Carmen's husband."

Trae was stunned. "I...umm...I want to turn myself in."

"Good because you just saved me from having to hunt your ass down."

Trae almost hung up the phone. "Shorty, I ain't doin' this shit for you. I'm doin' this my sister. I guess that makes me your brother-in-law...huh."

"You are nothing to me, you piece of shit. You shot my wife, and as soon as we have you in custody, I'm going to make sure we get to spend some one on one time."

"Whatever, man. None of that shit you talkin' gonna bring her back, so shut the fuck up. You think I ain't hurtin'. I had a sister I never knew about, and now I'm never get the chance to sit down and talk to her. I'll never know why my mother never mentioned having another child or why we grew up in two different places. You know why?

Because I killed her…that's why. So there ain't nothin' you can do to me that's gonna make me hurt anymore than I already do," Trae said, on the brink of tears.

"When do you plan on turning yourself in?" Damien asked.

"My planes arrives at six tomorrow…BWI airport," Trae said, before he hung up.

Damien immediately got on the phone and called the new Assistant Director. He explained to him how Trae wanted to turn himself in, but he wasn't sure if he was serious or just messing with his head.

The Director was shocked. "Do you know this will be the arrest of the decade? Look, get some people out to the airport first thing in the morning. We might even have to shut it down."

"Is that possible?" Damien asked.

"I don't know. Let me check on a few things."

Damien put the phone down on the receiver. This was turning out to be a good day after all, and tomorrow was going to be even better.

At five o'clock, the Baltimore Washington International airport was on lockdown. The FBI wasn't sure which airline Trae was coming in on, so they had every airline gate covered. There were several planes arriving around six o'clock, so they had extra men at every gate. Damien was so nervous he could barely keep his lunch down. He was finally gonna be face to face with the man who shot his wife.

It was exactly 6:15 when one of the agents phoned in that a man fitting Trae's description was walking down the corridor at gate seven.

"Team one…team one, come in," Damien shouted.

"This is team one," the man answered.

"Suspect is at gate seven…I repeat…suspect is at gate seven."

Damien ran to the gate. By the time he got there, Trae was lying on the ground in handcuffs.

"Get him up on his feet!" Damien yelled.

The agents helped Trae up to his feet. "Nice to finally meet you, brother-in-law," Damien said. Trae held his head down as Damien read him his rights. "Get him out of here," he said.

As soon as Trae walked out the airport doors, cameras started flashing. He looked around and saw that there was a news crew from almost every major network. He never thought in a million years that he would be the most wanted man in America. Even though he knew

DEEP

he was on his way to jail for the rest of his life, he was glad he'd turned himself in.

Before he was placed in the car, Trae turned slightly to the left and saw a familiar face. "Oh my God!" he said, in shock.

The woman walked over to him. "I'm glad you decided to end this the right way."

"I thought…"

"I know what you thought, but as you can see, you thought wrong. I always wear a bullet proof vest."

Trae smiled. He felt like the weight of the world was lifted off of his shoulders. His sister, Carmen, was alive and still feisty as ever.

The agent put his hand on top of Trae's head and shoved him into the car. Before they pulled off, Trae and Carmen locked eyes.

As Trae was driven off to jail, Carmen silently mouthed the words, "I still love you…brother!"

A NOVEL BY DANETTE MAJETTE

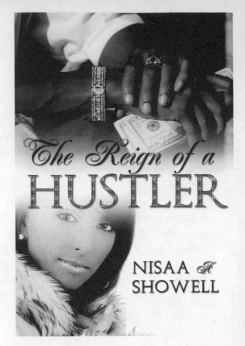

As a young girl Karen Whitaker dreamed of becoming rich and famous, promising to buy her mother that huge house on the hill with a Rolls Royce parked in the driveway. Her desire for material things turns into a grown woman's obsession with money, power and sex. Now of age, Karen possesses the brains of a scholar, beauty of a diamond, and a body that a Coca-Cola bottle would envy. She knows how to get what she wants even if it means taking advantage of those who trust her most. Greed and passion for tantalizing sex throttles her into compromising situations that may destroy her career and crumble her picture perfect relationship with a multi-millionaire. Take a journey into her intriguing story as demons from her past strike to unravel her fairytale life thread by thread. In the end, will she escape her dark clouds or be exposed as one money-hungry, conniving vixen?

Visit Nicolette Online @
www.myspace.com/paperdollthebook

**Available At Borders, Waldenbooks and
Independent Bookstores Nationwide**

The choice between love and life is never an easy one. Just ask Quinnzel "Supreme" Sharpe. Quinnzel has led anything but a charmed life. After shattering his knee in high school and ruining a chance at a college scholarship, his brother finances Quinnzel's way through school. But everything has a price. After graduating at the top of his class from Georgetown, Quinnzel takes his business degree and uses it to run his brother's drug dealing operation.

Imani Heaven Best is everything Supreme has been looking for. She is Beyonce, Oprah, and Eve rolled up into one. Her business savvy, as well as her street smarts, makes her wifey material and she has his nose totally open. After losing her first love to the streets, Imani is not really feeling another ride down heartache lane. But there is just something about that man they call Supreme.

Experience thug life and gangsta lovin' as a steamy connection ensues between two effervescently brilliant identities in this pictorial tale of raw urban hooks.

**Distributed by: Afrikan World Books,
Ingram,
Baker and Taylor, Life Changing Books.
and Amazon**

Life Changing Books Titles

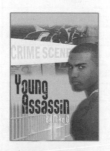

MAIL TO:
PO Box 423
Brandywine, MD 20613
301-362-6508

FAX TO:
301-579-9913

ORDER FORM

Date	
Phone	
E-mail	

Ship to:	
Address:	
City & State:	Zip:
Attention:	

Make all checks and Money Orders payable to: **Life Changing Books**

Qty.	ISBN	Title	Release Date	Price
	0-9741394-0-8	A Life to Remember by Azarel	08/2003	$ 15.00
	0-9741394-1-6	Double Life by Tyrone Wallace	11/2004	$ 15.00
	0-9741394-5-9	Nothin' Personal by Tyrone Wallace	07/2006	$ 15.00
	0-9741394-2-4	Bruised by Azarel	07/2005	$ 15.00
	0-9741394-7-5	Bruised 2: The Ultimate Revenge by Azarel	10/2006	$ 15.00
	0-9741394-3-2	Secrets of a Housewife by J. Tremble	02/2006	$ 15.00
	0-9724003-5-4	I Shoulda Seen it Comin' by Danette Majette	01/2006	$ 15.00
	0-9741394-4-0	The Take Over by Tonya Ridley	04/2006	$ 15.00
	0-9741394-6-7	The Millionaire Mistress by Tiphani	11/2006	$ 15.00
	1-934230-99-5	More Secrets More Lies J. Tremble	02/2007	$ 15.00
	1-934230-98-7	Young Assassin by Mike G	03/2007	$ 15.00
	1-934230-95-2	A Private Affair by Mike Warren	05/2007	$ 15.00
	1-934230-94-4	All That Glitters by Ericka M. Williams	07/2007	$ 15.00
	0-9774575-2-4	The Streets Love No One by R.L.	05/2007	$ 15.00
	0-9774575-0-8	A Lovely Murder Down South by Paul Johnson	06/2006	$ 15.00
	0-9791068-2-8	Changing My Shoes by T.T. Bridgeman	05/2007	$ 15.00
	1-934230-93-6	Deep by Danette Majette	07/2007	$ 15.00
	1-934230-96-0	Flexin' & Sexin by K'wan, Anna J. & Others	06/2007	$ 15.00
	1-934230-92-8	Talk of the Town by Tonya Ridley	07/2007	$15.00
	1-934230-89-8	Still a Mistress: The Saga Continues by Tiphani	11/2007	$15.00
	1-934230-91-X	Daddy's House by Azarel	11/2007	$15.00
	0-9741394-9-1	Teenage Bluez	01/2006	$10.99
	0-9741394-8-3	Teenage Bluez II	12/2006	$10.99
			Total for Books:	$
		Shipping Charges (add $4.00 for 1-4 books*)		$
		Total Enclosed (add lines)		$

*For credit card orders and orders for over 25 books
please contact us @ orders@lifechangingbooks.net
(cheaper rates for COD orders)*

**Shipping and Handling on 5-20 books
is $5.95. For 11 or more books, contact
us for shipping rates. 240.691.4343*